FURIOUS
SAILING INTO TERROR

JEFFREY JAMES HIGGINS

Black Rose Writing | Texas

ISBN: 978-1-68433-696-8 (Paperback); 978-1-944715-96-0 (Hardcover)
PUBLISHED BY BLACK ROSE WRITING
www.blackrosewriting.com

Printed in the United States of America
Suggested Retail Price (SRP) $19.95 (Paperback); 24.95 (Hardcover)

Furious is printed in Sabon

*As a planet-friendly publisher, Black Rose Writing does its best to eliminate
unnecessary waste to reduce paper usage and energy costs, while never
compromising the reading experience. As a result, the final word count vs. page count
may not meet common expectations.

For
Cynthia Farahat Higgins,
the bravest woman in the world.

ACKNOWLEDGMENTS

Writing a novel involves long hours alone with a manuscript, but no author succeeds without help. I could not have completed this novel without the support of Cynthia Farahat Higgins—my love, my wife, my life. She is the strongest person I know, and I write my books for her.

My parents, James and Nadya Higgins, read to me at an early age and have supported all of my endeavors. I credit them with kindling my imagination and instilling in me a love of story. I could not have asked for better parents.

Authors must learn the craft of writing, but the gift of storytelling is also genetic. With that in mind, I would like to acknowledge my grandfather, Nejm Aswad, an author, poet, philosopher, sculptor, and painter. I wish he had lived to read my first published novel.

My beta readers bravely faced early drafts of *Furious,* and I am eternally thankful for their feedback. Thanks to Cynthia Farahat Higgins, James Higgins, Nadya Higgins, Adam Meyer, Stacy Woodson, Dr. John Hunt, Stephen Cone, Susan Stiglitz, Matthew Stiglitz, and Richard Elam.

A good writing group is an author's most valuable asset, and I appreciate the skillful critiques of my fellow scriveners in the Royal Writers Secret Society. I am honored to be a member of such a talented group. Also, thanks to International Thriller Writers for their continued support of mystery and thriller writers everywhere.

I was honored to have my author portrait taken by Rowland Scherman, a Grammy Award winner and a talented photographer who has captured icons of American culture. View his work at www.rowlandscherman.com.

Finally, thanks to Reagan Rothe and everyone at Black Rose Writing for taking a chance on a debut author.

FURIOUS

SAILING INTO TERROR

CHAPTER ONE

I wanted to die.

I leaned into the crib and brushed my fingers over Emma's teddy bear, a stuffed animal larger than she had ever been. The velour fabric felt cool and still—the opposite of Emma during her short life—her three-month, impossibly brief existence. She had come and gone so quickly; it was almost possible to imagine she had never lived at all. Almost. Some mornings, I awakened and experienced a few seconds of peace, before remembering what had happened, then reality would rush into me like a cold wind.

My baby girl is dead.

The teddy bear's stitched eyes stared back at me. I had been so careful buying non-toxic bath toys and dolls free of choking hazards. Every object in the room was childproof, from the one-inch gaps between crib slats to the electrical outlet covers. I had given it all so much thought.

A tear wet my cheek, smearing my mascara, and I hugged the teddy bear against my chest. I could still smell the sweet, floral scent of baby powder, and I pictured the first time Emma smiled at me—her cheeks fat and rosy.

My eyes burned, and the crib blurred in my vision. The floor shifted under me, as if the carpet had transformed into desert sand, and the world rushed past me, moving on without me, jostling me like a leaf blowing down the side of the road, without direction, without hope.

I reached over the crib and caressed a cloth elephant dangling from a mobile. I flicked it and the mobile spun in a circle—going nowhere—as it chimed *Twinkle, Twinkle, Little Star*. Emma had giggled every time she heard it.

My pregnancy had been unplanned and the months before Emma's birth had been a flurry, a frantic rush to prepare for motherhood. We painted the nursery and purchased a crib, stroller, and pacifiers. I took vitamins and read how-to books, all so we would be ready when she came. Then she arrived, and everyone wanted to see her, touch her, share our joy. For three months she consumed our thoughts, our every waking moment. Then she was gone.

She had my blonde hair.

My knees buckled, and I wanted to fall through the floor, sink into the earth, lie with Emma in her grave. I wanted to hold her, kiss her, love her. I could not comprehend the unfairness of it, the cruelty. She had been healthy and full of life until the morning I found her cold and still.

Sudden Infant Death Syndrome. How could that be a real thing? How could anyone allow it to happen?

I gripped the crib to steady myself.

"Are you okay?" Brad asked from the doorway.

My body stiffened. I had forgotten my husband was home and the need to hide my weakness from him overwhelmed me. I turned away so he would not see my tears. I pulled my shoulders back and straightened, hoping I would not topple over.

"What do *you* think?" I asked. My voice sounded foreign, like a soundtrack dubbed by an actor.

"I have something to show you."

"Not now."

"Dagny, this isn't helping."

"I said, not now."

He touched my hand, and I pulled it away.

I knelt and ran my fingertips over the crib bumpers, designed to keep Emma from banging her head against the wood. I had chosen the tea rose color for its calming effect. Had they contributed to her death? Brad and I were both surgeons, but we had not seen it coming, could not save her. I wanted to climb into the crib and pull the blanket over my head until the world disappeared. Until I disappeared.

"Did I lay Emma on her back?" I asked, still not making eye contact.

"We've been through this."

"Was the baby monitor turned up?"

"You know it was."

"Did I do something wrong?"

"Dagny, please."

"Did you?"

Brad glared at me. "You have to stop."

Bunny rabbits smirked at me from a mural painted on the wall. I had been overconfident, unprepared. What did life mean if an innocent child could die for no reason? My life became a pause, a question mark, a purgatory waiting for an explanation.

"I could call the medical examiner's office or Detective Fuller again," I said.

"You've called them at least once a week for months."

"They've stopped returning my calls."

"Their investigation is over. Sometimes children die and we never know the reason."

"I still need answers."

I had always been an optimistic person, able to see the positive side of things, instinctively searching for ways to be happy. Not now. I still had that person inside me, but she was underwater, struggling to reach the surface, thrashing her arms and legs as her air ran out, trying to reach the light. All I could do was watch her, like a disinterested passerby on the beach, not knowing if I wanted her to make it or not.

Groaning emanated from somewhere, deep and guttural, and it took a moment to realize the sound came from me—as if my soul had taken control of my body and cried out for this nightmare to end. Life had broken on an elemental level, beyond repair. My baby was gone forever.

"Come on," Brad said.

He took my hand and led me out of the nursery.

I did not resist.

He turned to me. "There's something I need to talk to you about. Wait for me in the sitting room."

"Talk about what?"

"I have to get something from my office. Wait for me." An order, not a request.

I walked downstairs and stood in front of our bay windows, not out of curiosity or because Brad had asked me, but because I could not think of anything else to do.

A minute later, Brad hurried into the room with an envelope in his hand. He smiled. Not really a smile, but more of a failed attempt at one. His lips pressed together, and his cheeks rose, but the corners of his mouth turned down—both a smile and a frown—his frustration molded into a mask. His expression told me he had reached the boundary of his patience. He wanted my grieving to stop, needed my pain to end, craved his life back. He had found a way to move on, the ability to breathe again, and I had not.

"Hey, Dagny. How are . . . uh, I think you will like this."

I glared at him. Emma had only been gone for six months, twice as long as she had lived. I resented his resiliency, which was not fair to him, but I did not care. Life was unfair. Emma's death was unfair. The end of my happiness was unfair.

"Have a seat," Brad said, his voice gentle, solemn, like the funeral director who had helped me pick out the casket. "I think I know how to help you . . . to help us. I have an idea to break you out of this—"

"Break out of this? What makes you think there's a way out?"

"Come and sit down."

I followed him to the couch in the center of the room. It was a cavernous space, in a massive house, on an expansive estate. Brad had bought this mansion with his family's money and surprised me the week before we married, four months before Emma's birth. The beauty and opulence of the house matched the other homes in Newton, Massachusetts, but it was not Boston, not the city where I had spent my entire life. Not my home. It had all happened too fast—the dating, the unexpected pregnancy, the house, the marriage. The death.

I sat on the couch and peered out at the autumn tableau. The leaves had turned crimson, vermillion, arsenic-yellow. They were dying too.

"What is it?" My voice sounded distant, cold.

"It's been six months, and you're almost finished with your surgical fellowship," Brad said. "You need to . . . *we* need to dig our way out of this and live again. We need to—"

"How long am I allowed to be sad, Brad?"

"I'm not saying you can't grieve, but you have to move on. This has been hard for me too."

"Has it? You seem to have recovered quickly." What a mean thing to say. Who was this person who had taken over my body after my soul departed?

"It's been awful, unthinkable, but I pushed through the pain. Damn it, she was my daughter too. I'm trying to help you."

"Sometimes I think about taking pills, making it all stop," I said.

He slammed his hand on the back of the couch. "Fuck this. You don't think I've felt like dying too?"

I glared at him, silent. There it was. The anger always bubbling just below the surface. It had broken through and filled the room, like gas from a tar pit—foul, ugly, toxic.

"I . . . I didn't mean to yell," Brad said. "This has been unbearable. We have to do something."

He rolled his eyes to the ceiling.

I used to see that expression as a window into the mind of a brilliant doctor, but no longer. That was probably unfair too. Maybe I wanted someone to blame, and Brad's proximity made him a convenient target. Maybe not.

He held the envelope out for me, but I did not take it.

"What's that?"

"Plane tickets. Tickets to Bali. I leased a sailboat . . . a yacht, actually. We will sail from Indonesia to the Maldives, off the coast of India. Just the two of us."

I gawked at him and blinked. "You think I want a vacation?"

"It's not a vacation. It's one month at sea, away from Boston, away from our lives . . . away from all of it."

"You know I'm afraid of the water."

"You don't have to swim. We'll be on a sixty-two-foot yacht."

"I haven't sailed since I was a child."

"I've been sailing my family's yacht since I was twelve years old. I can do the heavy lifting, and if you're interested, I'll give you a refresher."

"They're expecting me back at Boston Pediatric," I said.

"They've been expecting you back for months, and I don't see you returning anytime soon. You need to get your head together before you can finish your fellowship and pass your boards."

Brad's answers came fast, as if he had given his plan great thought, prepared for my objections. I wobbled on my feet like a punch-drunk boxer, unable to respond to his counter-punches.

"I don't know."

"Trust me, the change of scenery will be therapeutic. I need this. *We* need this. You have to come."

I looked out the window at the fallen leaves swirling on the lawn. Swirling and swirling. Going nowhere. Decomposing.

"When?"

"We're leaving next week."

He stood, set his jaw, and stormed out of the room. Conversation over.

I opened my mouth to yell, to tell him not to leave, but instead, I leaned back on the couch and gazed out the window. How could Brad plan a month-long voyage without my consent? I felt like I had no say in the matter, no right to object. Adversity seemed to have brought out the worst parts of his character. He had grown more pedantic in recent months, assuming an unearned authority in our relationship. It seemed as if by succumbing to depression, I had abdicated my standing in our partnership. He had grown more domineering, consulted me less, treated me like a child, as if he knew best. I had serious doubts about that—serious doubts about him.

Outside, the car door slammed. The engine started and Brad drove past the windows and down the long driveway. The iron gates creaked open, and I watched him turn left, driving past brick mansions, stone walls, and velvet lawns. Leaves fluttered in his wake.

I did not care where he went.

I had done nothing but mourn for six months, the longest period of inactivity in my thirty-two years. I did not recognize the weeping woman

I had become—unable to work, unable to socialize, unable to cope. I had always used my mind to overcome obstacles, but I could not think my way out of this depression. I could not move on after Emma's death.

Maybe Brad's sailing trip would give me distance from the psychological trauma, the space to get my emotions under control. If I did not recover soon, I would lose my pediatric surgical fellowship, lose everything I had worked my entire life to achieve. Forcing myself onto a sailboat would also make me confront my biggest fear, and if I could do that, I would become a stronger person. My trepidation entailed more than an irrational phobia—sailing across the Indian Ocean carried genuine risks. Ships sank, accidents happened, people died.

But I was desperate. Maybe *this* time, Brad knew best. He loved me and sailing across an ocean could be the change I required to recover. Maybe I needed this voyage.

I sat on the couch and pictured my father, the sun reflecting off the water, moments before it happened—twenty-one years ago. The day that defined my life.

I blinked the thought away and focused on the front yard. Leaves blew in circles across the driveway. The sun sank lower in the sky and shadows crept across the floor. The umbra climbed my legs, covering me, plunging the room into darkness. I watched myself sitting there, like I was that bystander on the beach.

I waited to see what I would do.

CHAPTER TWO

"Your husband is an asshole," Jessica Golde said.

I slid into the passenger seat of her Toyota Corolla, which she had double-parked in front of Boston Pediatric Surgical Center, waiting for me under a no-parking sign. Jessica had never cared about rules.

"Good morning to you, too," I said.

"How can Brad ask you to go sailing for a month? You know I've never liked him, but dragging you into the middle of the ocean, it's really too much."

"I don't know if that's fair. Brad's suffering too. Maybe this is how he's dealing with it. I haven't been fun to live with, since . . . it happened."

"He knows you've been terrified of the water since you were a little girl and he still asked you to sail across the Indian Ocean. What a prick."

I had feared the water since that day in July—a memory forever imprinted on my mind. The scent of sunscreen and chlorine hung on the warm summer breeze. Women wore bikinis and enormous hats, and men sported colorful swimsuits and flip flops. Children screamed and laughed. Then the crowd quieted and gathered around something on the ground. Ice cream melted down the side of my cone, slid between my fingers, dripped on the concrete. I felt it in my stomach, knew what I would see laying there.

"Dagny?" Jessica asked. "Did you hear what I said? Are you still with me?"

I turned to her in the car. Goosebumps had risen on my arms. "Sorry, I was thinking. What did you say?"

"I said Brad knows about your phobia, but he still asked you on a sailing trip. Why did he do it?"

"I don't know," I said.

I contemplated my hands. I had thought about that too and concluded Brad's offer had been a challenge. He had always competed with me. I had not noticed it at first, but we had only dated for three months before I got pregnant. My decision to marry him had been rash, driven by surging hormones and a desire to create a stable home for my unborn child.

"I think Brad asked you to take a sailing voyage to make you admit your fear, confess your weakness, concede he's stronger than you," Jessica said.

"That would be cruel."

"Brad's always worried that you're smarter than him, a better surgeon. He wants this trip to be a competition."

Maybe it's time to prove he's right.

I turned back to Jessica but did not meet her gaze. "What if he chose a sailing trip to challenge me, to help me confront my fear? He knows I can't accept failure. Maybe he's using my childhood phobia to distract me from my grief and force me to heal. If that's what he's doing, he's playing three-dimensional chess—a master motivator."

This trip could save me.

"Or he's a master manipulator," Jessica said.

"Our marriage is in trouble. Brad thinks the time away from our routine will help me mend, and exposure therapy is an effective intervention for aquaphobia. Maybe he's right."

"Brad's a narcissist, and you know it," Jessica said. "He's a spoiled, handsome, rich kid who can't be bothered with your pain. He didn't even ask you before he planned the trip."

That was true, but I was not going to bad-mouth Brad to her. I owed him that much. Brad was my husband, and I had to be loyal. Besides, Brad could also be sweet and persuasive. His charisma pulled people toward him, made them want to follow. He probably did not intend on being insensitive. It was more a byproduct of his narcissism. He needed me to recover from Emma's death so he could be happy again, and if he had to force me to get onboard with his plan, so be it.

"I have to do something," I said. "I'm lost. Sometimes, I don't think I'll make it through the day."

"You can do anything you put your mind to, sweetie. You are the most driven person I have ever known. You thought Harvard would be impossible, but you graduated near the top of your class. You doubted you would become a surgeon, but you did. You thought you would never get this fellowship, but here you are. You're a winner."

Jessica had been my best friend since we sat next to each other in our Intro to Philosophy class during our freshman year at Boston University. That was fourteen years ago, before Harvard Medical School, before my surgical residency at New England General Hospital—where I met Brad—and before Boston Pediatric Surgical Center.

Jessica was short, plump, and brunette—the opposite of me. She was an Italian Jew from New Jersey, and I was a Scottish-Irish Catholic from Boston. We looked nothing alike and came from different cultures, but we had become fast friends. Jessica had gone into nursing; a career move she said I had inspired with my passion for medicine. We had even worked together briefly before I left New England General Hospital. She felt like the sister I never had, and I missed seeing her every day.

"Thanks, Jess. I wouldn't have made it this far without you."

"I'm glad you called. Stop acting like a hermit and come down the shore with Jimmy and me. He thinks you're a hottie."

"I like your husband, but I haven't been out at all. You're the only person I can talk to anymore."

"Yet you think spending a month on a boat with Brad will be fun?"

"*Fun?* Not exactly, but it may help me. I don't know."

"What were you doing at the hospital today?"

"I had a session with the staff psychiatrist."

Jessica's eyes widened. "You're kidding? I can't believe you went to a psychiatrist. What happened to the Dagny who said, 'I can solve any problem with my mind?'"

"The hospital administrator strongly recommended I see him, and she has been so good to me by allowing me to take this sabbatical. I felt like I couldn't decline her offer."

"What did your psychiatrist say?"

"The usually touchy-feely stuff. I told him about the sailing trip, and he thought it may be a good idea to get away, to put some space between myself and the house. He said a change of scenery may help, as long as I don't suppress my feelings."

I did not mention that I had also told the psychiatrist about my doubts about Brad and our marriage. The psychiatrist had suggested my feelings about Brad had nothing to do with Emma's death. He said they were probably a separate issue brought to the forefront by our tragedy—concerns born from unrelated problems—and I had not told him everything. Not the worst of it.

"What are you going to do? Will you go?"

"I just gave the administrator official notice that I'm extending my leave of absence. I told her I'll return in January. I think she'll allow me to finish my fellowship, but if I can't resume work by the new year, I may have to find another job."

"You're going on the trip to prove how brave you are. You agreed because you're afraid."

Jessica knew me better than anyone. I could never ignore a challenge, and this was an opportunity to confront my childhood phobia, an enduring source of weakness and shame. I swelled with pride at making the hard decision—a flicker of my former self.

Maybe I'm still in here.

"I'm going, because I'll die if I stay here. I need to get away and I can't get farther away than the middle of the ocean."

Someone knocked on my window and I whirled around. Eric Franklin smiled at me through the glass. I lowered the window.

"Hey Dagny, I'm glad I caught you. I've been thinking about you."

"Thanks, Eric. It's good to see you too."

"When do we get you back? It hasn't been the same without you."

"January, I think. I'm going away for a month. I gave notice."

"I can't say I'm happy to hear that, but I understand. If there's anything you need, anything at all, you have my number."

Jessica leaned across me. "Hi, I'm Jessica, Dagny's friend."

My cheeks warmed. "Sorry. Jessica, this is Eric. He's an infectious disease specialist with a pediatric specialty. Eric's great with the kids. We've consulted together on several patients.

"Nice to meet you, Jessica," Eric said.

"You remind me of Jude Law. Has anyone ever told you that?"

Eric blushed. "Uh, maybe."

"Are you single?" Jessica asked.

"Jessica, stop," I said, turning to Eric. "We have to get going. Nice to see you."

"Remember, call me anytime," he said.

I watched him walk into the hospital.

Jessica raised her eyebrows. "Call you anytime?"

"Knock it off. He's a colleague."

"I wouldn't mind having him examine me."

"Let's go. I have to pack. Brad and I are leaving in two days."

"Shit. How can I change your mind?"

"If I keep floundering like this, I'll die. I have to try something." I took Jessica's hand and met her eyes. "Support me on this one."

"I always do, sweetie, but I don't have a good feeling about this trip."

"I know. I'm scared, for a lot of reasons, but this trip could help me . . . I think."

"Don't say I didn't warn you."

CHAPTER THREE

I stood in my foyer after Jessica dropped me off. The house felt different. I felt different. Accepting Brad's challenge had done something to me.

I could not wait for Brad to come home to tell him I would go on the voyage. I picked up the phone and called his office to give him the news.

"Surgical Associates, this is Ellen," his group administrator said.

"Hi Ellen, it's Dagny Steele. Is Brad available?"

"Oh, Dr. Steele. How are you?"

How should I answer that? "May I speak with Brad?"

"Dr. Coolidge?"

"Yes, is my husband out of surgery? I need to speak with him."

"Uh, no. I mean, he's not in surgery. He's, uh, not here."

"Not there?" I asked. "Where is he?"

"I don't know. You'll have to try his cell phone."

She sounded hesitant, odd. I thanked her and hung up.

I dialed Brad's cell, and the call went right to voicemail.

Where is he?

I gazed through my living room window at the branches of our oak tree swaying in the wind. *His office is filled with beautiful nurses.* Dark clouds floated by, blotting out the sun.

Deciding to go on the trip—being proactive and taking action—felt right. I had always been driven to achieve, motivated to accomplish my goals. My calling to medicine came when I was eleven years old, after the incident that changed my life forever. Since that day, I had known I was meant to become a doctor, known it with absolute certainty, the same way I knew I was a girl, or that I lived in Boston. I remembered sitting on the edge of my bed, rocking my legs back and forth, trying to burn off my frustration at having to wait to become a physician. I had pictured a clock over my head, its hands ticking, counting the seconds and minutes I wasted while I finished school. Every day I was not a doctor, some other little girl could suffer the same fate as I. Every day, I missed another opportunity to save a life. Tick-Tock. Every day. That sense of urgency had driven me to excel for my entire life.

Until Emma died.

My phone rang, and I answered.

"Hi Dagny," Brad said. "Sorry, I missed your call. Is anything wrong?"

"Where are you?"

"At work. Is there a problem?"

"You're at the hospital?"

"What's going on?"

"I called your office and Ellen said you weren't in surgery and she didn't know where you were. I thought—"

"I'm in a pharmaceutical meeting on the second floor. I guess I forgot to tell her."

A gust of wind ripped several dead leaves free of the oak and they swirled in the air, fluttering to the ground.

"Really?" I asked.

"Are you checking on me?"

"No, I . . . sorry. I called to tell you I've decided to go on the voyage."

"That's marvelous, really great." Brad said. "This trip will do wonders for you; help you get your life back."

"That's my hope."

"I promise, you won't regret it."

CHAPTER FOUR

The dock swayed beneath my feet as Brad and I followed Ali, our facilitator, through the Bali International Marina. A variety of pleasure craft bobbed beside the narrow piers. Million-dollar yachts looked out of place tied to weathered planks, like Ferraris in a trailer park. Steady maritime traffic flowed in and out of Benoa Harbor, off Bali's southern peninsula.

I sipped my third coffee of the day, a double espresso, having nursed it on the way over from the Royal Indonesian Resort in Nusa Dua. Brad had scheduled us to depart the following morning, and we had to prepare the yacht. The trip from Boston to Bali had taken over twenty-six hours and had felt like an all-nighter in medical school. I remained groggy, fuzzy, as if I stumbled around inside a dream.

"There she is," Brad said, eyeing the end of the dock.

"Yes, yes," Ali said, and flashed a toothy grin.

We crossed an arched bridge onto a long pier which jutted sixty yards into the harbor. I surveyed boats moored in perpendicular slips on our right. Gorgeous cruising sailboats averaged forty to fifty feet; their sails lashed to booms beneath soaring masts, like a forest of redwoods. As we passed, I read the model names painted on their hulls—Gulfstar 50, Jeanneau Sun Odyssey 49, Oyster 56, Bavaria 42, Bristol 40—all floating vacation homes. On our left, twin-hulled catamarans docked parallel to the pier to accommodate their width. I admired them, but my stomach clenched at the thought of taking to sea.

"Which one is it?" I asked, unable to contain my curiosity.

"There, Mrs. Coolidge," Ali said.

"It's Steele," I said. "I kept my name."

Why did I need to explain that to him?

Ali gave me a funny look and pointed. I followed his outstretched finger to the end of the pier, beyond the catamarans, to the longest of all the boats—a Beneteau Oceanis Yacht.

"You're kidding," I said.

"What do you think?" Brad asked.

"You're going to sail that behemoth?"

"*We're* going to sail it. You're my first mate. We can control everything from the helm, and it practically sails itself."

A chill crawled across my skin, followed by a wave of nausea. I rubbed my neck and stared at the yacht, the vessel which would deliver Brad and me across thousands of miles of open ocean, and the only thing protecting us from my worst fear. Well, the yacht and Brad's sailing ability. I shivered and gnawed on a fingernail.

The deck stood eight feet above the waterline, with expansive freeboard over a gleaming white hull. A band of tinted windows bisected the topsides and ran the length of the boat. A white hardtop covered the cabin, and a carbon mast towered ninety feet over the deck. The yacht looked contemporary, elegant, and efficient.

"How long is it?" I asked.

"Sixty-two feet and almost eighteen feet wide at the beam. She's a beauty, isn't she?"

"It's huge."

The yacht was much more than I had expected, and the idea of living on a boat for a month was tangible now—real for the first time. My hands grew clammy.

This is happening.

"I was lucky to get it," Brad said. "The French only made thirty-five of these, but my father's friend owns this one."

"It seems like a Bond villain should live on it. I have to ask, how much did it cost?"

"This hull sold for $1.4 million and I rented it for $24,000 for the entire month of December."

"That's a third of my salary."

"You don't have to worry about money anymore."

The name "*KARNA*" adorned the stern in gold letters.

"What does *Karna* mean?" I asked.

"I asked too," Brad said. "The owner spends a lot of time in the Indian Ocean, so he named it after a mythological Hindi hero. Karna was a moral champion blessed with strength and ability. He suffered betrayal and attacks but stayed true to himself and overcame adversity."

"It must be good luck to name a boat after a hero, right?"

"It's a yacht," Brad said.

"Come, come," Ali said. "Let me show you. You ready for sail now."

I had sailed with my father and taken lessons as a child, often navigating Boston's Charles River by myself, but those lessons had been on an eleven-foot Sailfish—essentially a surfboard with a small sail, centerboard, and rudder. This yacht was a leviathan. I still remembered how to sail and had refreshed my memory by reading a sailing manual on the plane. I had a decent grasp of nautical terminology and knew enough not to call a line a rope, but the list of sailboat parts seemed endless. Sailing jargon was almost as complicated as medical terminology.

Ali leapt off the pier, climbed onboard, and hydraulically lowered the transom door. The door unfolded and extended ten feet behind the boat, forming a swimming platform. Behind the open transom, a nine-foot inflatable motorboat rested inside a tender garage.

"Come," Ali said, and waved us onboard.

I hesitated, panic building.

Brad grabbed my hand.

"I can't," I said.

"You can." He lifted me off the pier and onto the diving platform.

My head swam, and I stuck my arms out for balance. "I don't know."

"This trip will be an adventure," he said. "I'm excited."

"I'm nauseous."

Twin companionways bracketed the stern, and Brad guided me up four teak steps to the deck. I had not been on the water since the incident, and a cool sweat broke out on my forehead and back.

Brad did not seem to notice my discomfort. He was giddy, like a child with a new toy. He grinned and surveyed the length of the boat, excited to show off his acquisition.

"We have twin helms, starboard and port, with duplicate sailing controls," he said. "You can raise and lower the sails, steer, and navigate from either side."

I glanced at the bay, light-headed. "I have no intention of piloting this boat."

"It's still a yacht, and it's easy. You'll figure it out in a day or two."

"I don't know."

"Trust me."

The cockpit lay in front of the steering wheels, with white-cushioned couches and teak tables on either side. Two feet of deck space ran along the gunwales all the way forward to the bow, and metal lifelines extended two-and-a-half feet above the deck, but they did not make me feel any safer. A composition arch and Bimini hardtop hung over the cockpit, and a covered companionway led below to the cabin.

I glanced back at the pier and dry land.

"Follow me," Brad said, walking toward the bow.

"There's a lot of deck space," I said, gripping the lifeline as I followed.

"It will seem smaller after a month at sea." Brad stopped between two small hatches in the deck and a larger one near the bow. He bent and opened the large plexiglass hatch. "This is the foresail locker, it's been outfitted as crew quarters, but we'll store emergency gear in it."

I peered into a small, claustrophobic space containing a bed, sink, and storage cabinets. "I'm glad we're not sleeping in there."

"The galley is stocked, as requested," Ali hollered from the stern. He disappeared down the companionway into the cabin.

"Come on, Dags. We'll have plenty of time to hang out on deck tomorrow. Let's make sure he loaded our food onboard and topped off the water and fuel tanks."

We walked aft, and I took a deep breath before descending six wooden steps into the cabin. To my left, a swivel chair had been bolted in front of a chart table, with communication, navigation, and control equipment recessed in the wall. A large dining table ran parallel to the port side, bracketed by couches. To starboard, a galley contained a freezer, refrigerator, stove, oven, microwave, and sink. Tinted windows extended to the bow, with white-lacquered cabinets above them.

"Behind you are two berths, port and starboard, each with its own head," Brad said. "That's a *bathroom* in sailor-speak."

"Thanks, captain."

"Our stateroom is in the bow."

"So, two bedrooms in the back and a big one in front?"

"Two cabins in the stern and the stateroom in the bow; and we say *fore* and *aft*, not *front* and *back*."

Brad led me forward through the galley to a small passageway. He paused and opened two cabinets, containing a refrigerator and a washing machine. The passageway opened into the largest berth—our stateroom. A queen-sized bed sat atop a raised platform and light streamed in from two overhead hatches and rows of windows along the sides. Cabinets lined the starboard side, and a forty-inch digital television hung from the bulkhead.

"It's more luxurious than I expected," I said, "but it's a smaller space than we're used to. Won't we get cabin fever?"

"We have three berths with locking doors, a comfortable salon, and plenty of room on deck. You won't have any difficulty getting away from me."

"Do you ever want to get away from me?"

"I didn't mean—"

"I know, but . . ."

"But what?" he asked.

"I called you the other day, and you weren't at work."

Brad put his hands on his hips and scowled. "I already explained that. I was in a pharmaceutical meeting."

"You work with all those pretty, young nurses . . . women without my depression."

"You're being ridiculous," Brad said.

"I feel like you're not telling me something."

"You have nothing to worry about," Brad said, avoiding my gaze. "Let's finish the inventory and head to the hotel. I want an extravagant dinner before we shove off tomorrow."

I followed him into the galley where Ali had opened cabinets filled with canned goods. The freezer overflowed with meat in vacuum-sealed packages, and fruit and vegetables packed the refrigerator.

Ali bent over, pulled a panel off the deck, and opened a hidden compartment below. I peeked over his shoulder at rows of canned goods, oils, dish soap, shower gels, shampoo, bottled water, beer, sodas, flour, sugar, cornmeal, condiments, spices, oils, butter, rice, crackers, pasta, beans, nuts, granola bars, chips, jelly, tuna, and soup. Too much food for land and barely enough at sea.

"We could feed a navy," I said.

"You'll be surprised how fast we go through it. Once we enter the Indian ocean, if it didn't come with us, we won't have it."

Brad turned to Ali. "Everything appears to be here. I won't count all the cans."

"Not necessary, Mr. Coolidge. I checked them myself."

"Good," Brad said. He pulled a stack of Indonesian rupiahs from his pocket and handed them to Ali. "This is for your efforts, my good man. Please give me a minute alone with my wife."

Ali thanked him and climbed the companionway.

Brad took my hands in his. "I know I surprised you with this trip and you did not have time to prepare, but I'm the captain and I'll take care of everything. You're in expert hands."

"Okay." I almost thanked him, but this trip was something he wanted to do, something he had challenged me with, and he had waited until the last minute to tell me about it. Thanking him for being my knight in shining armor seemed wrong.

"Listen, if this is too hard for you, I won't force you to go. We can stay at the resort and lie on the beach for a few days."

"Really?" I asked.

"I'm not a monster."

"But the lease?"

"It's only money."

I exhaled. "Thanks for saying that, but no. I said I'd go, and I will. I need to do this."

Brad smiled. "You'll be glad you did. This is one of the best yachts ever constructed. Tomorrow, after we clear the harbor, I'll explain all the emergency procedures to you."

"Emergency procedures?"

"What to do if I fall overboard, operating our communication equipment, basic skills."

"You better not fall overboard. I could never sail this alone.

"Don't be paranoid. I'll take care of you. Nothing bad will happen."

CHAPTER FIVE

I padded across the teak floor in our bungalow at the Royal Indonesian Resort and stepped onto the balcony. I gazed past a stand of swaying palm trees and across the beach to the Indian Ocean. The sun melted and spread across the horizon as the water darkened and the sky burned shades of amber and scarlet.

"This may be the most beautiful island in the world," Brad said, coming up behind me.

I nodded but stayed silent. It did not feel right staying in a five-star hotel on a tropical beach while Emma lay dead in her grave. Would that ever change?

"Are you okay?" he asked. The muscles in his jaw tensed as he awaited my answer.

"Being on the water scares me, but I would rather be out there than here. Somehow, spending a month on a sailboat seems more appropriate. Maybe my aquaphobia makes it a punishment, my penance for failing my daughter."

"You'll get your wish tomorrow."

"I have no choice. If I lose my fellowship, I don't know what I'll do."

"I'll check the forecast then let's get some sleep. I want to leave at dawn."

Brad undressed and climbed into bed with his laptop while I sifted through clothes in my suitcase. I had packed in a hurry, not knowing what I would need. The island heat lingered throughout December, so I brought bikinis, shorts, and short-sleeve shirts.

Thinking about the yacht raised my blood pressure. I had not been on a sailboat in twenty-one years. I remembered sailing on the Charles River with my father, when he had borrowed his friend's thirty-one-foot Catalina and we had navigated out of the river into Boston Harbor. A perfect day, with no clouds, no humidity, and no worries. At least that was the picture frozen into my memory—before everything changed.

I closed my suitcase and sighed. Whatever I had packed would have to suffice. I washed off my makeup, brushed my teeth, and changed into a long tee shirt. I carried my laptop with me and slipped into bed beside Brad.

"Shit," Brad said.

"What?"

"There's a monsoon moving into the Bay of Bengal."

"That doesn't sound good."

"We're taking the northern route to India, passing south of Thailand, because the northeast winds will be behind us, but if they reach gale force in the bay, it'll be dangerous."

The weather looked perfect outside. The monsoon had to be far from Bali.

"I thought you said monsoon season was over," I said.

"The northeast monsoons peak between June and September and die out in the fall. They're supposed to be finished by now, and the southwest monsoons don't begin until mid-May."

"So, we won't hit one?"

"We shouldn't."

"I'd feel better if you were more certain," I said.

"The Bay of Bengal gets them, but the wind will diminish as we get closer to the equator."

"Could we take the southern route instead?"

"The winds are slower there, and we would have to sail south of the equator to use the westbound equatorial current. I'd prefer to use the northeast winds."

"What do we do?" I asked.

"There's nothing we can do. Let's stay an extra day and let the monsoon pass. We can leave the day after tomorrow."

The thought of sitting in the hotel, like some honeymooning couple, made me sick. I ran my hands through my hair.

"We have to sit here and wait?" I asked.

"Bali is an international tourist destination. Let's hike through the jungle or visit a temple."

I should be grieving.

I touched my abdomen, remembering Emma growing inside me. I could still feel her suckling at my breast, the way an amputee feels the tingle of a lost limb. Whenever I thought about her, my depression took on a life of its own, tugging behind my eyes, pulling on my body, as if I had weights attached to my limbs. Emma's life had been short, but I had bonded with her while she grew in my womb. Maybe hormones had driven our connection—a chemical compulsion to ensure I cared for my infant—or maybe it came from something greater, something ethereal, something metaphysical. I did not know how long I should suffer, but I could not see the end.

"You explore the island and I'll stay in the room."

"You need to take advantage of our extra day here."

"Please don't tell me what I need to do. I agreed to follow you halfway around the world. Isn't that enough?"

Brad scowled, like a child I had punished. He rolled over and turned his back to me.

I glared at the back of his head and could almost hear his synapses raging. Brad had grown accustomed to getting what he wanted. His wealthy parents had spoiled him as a child and their behavior had not changed. Brad had spent his childhood in private schools, taking vacations in Europe, receiving nothing but the best. He came from a blue-blooded family and acted like it. He was handsome, rich, and confident. I may have been the first woman to refuse him.

I powered up my MacBook Air and checked my email. The first message was from Eric, and my mood brightened. Eric had become a close friend during my two years at Boston Pediatric Surgical Center, and he cared about me. He exhibited a sharp intellect, keen judgment, and empathy with his young patients. The entire staff respected him, and I felt honored when he consulted me.

Eric always listened when I spoke, but we were only friends and colleagues, nothing more. I had just started dating Brad when I met Eric and while I had found him attractive, I could never date more than one person at a time. Eric never expressed romantic interest in me, but I believed he harbored more than platonic feelings. That was before the surprise pregnancy, before the hasty marriage, before my life crumbled. After my wedding, Eric had congratulated me, saying he had waited too long to ask me out. That kind of comment would have been inappropriate, but he had laughed when he said it, and we were comfortable teasing each other, so I had shrugged it off. I had married Brad, and that was that.

I read his email.

Hi Dagny. Everyone here misses you. I hope your voyage gives you the time and distance you need to regroup and gather your strength. Don't expect miracles. These things take time, so don't rush yourself, but I hope you return to complete your fellowship after your trip. You're a bright, rising star, and the children need you. We all do. If you want to talk, email or call anytime. Give my regards to Brad. - Eric.

The email was sympathetic and kind. I had worried what people at the hospital thought about my lengthy absence. Did they judge me for not returning to work? Did they think I had lost my mind? Knowing Eric stood behind me gave me confidence, and I enjoyed interacting with someone who considered my feelings—without the competition, without the impatience.

I shut my laptop and eyed Brad, who tapped away on his laptop.

"What are you working on?" I asked.

Brad look up startled, like he had forgotten I was there. He slammed his laptop shut. "Nothing. Checking the weather again."

"I'm trusting you," I said.

"I wasn't doing anything."

"I'm talking about the trip. I agreed to come, to put myself in your hands, because I want to get through this. I want *us* to get through this."

"Me too. Let's get some rest. We will need it." He rolled over and went to sleep.

I stared at him for a long time before I shut off the light.

CHAPTER SIX

The sun streamed through a part in the curtains, assaulting my dry, irritated eyes—sore from crying through the night. On the verge of sleep, my mind had conjured the image of my baby and I had thought about the life Emma would never live. That was all it had taken for me to breakdown. I had fallen apart and sobbed until my stomach hurt, burying my face in my pillow to avoid waking Brad. I had slept less than two hours.

The hotel room door opened, and Brad walked in carrying coffees. Caffeine had become medicine for me. Caffeine and Xanax. I could not function without them, or at least I did not dare to try.

"Good morning, Dags," Brad said, setting my coffee on the nightstand.

"Morning."

"I know you had a dreadful night, but I won't let you sit in the room. Come with me."

"I . . . I can't."

"You can. If you take a shower and get dressed, you'll feel better. Let's go to one tourist site and if you hate it, we can come back."

"I don't know," I said.

My will to resist waned. Depression exhausted me. The constant emotional turmoil depleted my energy, but even the physical act of sitting in a room and crying ate away at my life force. I had grieved nonstop for six months, and the thought of spending the day inside the hotel room was too much, even though I deserved the pain for failing my daughter.

"If you don't come, I won't go either, but we're about to spend thirty days in an enclosed space. Let's not waste our last day on land by sitting around in a cramped hotel room.

"Last day? The weather improved?"

"The monsoon is moving fast. It'll be far in front of us by the time we reach the Bay of Bengal. We leave at dawn."

I perked up at the news. I would not have to stay in this hotel room, this purgatory, for much longer. Tomorrow, I would take a proactive step and attempt to snap out of my psychosis. It was time to confront my fears, to see if I had anything left worth saving.

Brad scrutinized me—cocking his head and raising his eyebrows—wanting an answer.

What the hell was I doing in Bali? What was I doing with my life? I was lost, uncertain. Was I making intelligent decisions or acting out of desperation?

"Okay, give me thirty minutes."

CHAPTER SEVEN

Our taxi stopped on the road outside the *Pura Goa Lawah* temple. I wore shorts and a short-sleeved blouse, and Brad had on jeans and a tee shirt. Before we exited the car, I wrapped a *kain kamben*, a Balinese sarong, around my waist and draped a *selendang*, a temple scarf, over my shoulders. Brad slipped on similar garments, which we had purchased in the hotel gift shop. The concierge had insisted we cover ourselves before we entered the temple, and I had wondered if he lied to make a sale, but now I saw dozens of tourists wearing the coverings, and I doubted the whole Balinese population had conspired to scam tourists.

"This is it," Brad said, beaming.

"It's a beautiful setting."

I had been miserable company, and I attempted to sound upbeat for him. Besides, the stone shrines fascinated me. I opened the door of our Bali Taxi, known as a *Bluebird*, because of its color and the winged emblem on top. A horde of aggressive hawkers descended on us, selling sarongs, Balinese calendars, and an array of trinkets. Women grabbed at my arms and one of them slipped a shell necklace over my head. I had not asked for it, but I gave her eighty thousand rupiah. It sounded like a lot of money, except the exchange rate was close to fifteen thousand rupiah to one dollar.

Brad paid our entrance fees, and they forced him to pay more for a guide. Nothing cost much, but I felt like a rube, there to be fleeced.

"I hired a guide, but the site is small, and I have a guidebook, so let's explore it alone," Brad said.

"Aye aye, captain."

Brad read from the guidebook as we walked. "Goa Lawah is an early eleventh-century Hindi temple built to protect the Balinese from dark spirits invading from the sea. There are twenty-five stone shrines and pavilions on the grounds."

I surveyed the area. "It looks like the set for an Indiana Jones movie."

"It does, but it's a significant holy site for the Balinese."

The sprawling temple complex nestled against a jagged hill, with Mount Agung looming in the distance. A black sandy beach, bordering the Bali Sea, peeked between the trees behind us. The jungle surrounded the temple, poised to overtake the site the moment the groundskeepers turned their backs. Fig and bamboo trees dotted the grounds and two massive Banyan trees towered above the main temple. Wind rustled through the leaves and perfumed the air with a sweet fragrance.

"Why do they call these sites *puras*?" I asked, reading over Brad's shoulder.

"The book says a pura is an open-air Balinese Hindi temple, with smaller shrines to various Hindu gods. The Goa Lawah complex is one of the six holiest worship sites on the island."

Brad narrated as we moved inland toward the main shrine. We passed through a portal into the inner sanctum containing three primary shrines. Beyond it, long stone steps rose to traditional Balinese *candi bentar* gates, which bracketed an enormous entrance to a cave, like ornate stone bookends.

"According to legend, tunnels lead from the cave, all over the Island and to the Besakih Temple at the foot of Mount Agung. That cave is home to *Basuki*, the snake king. There's a shrine somewhere on the grounds with a sculpture of the serpent."

"There are worshipers here among the tourists," I said.

Two dozen Balinese sat in front of the temple, with their feet tucked under their thighs and their palms pressed together. We watched the ceremony from a distance, and when it ended, we approached the elaborate shrine. We slipped off our shoes, mounted the steps, and stared past the gates into the mouth of the cave.

Shadows bathed the interior of the cave, and its walls vibrated and pulsed with tens of thousands of black bats.

"Goa Lawah literally means *bat cave*," he said.

"Yuk. They're disgusting."

"Come on. They're cute."

I examined a bat near the edge of the cave. It slept inverted, hanging from the rock with its black wings folded and tucked against its body. I leaned in closer. Its head resembled a dog, with a pink nose, long snout, and brown fur. Its chest heaved with respirations.

"They're creepy."

"If we wait for nightfall, we can watch them fly out to feed."

"I'll take a hard pass."

Brad hovered over my shoulder and craned his neck to see. "They look soft. Want to pet one."

"Gross. They're filthy and probably diseased."

"That's the city girl coming out of you."

I caught movement out of the corner of my eye, and a bat darted out of the cave right at us. I screamed and ducked. Brad toppled over backwards.

"What the hell was that?" I yelled. "Where did it go?"

"It's gone."

"Are you okay?"

"I'm fine," Brad said, climbing off the ground. He seemed shaken.

"Are you sure?"

"It bounced off my head as it flew by," he said.

"Did it bite you?"

"No." He ran his fingers through his hair and inspected them.

"Did it?"

"I said *no*."

"Let me check."

"Damn it, Dagny. I said I'm fine. Stop treating me like a child."

I glared back. The bat had startled us, but that was no reason for him to berate me. It had unnerved him, so I let it go.

"That scared the hell out of me," I said. "I thought bats only flew at night."

"Maybe we scared it."

"How did we do that? We were the only ones frightened."

"I don't know. Maybe it's sick."

I peered into the cave, unsettled. "That freaked me out."

"What's wrong?" Brad asked.

"I'm not sure. Maybe it's just my worry about the trip, but that felt like a bad omen."

Brad frowned and put his hands on his hips. "You're being silly. Do you want to back out?"

"I didn't say that."

Brad scratched his head and ruffled his hair. "Come on, let's go back. I need to take a long shower."

"And check the weather again?"

"What's that supposed to mean?" Brad asked. He stomped away before I could answer.

I turned and gazed at the cave's throbbing walls. It seemed as if the rock itself was alive, and I was looking at the snake king. I shivered and followed Brad.

CHAPTER EIGHT

I stood in the starboard helm with my fingers wrapped tight around the wheel and watched Brad untie the stern line. The harbor looked as flat as a pond, and for a moment, I felt like a child pretending to be a ship's captain, but the red life vest, pulled tight around me, did not support my fantasy. I had no idea what I was doing, and I might as well have been holding the wheel of a 747 jumbo jet.

Brad coiled the line and took the helm, and I sat on a bench behind him, relieved to yield my responsibility. He turned the key in the ignition and the diesel engine purred to life, sending vibrations through the soles of my sneakers and into my feet. When the engine warmed, he activated the side thrusters and pushed the yacht away from the dock, then fired the bow thruster and pointed us toward the channel.

Here we go.

My heart threatened to pound out of my chest, and I broke out in a cool sweat, despite the Xanax coursing through my system. I had not known until this moment, until we shoved off, if I had the courage to accept Brad's challenge. It would have been easy to climb back on the dock, hail a cab to the airport, and fly home. It would be simple to go back to my life, avoid my aquaphobia, ignore our marital problems—refuse to confront Emma's death. But if I gave up now, I could not see a way forward.

I stood, leaned over the gunwale, and gazed at water separating our boat from the dock—a saltwater moat imprisoning me onboard. A chill ran down my spine and my muscles tightened. We floated ten feet away, and I could almost reach out and touch it, but we were no longer tethered to terra firma.

We were at sea.

Brad saw the apprehension in my face and smiled. It was not a pleasant smile, but a smug and arrogant one, and I wanted to push him overboard.

"I know you're afraid of the water, but don't worry," Brad said.

"I'm not afraid of the water. I'm afraid of drowning."

"You're safe. We have the dinghy in the tender garage and an inflatable four-man life raft stored in the port berth. Besides, this boat is all but unsinkable."

"They said that about the Titanic."

Brad navigated past yachts bobbing on moorings and steered us into the channel toward open water. We fell in line with other craft departing the harbor, a few hundred yards behind a fifty-foot yacht. The temperature hovered around eighty degrees, and white cumulus clouds billowed overhead—a perfect day—except for my paralyzing fear.

I sat on the bench and held on with both hands, trembling, afraid to venture near the edge. The sea pulsed with meager one-foot swells, but I still felt the motion as the bow rose and dipped. The sensation started in my feet and moved through my body. Up and down. Relentless. I held my stomach and hoped I would not get seasick.

"How bumpy will it be?" I asked.

"Depends on the weather and the direction of the wind and current."

"Could it get bad?"

"Of course. We're sailing across the ocean." He spit the words out, annoyed at having to explain.

"This is hard for me."

Brad stayed silent for a full minute, before he spoke. "You're right, I'm being cranky. I've had a splitting headache all day. I'll be more patient."

"Thanks," I said.

"This yacht weighs over fifty-three thousand pounds, fully loaded. She won't get tossed around like smaller craft."

"I can feel the motion now."

"You need to get your sea legs. By the time we disembark in the Maldives, solid ground will feel awkward. Don't worry about it."

"That's not how phobias work."

Brad stiffened.

I shut my eyes and tilted my face to the sun, letting the rays warm me. The air smelled salty and fresh. Water splashed against our hull, the motor rumbled, seagulls cawed. My trembling dissipated.

We motored southeast and Brad followed the buoys into the harbor. We passed between Tanjung Benoa and Seragan Island then cleared the harbor reef. The island grew fuzzy, its detail fading to a brown smudge until only Mount Agung remained visible in the distance. Bali was one of a thousand islands forming the Republic of Indonesia, which cut across the Java Sea like a giant slash and separated Australia from Southeast Asia.

"Now that we're clear of the marina, I want to give you a sailing refresher," Brad said.

"You told me you would do everything."

"You need to know the basics, so you're comfortable taking the helm when I'm asleep or if we have an emergency."

"The wind blows the sails and pushes us across the water, right?" I asked, attempting sarcasm.

"Actually, no. The wind pushes from one direction and the water impacts the hull from the other. We move forward because we're squeezed between the two forces, like a watermelon seed pinched between your fingers."

"Watermelon seed. Got it."

"I'm explaining this for your own good. If I fall overboard, you will wish you'd paid attention."

My stomach hardened as if I had swallowed a rock. He was right. We were sailing three thousand miles across four seas and the Indian Ocean. I needed to recover my sailing skills.

"Sorry. I'm listening."

"The most important thing in sailing is the wind. We have an east-southeast wind blowing off our starboard side, at about seven knots, but once we pass Indonesia and head toward India, the winds will be north-northeast and more intense."

I surveyed the giant black mast towering over the deck. "I didn't realize geography dictated wind direction."

"Trade winds are tied to geography and seasons affect wind speed. Around the equator, winds collide and swirl, canceling each other out. We could even hit westerly winds when we cross the Indian Ocean."

"Can we sail into the wind?"

"Pointing the bow at the wind puts us in irons, meaning we don't move, but we can still sail into it by shifting a few degrees in either direction."

"Moving toward the wind always seemed counterintuitive."

"When the wind blows over one side, it's called reaching, and when it's behind us, we're running."

"I remember the points of sail."

"If you remember nothing else, remember this—sailing is all about the wind direction and speed."

I shuffled to the edge of the gunwale, wrapped my fingers around the safety line, and watched the water slosh against our hull. It left a frothy wake behind us as the yacht pitched over the swells. The motion was not violent, but it was unnatural to feel the deck shifting below me. My knuckles whitened on the line.

I closed my eyes and exhaled then opened them and focused on the horizon. "It's coming back to me. It's simple enough."

"It can get incredibly complicated, but we're not racing, so we don't need to study algorithms. Our hull will heel over in a close reach. Heeling more than thirty degrees is dangerous and we risk capsizing, so pay attention, because winds shift, waves grow, and currents change."

"What if the boat leans too far?" I said, crossing my arms over my stomach.

"It's called *heeling*, not leaning, and if it's too extreme, let the sails out or turn into the wind. Either maneuver will right the yacht and slow us."

"I understand . . . in theory."

"I can talk all day, but it's easier to show you."

Brad turned off the motor, and the deck stopped vibrating. The whoosh of the winds and the lapping of water replaced the throaty growl of the engine. I could have been on the deck of an eighteenth-century whaler, except more electronics surrounded me than had been on the Starship Enterprise.

A hollow feeling settled in the pit of my stomach.

"The mainsail is almost eight hundred square feet. We can furl and unfurl it from the control panels at either helm. A genoa hangs off the forestay in the bow and gives us close to nine hundred more square feet of sail. We control it with this switch."

"You memorized the square footage?" I asked.

"The sails and the wind mean everything."

"It sounds like we need a crew of four."

"Not with this beauty. They automated everything on this yacht. Electric winches control the sheets and pull them through the cockpit coaming until they converge at the helm."

"I'll take your word for it," I said.

"Watch me."

Brad flipped through the control screens on the sixteen-inch display behind the steering wheel. The labels read: chart, echo, structure, radar, sail steer, race, instruments, video, auto pilot, time plot, and wind plot.

"I imagine the space shuttle has controls like this."

Brad smiled.

He hit a switch, and the mainsail unfurled above us—a massive sheet of carbon gray, almost black. The wind was light, but the sail caught it and filled. The breeze came over the stern from our five o'clock, and we heeled a few degrees to port. I grabbed a chrome handle on the side of the instrument panel to steady myself. My body tingled.

"You'll get used to the tilt. When we're flying, we'll heel about twenty-five degrees more."

"I feel like I could fall overboard," I said, my voice a whisper.

"Always use one hand to hold on to something, and when the wind picks up, wear a safety harness and clip onto the lifelines."

Above me, the boom swung the main sail to port. Brad hit another switch and deployed the genoa in the bow. It filled and rounded like a giant balloon. An image of the Macy's Thanksgiving Day Parade flashed in my mind.

"The key is to trim the sails and keep them as full as possible, without allowing the wind to slip off. When the edge of the sail shakes, we call that luffing, and it's a sign to pull in the sheet. If we heel too much, let the sail out."

Sailing was complicated and even the basic concepts Brad explained involved deep levels of nuance—half science and half art. I had thought Brad would chauffeur me around on our voyage, but as I scanned the expansive sea around us, it became clear he would need me.

"The yacht looked enormous docked against the pier," I said, "but now, it feels insignificant compared to the size of the sea."

"Wait until we hit the Indian Ocean. It's the third largest ocean, with over twenty-six million square miles. Come on, let me show you the best view onboard."

Brad sounded professorial, pedantic. He had been unbearable at home, and now, I was stuck on a boat with him for a month. *What was I thinking?* At least he was an expert sailor, capable of keeping us safe. He seemed more confident at sea, as if the boat brought out the best in him.

I followed him to the bow. He unlatched the hatch leading to the foresail locker and descended the ladder. I peered after him and watched him dig into a canvas bag on the bunk bed. A minute later, he climbed up carrying a harness.

"This is a mast climber. If the electronics pods need fixing, we can use it to get up there."

"Get up where?"

Brad pointed at the ninety-foot mast and grinned. "Up there."

I had to bend backward and stretch my neck to see the top of the mast and the attached satellite and communications pods. "You're using that flimsy piece of material to climb up there?"

"One of us may have to, if something breaks."

My stomach fluttered. "Let me make something clear, Dr. Coolidge. The only thing close to my aquaphobia is my fear of heights. You will never see my feet leave this deck."

"I'm teasing. You don't have to go up there, but if something goes wrong, I may. They designed the mast ascender for solo sailors. I'll show you."

"Don't do it. Just imagining it scares me."

"Heights don't bother me," Brad said.

He did not have to climb the mast, but he would do it to prove he was not afraid. For a moment, I saw him as a teenager, trying to impress a girl. His one-way competition with me never seemed to end.

Brad untied a line, which ran the length of the mast, and secured it to a cleat. He clipped a small climbing mechanism to it—a one-way jammer like rock climbers used—and fastened it with a metal pin. He hung a harness off the mechanism and a swing dangled below it.

"You sit in that swing?"

"It's a bosun's chair, and yes, it's perfectly safe."

Brad stepped into it, resting his butt against the chair and dangling his legs through the straps. He tightened a seatbelt around his lap until he was secure in the seat.

"How do you raise the seat?" I asked.

"Like this."

He attached a second climbing mechanism below the first, with two stirrups hanging off it. He stuck his feet into the stirrups and raised the mechanism until his feet were as high as his seat. Brad stood in the stirrups, taking his weight off the seat, and raised the seat's jammer up the line. He sat back into it and raised the lower mechanism. He shifted his weight back onto the stirrups and elevated the seat again. A simple, ingenious design.

He climbed for several minutes, his body getting smaller as he ascended. Ninety feet was high—close to nine stories. My head spun and my legs weakened, and I had to look away.

"I can see for at least ten miles," Brad yelled, his voice almost inaudible over the wind. "The curvature of the earth is so pronounced up here."

"Be careful. I can't sail this thing alone."

What if something happened to Brad? I appreciated his skill, but I did not like having to depend on him. I looked up, and he waved. He seemed comfortable in his element, enjoying the experience, proud to protect me.

I stared out at the blue water and inhaled the salty air. The sea was gorgeous, vast, powerful. Beautiful but deadly. A shiver of fear passed through me, and I clutched my elbows against my body.

I wanted Brad to come down.

CHAPTER NINE

The other boats dropped from sight after a couple hours, leaving only the distant Island of Penida visible on the horizon. The wind strengthened as the sun rose higher and the yacht bounced with a gentle rhythm. The motion made me sleepy, and I laid down on a bench in the cockpit and fell asleep.

I awoke with the sun further to the west, over our port side. My skin felt dry and warm and my throat had parched. I looked behind me at the unmanned helm and bolted upright.

"Brad? Where are you?"

I looked around the deck, frantic, on the verge of panic. Had he fallen overboard? What should I do?

"Hey Dags," he said, sticking his head out of the companionway. "I went below to use the head. I'm not feeling very well."

"You can leave the helm unattended?"

"I have her on autopilot. Taking quick breaks is fine, but not too long. Ships travel fast out here, and we have to remain vigilant."

"You scared me."

"I didn't want to wake you. I haven't seen you sleep that soundly since . . . since before."

"How long was I out?"

"Two hours."

That surprised me. I could not remember the last time I had napped or had slept without having nightmares.

"It must be the salt air and the motion of the boat," I said.

"It does that. We will both sleep better here. Everything will be better."

"You said you're sick. What's wrong?"

"I don't know. I still have a nasty headache, and it's making me nauseous. I may vomit."

"Sea sickness?"

Brad scowled at me. "I don't get seasick."

"I'm concerned about you. Don't bite my head off."

"I don't need mothering. I'm fine. It's jet lag."

"What can I do to help you?"

"Let me explain our route again," Brad said, avoiding my question. "Follow me."

He was always too proud to accept my help. I descended the stairs behind him. He opened a cabinet under the chart table, retrieved a pile of maps, and spread them on the table.

"I'm not great with maps . . . or directions," I said.

"It's easy. We're heading north, off the east coast of Bali. We'll pass through the Bali Sea and head northwest through the Java Sea, between Jakarta and Borneo."

I followed his finger on the chart. We headed toward Thailand on the mainland of Southeast Asia.

"I see."

"We'll continue northwest along the coast of Sumatra, pass Singapore, and enter the Strait of Malacca. We'll sail into the wind as we pass Kuala Lumpur in Malaysia."

"Will we stop anywhere?" I asked.

"We could, if we had a problem, but our plan is to sail directly to the Maldives."

"What's after Kuala Lumpur?"

"We enter the Andaman Sea and turn hard to port at the end of Sumatra. From there it's a straight shot west to the Maldives."

"That's the real open ocean, right?"

"It will all feel like open ocean, but yes, the last leg is blue-water sailing. We will have the Bay of Bengal to starboard and the Indian Ocean to port."

"How far is it to the Maldives?"

"It's seventeen hundred miles from Bali to Banda Aceh, on the tip of Sumatra, and another thirteen hundred nautical miles to the Maldives."

"That part of the trip intimidates me the most."

"It's the longest long leg of our journey and the most dangerous."

"Dangerous?"

"The most remote. We'll travel the vast expanse of the Indian Ocean, on our own. Our course will take us south of India, about five degrees north of the equator. The next land we see after Sumatra will be the Maldives."

I studied the map. The Indian Ocean was massive. The oceans had been a mystery to man for millennia, and now I understood why. Uninhabited blue space painted the chart.

"How long for the entire trip?" I asked.

"It depends on the wind speed, current strength, wave size, and our sailing ability. If we average five to seven knots, we should be there in about nineteen days—assuming everything goes smoothly."

"Less than three weeks for the entire trip?"

"Best case."

"What's the worst case?"

"We sink and sharks eat us," Brad said.

"Not funny."

"I'm kidding, but things happen."

This trip entailed risk, and I needed Brad. He was better at this, and I had to put my faith in him, but I had doubts, difficulty trusting him.

"Can I ask you something?" I asked.

"Sure."

"Will you tell me the truth?"

Brad narrowed his eyes. "Okay."

"Who were you emailing last night?"

"When?"

"When we were in bed. When I asked what you were doing."

"I told you I was checking the weather forecast."

"You slammed your laptop shut so fast."

"What do you think I was doing?"

I wet my lips. "Did you date a lot before we met?"

"I told you I did."

"Did you date any of the nurses at General Hospital?"

Brad's eyes darted to the companionway. "A few."

"When you were married before, did you cheat on your ex-wife?"

He folded his arms across his chest. "Where's this coming from?"

"Lately, you seem secretive."

"No, I didn't cheat on my ex-wife, and I'm not cheating now, if that's what you're insinuating."

"I just want us to be open with each other," I said, searching his eyes for the truth.

He turned away. "Over the chart table you have a radar screen, which gives us our exact position on a map."

I saw no point in pushing it. I inhaled and let it out then walked to the instrument panel. The screen looked like Google Maps on steroids.

"And this is a satellite phone?" I asked, pointing at the wall unit.

"Yep, and you have access to most of our data here on these instrument panels."

"We can control the boat from here?"

"We can monitor it, but we need to steer and control the sails from the helm. Here's something you'll love. We have a TracPhone V7-HTS satellite system."

"Just what I've always wanted. What the hell is that?"

"The entire yacht is a Wi-Fi hotspot. You can access the internet from your Mac and email, surf the net, even make Skype calls. It's a crazy expensive system, but it's better than relying on a satellite phone. This yacht has all the creature comforts."

That excited me. We were not as disconnected as I had thought. "We can call for help if we need it?"

"If we're sinking, sure. The question is, would anyone come?"

My stomach rolled, and I turned away from him.

"What's wrong?" He asked.

"Let's not talk about sinking."

"We're almost unsinkable."

"Don't jinx us."

Brad walked around the chart table and touched my shoulder. "I shouldn't have said that. It will be fine."

I turned to him and smiled, thankful for the human touch. "I'm glad you're comfortable on a boat. You know I wouldn't have come without you."

"I'm doing this for you."

"This trip must have caused you problems at work. How did you wrangle a month off?"

Brad lowered his brow and pulled his hand away. "It wasn't hard, and we needed to do this."

"Who's taking care of your patients while we're gone?"

"The surgical team split them up."

"Were they okay covering your shifts for this long?

He rubbed his neck. "It's a hospital. They can handle any emergencies."

"I didn't mean to stress you out," I said. "Speaking of emergencies, do we have a medical kit? I brought Dramamine and aspirin, but nothing more serious. I guess I didn't think about how isolated we would be, and I didn't have time to plan."

I immediately regretted the barb which sounded passive aggressive. If Brad had noticed, he did not mention it. He walked into the port berth, opened a cabinet, and dragged out a large medical bag.

"This is a maritime medicine bag. It contains a standard first aid kit, larger dressings for deep wounds, and a module with airways, neck collars, splints, needles, homeostatic clamps . . . all the gear we need for serious trauma."

"No prescription meds?"

"I couldn't get them without jumping through a lot of hoops. Indonesia has strict narcotics laws."

"I'll try not to get injured," I said.

"If either of us has a serious problem, we can contact local authorities, wherever we are, and head to port."

"Contact them how?"

"Use the sat phone or the radio. The directions are next to them. In a catastrophic event, like a life-threatening accident, we can request an evacuation. The yacht's owner has a contract with Medevac Worldwide Rescue. Their numbers are in the manual."

"If two surgeons can't handle it, we're in trouble," I said. "Anything else?"

"There's a fire extinguisher under the sink in the galley. Fire on a boat is bad."

"Got it. No arson."

"If I fall overboard, I'll be out of sight in thirty seconds, so throw over as many inflatables, cushions, whatever you can find. Make two ninety-degree turns and motor back to the debris field. It's hard to find someone drifting away and almost impossible in a storm which is why you need to wear your safety harness and attach your tether in high seas."

"Trust me, I won't be going into the water. I'd die of fear before I drowned."

"We should probably do a man overboard drill," Brad said.

"I think you've scared me enough for one day."

"Last thing. The flare gun is in the foresail locker."

"That only works if someone's out here to see it," I said.

"Don't worry. We will be fine. I promise."

CHAPTER TEN

My mind raced as I climbed into our stateroom berth. The trip horrified and challenged me at the same time. Scaring myself seemed like just desserts, but facing my fears also expressed my core personality. Whenever I had encountered obstacles, whether in school or the operating room, I had tackled them head-on. Man had become the apex predator, because of the human mind, and I believed I could reason my way clear of any predicament.

Brad climbed in beside me. He slipped his hand under the sheets and caressed my hip.

I froze. I had known this was coming. We had not had sex during the last two months of my pregnancy and only twice after my body healed from giving birth. Then my libido had died with Emma.

I pretended to be asleep—a cowardly response—but I did not have the energy to reject him again and explain why I was not ready. Maybe I did not wish to confront the possibility that my reluctance involved more than grief.

"Dagny? I know you're awake."

I rolled over and met his eyes. "I can't."

"It's been six months."

"Not yet, I'm sorry."

"You've always enjoyed our sex life," he said.

I looked away. "That was before."

"It'll be therapeutic for you, take your mind off things. If you—"

"I'm not in the mood. I—"

"Focus on your body, don't think about anything."

"It isn't right," I said, my chest tightening.

Brad leered at me. "Or is it exactly what you need?"

"I want to make you happy, really I do."

"It'll feel good. Relieve your tension."

"I'm sorry. Not tonight."

His expression hardened. "I understand, and I've been patient, but I have needs."

"Soon."

"I've heard that before."

He threw the sheets aside and stomped into the head. His outbursts had come more frequently since Emma's death.

Brad had joined the staff at New England General Hospital a little more than a year ago, and a few weeks later, I had completed my five-year general surgical residency and left to become a fellow in pediatric surgery at Boston Pediatric Surgical Center. Brad had courted me for almost ten months before I agreed to go out with him. I had not dated much, and he had movie-star looks, so I had thought, *why not?*

The answer arrived three months later when I got pregnant.

A month after Brad and I began dating, I missed my period. I had assumed it was stress, but then I had missed it again the next month. I had taken a pregnancy test and sat on the toilet staring at a blue cross on a stick. I had insisted Brad use a condom, for disease prevention and as a prophylactic measure, but I had become pregnant anyway. It had elated and terrified me.

I always believed a fetus was a life, so I had not considered abortion. Brad had proposed, both to his credit and to my relief. I had not known him well, but Emma had needed a father, and I had lacked the resources to care for my child and continue my fellowship. Brad's family had money, and he had seemed sincere, so I accepted.

Later, I tried not to judge myself for my rash decision, because hormones had hijacked my system. We had only been together for a few months, and everybody seemed shiny and flawless during the early stages of a relationship. At the beginning, everyone showed their best selves to their significant others. Dating was like a job interview, except with raging hormones and the future hanging in the balance. It only took a few months to discover the corrosion on Brad's spotless image.

I shook away the memories.

Brad muttered over the running water in the head. Sexual frustration made him crazy, and I doubted any other woman had ever refused the gorgeous doctor with the perfect body. He had charisma, sex appeal, and family money—all aphrodisiacs to single women.

So many pretty nurses around him every day.

Not having sex was difficult for him, but worse, this rejection came from his wife. It had been hard for him to swallow, but his anger sprang from deeper psychological roots. His experience had conditioned him to get what he wanted. His parents had spoiled him and when things did not go his way, his frustration turned into anger.

And violence.

The head door opened, and Brad glowered at me with a familiar glint in his eyes—wild, hungry—like a lion stalking its prey. The hair rose on my neck. I closed my eyes and pretended to sleep.

CHAPTER ELEVEN

On the seventh day of our voyage, I awoke on the couch in the salon. Afternoon naps had become part of my daily routine. The yacht pitched up and down, but I had my sea legs and barely noticed. Now, the motion relaxed me, and when I lay in bed, it lulled me to sleep like a child. I pictured Emma in her crib and stood.

It had taken six days for us to cross the Java Sea, longer than expected, because the winds had shifted and weakened. We sailed northwest toward Singapore, between the islands of Java and Borneo, with the South China Sea to our north. Brad said we should reach the Strait of Malacca, between Indonesia and Malaysia, sometime this evening.

The most dangerous part of our voyage lay beyond, in the vastness of the Indian Ocean.

The sun hung low on the horizon and the breeze cooled. It happened fast, like someone had thrown a switch. I slipped on a crimson Harvard sweatshirt over my bikini. The temperature hovered in the mid-seventies at night, but the sea breeze made it feel chillier.

I climbed the stairs to the cockpit with ease, now accustomed to the rise and fall of the bow, the tilt of the deck, a world in constant motion. I had grown acclimated to miles of shimmering blue seas, the salty air, the relentless sun. We saw an occasional sailboat or tanker on the horizon, but we were otherwise alone. My aquaphobia had diminished to background static, like a television in the next room. The tremors returned if I dwelled on it, but I concentrated on other things and kept my fear in remission.

"Good you're awake," Brad said from behind the wheel.

"Still have your headache?" I asked.

"It's worse."

"Should I worry?"

He massaged his temples. "I've had a headache and fatigue since we left Bali. It's jet lag."

"For a full week?"

"I take longer to recover than I did when I was twenty. That's all it is . . . jet lag."

"What about your nausea?" I asked.

"Still there."

"If you get sick, we're in real trouble," I said. "We should stop in port and have a doctor examine you."

"I *am* a doctor. There's no way I'm letting some island quack medicate me."

"Still . . . I'm concerned."

"Keep your eyes open for tankers while I get dinner," Brad said and disappeared down the companionway.

We had slipped into a routine, two sailors bonded by a shared mission and a mutual interest in survival. He cooked breakfast and dinner and did most of the sailing, and I made lunch, washed our laundry, and took shifts at the helm while he slept. My sailing ability improved daily. I also kept a lookout for other vessels in the shipping lanes, which meant I spent my days laying on sunbathing matts and soaking in sun and fresh air. My contribution to the crew involved staring at sea in sullen silence, but it gave me time alone with my thoughts and the space I needed to think things through.

I had unraveled after I found Emma cold and still in her crib. I still could not describe my pain. My greatest fear, the most horrible thing I could have imagined, had happened. I had lost my child. She had died without warning, not after a lengthy illness, but suddenly, without time to prepare.

The worst part, the thing I tried not to remember, was when she died, I had not immediately known. The day it happened, I had woken up, brushed my teeth, and put on a bathrobe. I had done all of that while my daughter lay dead in the next room. She had passed away, and I had not felt it. A part of me had gone forever, and I had puttered around my bedroom, as if my world still existed. I had felt rested, happy Emma had not woken me during the night. I had enjoyed my sleep while my baby girl died.

I had been inconsolable for at least a month after her death. I did not remember most of it—the paramedics, the doctors, the police and their questions. The funeral. Tragedy had brought an unending flurry of activity, a waking nightmare. I could not concentrate or work and had taken a leave of absence from Boston Pediatric Surgical Center. The staff there had been great. Eric had been great. They showed incredible understanding, but there was nothing they could do to ease my pain.

The hospital had provided me with a psychiatrist, and I had attended weekly sessions sitting in a cushy leather chair listening to him drone on about the stages of grief: denial, guilt, anger, bargaining, depression, and acceptance. I had started with shock, an inability to believe Emma had died, which I guess was denial, then I had gone numb and remained that way for six months. I had experienced depression, for sure, but anger too—anger at myself for not being able to keep my baby alive.

And guilt. So much guilt.

I knew children died from Sudden Infant Death Syndrome—SIDS. I also knew unexplained SIDS deaths happened about thirty-five times out of every one hundred thousand children. I had researched it. Now, doctors spoke about Sudden Unexpected Infant Death Syndrome—SUIDS. Who took time to think of better acronyms for the most devastating thing to happen to a mother?

Every day for six months, I had awakened and experienced a split second of blissful ignorance before I remembered, and the numbness returned. I fumbled my way through my days in a haze and when I thought about Emma, my denial turned to raw pain, as if my soul had been sliced open and bled through into my consciousness. I knew I had to accept Emma's death and get back to work, get back to my marriage, get back to being a person again, but that seemed like a betrayal of her memory, because being happy would diminish my loss. I needed to feel the pain, to show Emma how much I loved her, how much I missed her.

I was not ready for happiness. Maybe I would never be ready.

Brad banged around in the galley, and the smell of baked chicken drifted on deck. Night fell over Southeast Asia and the sky turned deep black in the east and fiery red to port. Lights sparkled on shore in the distance, far off the bow. They glowed miles away, but I felt like I could reach out and touch them.

"That's Singapore," Brad said, coming on deck with our plates.

"It's beautiful."

"We'll enter the strait soon, and it should only take four days to reach the Andaman Sea. After that, we won't see land again until we reach the Maldives."

"I'm still a little scared," I said.

"Nothing bad will happen."

I sat beside him, devouring a chicken breast and salad. The fresh vegetables would not last for the entire voyage, so we ate them twice a day and saved the frozen corn, peas, and carrots for the second half of the trip. The sea air, being outside all day, and the boredom had brought my appetite back for the first time in six months, and I ate with ravenous abandon.

Brad finished and got up. I watched him pull a long fishing pole out of storage and attach a thick sliver lure to a metal lead.

"What are you fishing for," I asked.

"Whatever's biting."

Brad tugged on the lure to make sure it was secure, then cast off the stern into our wake.

"That lure is huge."

"There are monsters down there," he said.

"Wonderful."

"The wind will be weaker here, coming from the north, and we'll have to tack back and forth across the strait," Brad said.

"That sounds like real sailing."

"The strait is wide, and we can sail in one direction for hours. Just keep your eyes on the sails in case the wind changes direction."

He locked the fishing line, set the pole into a holder, and wiped his hands on his shorts.

"I'll take the first watch and wake you around two o'clock," I said.

"If your eyelids get heavy, come get me. The strait is congested, and someone needs to stay on deck."

Since leaving Bali, we had taken shifts keeping watch at night. Brad said we could both sleep once we hit the Bay of Bengal, but there was too much maritime traffic in the Java Sea. He told me stories about tankers arriving in port with rigging wrapped around their bows. The crews of those commercial behemoths never felt the impact of a small sailboat.

"The time alone . . . it helps," I said.

"That's why we came."

I had to admit, despite his flaws, Brad was trying to save me. "I'll wake you if I see anything."

"Dagny?"

"Yes?"

"I'm glad this is working," Brad said.

"Thanks for supporting me."

Brad lifted the remains of half a chicken off his plate and tossed it over the transom into the sea. I had noticed him throwing scraps of food overboard after every meal.

"Won't the food attract sharks?" I asked.

"Fish need to eat too."

"I don't think it's smart to chum around our boat."

"You worry too much," Brad said.

"Please stop doing it."

"Don't be ridiculous."

"My concerns aren't ridiculous."

He opened his mouth to speak, then shut it and stood.

He confirmed the Automated Identification System was functioning and went below to sleep. The AIS transceiver broadcast our vessel's identification number and GPS location to any vessel within twenty miles. It also had a collision avoidance function, which sounded a loud alarm if another vessel came close. It was not foolproof, but it was a nice backup if we both fell asleep.

I cleared our plates, climbed back on deck, and sat on the bench behind the helm. The breeze blew across the starboard side, holding the main sail to port. The wind diminished, as it did every night after the sun set.

I watched the horizon. Sailboats had running lights at the tops of their masts, and cruise ships lit themselves like Vegas casinos, but we had seen a few fishing vessels with no exterior lights at all. I also watched for sea garbage. Hitting anything at eight knots could put a hole in our hull and sink us. When we left Bali, my fear had bordered on panic, but days of monotony had dulled my worry, like a sore tooth, always present, but possible to ignore.

I pulled a harness from the cabinet, stepped into it, and connected the tether to the instrument panel. I made a habit of wearing it when I stayed on deck alone. I tugged on the lifeline to ensure it held and rested my hand on the wheel. If a rogue comber hit us or the wind changed direction and I fell overboard, Brad would never find me. The thought of floating on a black sea waiting to be eaten or drowned raised gooseflesh on my arms.

My worst nightmare.

Darkness enveloped the night sky, veiled the textured sea, embraced us. The strait blackened, hiding the marine world below. The surface flattened, making the swells almost indiscernible, and our speed lowered to two knots in the nearly windless night. I leaned backward on the bench and stared at millions of stars filling the sky. The night at sea, away from the ambient light of civilization, turned the world into a planetarium, a canvas painted with awe and wonder, and it stretched to the horizon.

I had never seen anything like it.

As a city girl, born and raised in Boston, the natural world seemed foreign. I had grown up in a two-story, nineteenth-century brownstone near the corner of Commonwealth Avenue and Fairfield Street. Three, enormous bay windows faced the street, and as a child, I would watch the parade of humanity jogging and walking their dogs on the Commonwealth Avenue Mall. The city had soothed me, surrounded me with life, with love—as if the City of Boston had wrapped me in a hug. I remembered listening to the melted snow spinning off tires as cars hurtled down Commonwealth Avenue. The sounds of the city had comforted me like an infant listening to a mother's heartbeat. My father had paid the house off, and after my parents passed away, I stayed.

Until I married Brad.

We had moved to the suburbs, but I kept the brownstone. When I thought about it, I could smell the smoke from our burning fire, as if remnants of the past reached out to me. It reminded me I came from somewhere. It was my family home, my last link to my father, and I would never let it go.

I surveyed the horizon. We were alone. The moon reflected off the surface, like a giant spotlight shining down from heaven. I sighed. For the first time since Emma's death, I felt a measure of peace. Maybe I could learn to be happy again.

CHAPTER TWELVE

"Morning, Dags," Brad said, standing behind the helm.

"It's after seven. You let me sleep." I exited the companionway with a cup of coffee and walked across the cockpit.

"You needed rest. It's why we came."

"See any ships last night?" I took a long pull of French roast. The warm, aromatic liquid sloshed over my tongue, relaxing me and sharpening my mind. I could almost feel my synapses connecting.

"A sloop came up behind us from the east on course to intercept, so I tacked to port."

"You sound worried."

"No, not really, but the boat turned with us."

I stopped mid sip and looked at him. "Is there a problem?"

"Don't worry. I shouldn't have mentioned anything, but the sloop made several tacks with us. It's probably nothing."

"What are you thinking?"

"It was strange, that's all. Usually sailboats give other boats a wide berth, but this one took active measures to hang with us."

"Why would they do that?" I asked.

Brad sighed. "Don't freak out, okay?"

"You're scaring me."

"It's nothing, but there have been incidents of piracy around Indonesia," he said.

"Pirates? Are you kidding me?"

"It has happened. It's not as bad here as it is off the coast of Somalia or near the Persian Gulf, but Indonesia has their fair share."

"But pirates? This is the twenty-first century."

"I'm not talking about eye patches and parrots. They have AK-47s and meth addictions."

My fingers tensed around the coffee cup. "Wouldn't they use a motorboat?"

"Probably. I'm being paranoid."

"Should we call someone? Radio for help?"

"We can if they show up again, but I haven't seen them in hours. The Indonesian Sea and Coast Guard patrols the Johor Strait, and I doubt we would see pirates this close to Singapore. Their chance of capture is too high."

"But if they're pirates?"

"They're not."

"Humor me," I said.

"We call for help on the emergency channel and head towards the closest port. We shut off the AIS, so we don't broadcast our position and identify ourselves."

"Maybe we should turn it off now."

"I already did, two hours ago."

The hair on my neck stood. I swiveled on the bench and peered over the transom. Blue water stretched to the horizon. "I don't see anything."

"They're gone. It's nothing. Really. I shouldn't have mentioned it.

"Brad, if we have a problem, I want to hear about it. I can't help if I don't know what's going on."

Brad flashed a condescending smirk, like it was ridiculous for me to assume I could help. I had the urge to tell him his recent behavior bordered on misogyny, but why inflame his insecurity? It was too early in the morning for a fight.

"It's nothing. I'm going to rack out for a few hours. I'm feeling worse. Take the helm?"

"I'm worried about your health," I said.

"It's only a headache, fatigue . . . some joint pain. I'll be fine."

"You're sicker."

"I just need sleep." Brad walked to the companionway and stopped with one foot on the stairs. "Wake me if you see anything, uh, concerning."

I nodded, and he disappeared below. I scanned the horizon again. The idea of pirates seemed ridiculous. I poured myself another cup of coffee and settled in behind the wheel. The back of my neck tingled—as if someone watched me—part of the non-visual awareness everyone possessed. I examined the horizon in all directions, but saw nothing, except miles of sea.

I thought about the hospital and working again. Did I have the focus necessary to concentrate on my patients' needs? Returning to my routine would help, and it would be nice to see Eric again. I missed his company.

The air cooled, raising goose bumps on my arms and shaking me from my daydreams. Black clouds crept in from the east. The morning's nautical weather report had forecast clear skies with only a ten percent chance of precipitation. Ten percent was not zero percent. It would rain soon, at least a sprinkling.

I slipped below and found my Harvard sweatshirt in the starboard berth. I kept it there, along with a few paperbacks and other things, to avoid having to keep going into the stateroom and waking Brad. I climbed the stairs and stopped dead.

Two sails bobbed on the horizon behind us. I could only see the top of the sails, which meant it was over four miles away. I turned to get Brad and paused. Was I acting melodramatic? Was it even the same ship Brad had seen? He had called it a sloop.

What the hell is a sloop?

I would wait to see if it came closer. I took the helm, flipped off the autopilot, and turned the wheel to port. The wind poured across our starboard side, sending us into a beam reach, and the boat heeled. The deck slanted to port, and I gripped the wheel hard, spreading my feet to keep my balance. Years of childhood ballet lessons had finally paid off.

Brad had said the yacht could safely lean until it reached thirty-something degrees. I could draw a thirty-degree arc on paper with a compass, but it was another thing to estimate pitch on the deck. I extended my arm toward the horizon. Straight up was 180 degrees, meaning my arm was at ninety. Halfway between my arm and the horizon was forty-five degrees. I lowered my arm and compared the angle to the deck. We heeled less than that and the sea was nowhere near the gunwale, so we were safe. *Probably.*

I scrolled through the control panel. Our speed had increased to eleven knots and swells crashed against our hull. Brad had warned me about sailing parallel with the swells, but I wanted to see if the ship followed us. I flipped to the sail screen and eased the boom out. The deck righted, and the yacht slowed to six knots. The luff edge of the mainsail fluttered, and needed to be trimmed, but heeling scared me. I stared over the transom and the other boat's sails appeared farther away. Had they turned?

Clouds moved overhead, blotting the sun. Rain pattered on the deck and fog rolled across the surface with the leading edge of the cold front. Within minutes, a turbid stew shrouded us, limiting visibility to twenty yards. At least the other boat could not see us. Would they spot us on their radar?

The AIS was off!

Brad had turned off our radar signature. We would be invisible, or at least unidentified, to other ships. Worse, I would not hear an audible alarm if another ship was on a collision course. I hoped our path was clear, or if another vessel was nearby, that the crew monitored their radar. The rain continued for five minutes then stopped, but the fog remained. Thick white clouds hung close to the water. It reminded me of a Sherlock Holmes book—something in a cranberry bog—but I could not remember the title.

A foghorn blared twice in the distance, off our starboard bow. The sound resonated through the heavy air, like a monster moaning in the wilderness. It chilled me to the bone.

What now?

I flipped through the instrument panel and hit our air horn. One high-pitched yelp cut through the air. A moment later, the foghorn howled in response. The sound came from in front of us, off to port. Whatever kind of commercial vessel it was, it had seen us, or heard us, and knew we were there.

"What the hell is happening?" Brad yelled from below.

"We're in the fog,"

"No shit. Where's the ship?" He climbed the stairs and moved into the helm beside me.

"It traveled from starboard to port. I hit the horn, and it responded. I think it passed us."

Brad turned to starboard and elected the radar screen. "He's out of our path and heading south. It's probably a tanker or a container ship. Wait, why are we headed west?"

"I saw a ship behind us and wanted to get away," I said.

"What other ship?"

"There were sails behind us." I looked aft. The sky to the east and south had cleared and there was no sign of the ship.

"I don't see any sails."

"Maybe I outran it or lost it in the fog."

"Are you sure you weren't imagining it? I think I scared you before."

"Yes, Brad, I'm sure I saw it. I didn't hallucinate a set of sails."

He scanned the horizon. "If it was there, it's gone now."

"*If?*"

"There's nothing there now. I'm going back to bed." He went below.

I said nothing. Why had he been condescending? I had seen the ship. It had not been my imagination. It was probably a fishing vessel or maybe a family on a vacation cruise—not pirates. That would be absurd.

I shook the thought away but could not shed the feeling of dread. My fear of water had put me on edge since Bali, but there was something else too. I felt unsettled, as if I had left the stove on at home. I had missed something—something critical—and I could not put my finger on it. I wrapped my arms around my chest and watched the horizon. Whatever it was, I would figure it out soon.

CHAPTER THIRTEEN

By nine o'clock, the pirate threat had not materialized. I had not seen any other boats, and with the wind behind us, I did not have to trim the sails or change course. I sat behind the wheel, but my mind drifted six months into the past and thousands of miles away. I thought of Emma— her smile, her laugh. She had been happy, which meant I must have been a decent mother. She would giggle and scrunch up her face when I tickled her. I hung onto the image of her smiling, before letting my mind go blank and focusing on the sensations of the sun and salty breeze against my skin.

I felt more and more like myself each day, but guilt gnawed at the edges of my consciousness. I had not been a good wife these past six months, nor a good friend. I had been lost in my grief, consumed by my tragedy, and I had not shown concern for the people around me. I missed Jessica. I missed Eric too. They both deserved apologies.

I went below, lifted the satellite phone out of its cradle, and dialed Jessica's number. I wanted to hear her voice, and I longed for a piece of home. Boston was thirteen hours ahead, and I had to catch her before she went to bed. Jessica answered on the second ring.

"Dagny! Oh my God. How are you? Are you okay?" Her voice sounded tinny, echoing over the line.

"I'm fine. I feel better than I have in ages and I wanted to talk to you. Is this a good time?

"Jimmy was homesick for Jersey, so we're sitting here eating hoagies and disco fries."

"I'm on a boat at sea and *that* food still sounds bad."

"I've been thinking about you . . . and Brad."

"I didn't think you ever thought about Brad," I said.

"I don't know if I should tell you this, sweetie, but I heard something about him."

An icy wind blew through my chest. "About Brad?"

"I heard Dr. Emery talking after my shift last night. You remember her, right?"

"Yes."

"She was chatting with Dr. Manson in the ER, and I heard her say a patient filed a lawsuit against Brad for malpractice."

As soon as she said *malpractice,* I realized I had expected her to say Brad was having an affair. Subconsciously, I had been waiting to catch Brad sleeping around. I did not have evidence of infidelity, but I knew it, deep inside. Brad had cheated on me. I decided not to mention it to Jessica.

"Malpractice? For what?"

"I don't know," Jessica said. "I only overheard part of the conversation and I didn't want them to think I was eavesdropping."

"Did they say when it—"

The door to the stateroom opened and Brad walked into the salon. He met my eyes, and I turned away.

"What's that, sweetie?" Jessica asked.

"I have to go," I said. "I'll call you in a day or two."

"Are you upset? Was I wrong to tell you?"

"Not at all. I'm glad you mentioned it. Brad's awake. I'll call you soon." I hung up.

Brad stood in front of me. "You know that's like four bucks a minute."

"Money wasn't an issue when you spent twenty-four thousand to rent the yacht. Another twenty bucks won't bankrupt us."

Brad cocked his head. "Is something wrong?"

"Are we being sued for malpractice?"

Brad's eyes widened. "Who were you talking to?"

"Answer the question."

"Okay." Brad expelled a long stream of air. "Yes, I'm being sued."

"*We* are being sued. We're married, remember? What's the suit about?"

"I operated on a patient to remove an infection, and I guess I didn't get it all. I don't know. Something happened. He died."

"You never told me. When?"

"About two months ago."

"And they blame you?"

"They think it was my fault."

"We can fight it."

"The nursing staff complained too."

"What did they say?" I asked.

Brad took a deep breath. "That it was my technique, my lack of thoroughness. They alleged negligence."

"Allegations have to be substantiated," I said.

"This wasn't the first time."

"*What* wasn't the first time?"

"Another patient died a few months before."

I stayed quiet. Brad had not told me about that patient either. New England General Hospital had hired Brad before I left to take my fellowship at Boston Pediatric Surgical Center, but we had only worked in the same hospital for a brief time, and I had no firsthand experience to evaluate his surgical skill. I had heard rumors after we started dating, talk about incompetence, but I had shrugged them off as ad hominem attacks based on jealousy—catty attempts at career advancement. People could be competitive and cruel, and I knew doctors and nurses who thought demeaning the work of a colleague somehow made them appear more competent. Brad had done the same thing many times. But maybe the rumors were true.

My stomach twisted.

"Are we being sued for that one too?"

"Not yet," Brad said.

"Does the administration think there was negligence? Are you culpable?"

"It's only a simple lawsuit filed by the patient's family. It's frivolous."

"But the complaints from nurses. Did they—"

"Lawsuits happen all the time. You know that. I'm insured."

"Was there malpractice?"

"Everyone's exaggerating, trying to feel superior. The other doctors don't like me. It's all bullshit."

"That may be true, but is there any basis for this? Did you make a mistake?" I held my breath.

Brad shook his head and his eyes drifted to the floor. His shoulders slumped and his head sank. "Maybe . . . I don't know."

I glared at him and my anger gave way too empathy. "What are we going to do?"

"I don't know, dammit."

"Brad, I—"

"I said, I don't know."

"Relax."

"I *am* relaxed," he screamed.

Brad's eyes flared, chilling me. I wanted to speak but stayed silent. I had seen this mood before.

"I'll be on deck," I said, "if you want to talk."

Brad followed me with his eyes.

CHAPTER FOURTEEN

I paced on deck with one eye on the sails and my other on the companionway, unsure what worried me more—sailing or Brad's temper.

Brad always had an edge to him, an unpredictability, as if he lived on the precipice of fury, poised to erupt. Sometimes, he would grow quiet, his eyes would narrow, and the muscles in his jaw would bulge. In those moments, he would remind me of a lion, a predator in the bushes. He had controlled himself while we dated, but I had sensed a gathering storm.

Then, on a wintry day last January, the beast had broken free.

Brad came home smelling like perfume and whiskey and stormed around the house, angry about some problem at work. He had been drinking more since the pregnancy, and his intoxication only worsened his moods. When I asked him whose perfume I smelled, his eyes flared with rage and he grabbed me by the shoulders, hard enough for his fingers to leave bruises. I was eight months pregnant, and it scared me. He apologized profusely after the incident, saying he had been drunk and had not meant to do it. I made him sleep on the couch for a week, and he catered to my needs, waiting on me like a servant.

His exemplary behavior lasted for one month.

Two weeks after Emma's birth, I complained Brad was not helping enough around the house, and he threw a glass of scotch against the wall. That scared me too. He begged for forgiveness again and promised to stop drinking and see a counselor. My judgment told me to dump him, but I owed my infant daughter a stable home and Brad had not touched me—not that time—so I relented. Chalk up another decision to my hormonal imbalance. He stopped drinking and saw a therapist. Things improved, but I still considered leaving.

Then Emma's death trapped me in a fog of despair.

Now, Brad's dishonesty, my suspicion of infidelity, and his seething anger all left me disquieted. Had he always been like this? Had Emma's death opened a portal for his true self to break out? Brad had married once before, in his late twenties, to Helen Swift. Before Brad and I wed, I had looked her up online. She worked as a graphic artist, was a year younger than me, and still looked beautiful.

Helen may have the answers I sought.

I tiptoed down the companionway and listened to Brad's snoring reverberate inside the stateroom. I returned to the navigation table, opened my laptop, and Googled *Helen Swift*. My old research popped up, and I located her telephone number. I lifted the satellite phone and dialed.

Is this crazy?

"Hello?"

My eyes darted to the stateroom door. "Helen Swift?"

"Yes."

"My name is Dagny Steele. I'm sorry to bother you at this hour, but I wanted to talk to you about Brad Coolidge."

The line fell silent, and I looked at the instrument pad to make sure the call had not dropped.

"Hello?" I said.

"Yes, I'm here. I haven't thought about Brad in years. Is something wrong?"

"Brad's fine. I, uh, Brad and I were married."

"Okay," she said, her voice an impenetrable monotone.

"We had a baby, a girl."

"Congratulations."

"We lost her."

More silence. "I'm very sorry."

"Thank you. That's not why I'm calling. I'm concerned about Brad, and I—"

"What do you want to know?" she asked.

I summoned my courage. "I hope this isn't too weird for you, but I haven't known Brad for that long. He's been angry, stressed, lashing out."

"Has he hit you yet?" she asked.

"Yet?"

"Brad was perfect when we dated. He was handsome, charming, and rich. His parents accepted me. Only after we married did the real Brad show himself."

"The *real* Brad?" I asked. I wanted to know what she had done to make Brad's parents accept her, but I let it go. One problem at a time.

"Two months after our wedding he came home drunk, and we got into a fight. He told me he was having a cocktail with some colleagues, but when I pressed him, he admitted he had been alone with one of his nurses. I was jealous and overreacted, and when I accused him of cheating, he slapped me across the face. He—"

"Oh, my God," I said.

"Yeah, it was bad. I saw stars. My cheek swelled the next day, and I had a purple bruise under my eye."

I did not know what to say. "What did he do?"

"Oh, he apologized and blamed it on the booze, stress at work, that kind of thing—"

"That's awful."

"He hit me again two months later."

I clutched my stomach. Brad had a history of abuse. I was afraid to ask anything else, and I did not think she enjoyed reopening old wounds. Static hissed over the line between us—two women abused by the same man.

Finally, she broke the silence. "I left him after that. I assume you went through the trouble of finding me because of similar behavior."

"Brad grabbed me when I was pregnant. He hasn't done it again, but his temper is getting worse." I had not told anybody that, not even Jessica, but this woman knew what I was going through. Only she could understand.

"My advice is to leave while you still can. The Coolidge temper is infamous. He can be violent."

I thanked her and hung up.

I leaned backward in the navigator's chair and listened to Brad snore. He had an uncontrollable temper, a dark side, and it had always been there beneath a shiny surface.

Had he done something to Emma? I pushed the thought from my mind, hating myself for having it.

Brad's snoring stopped.

I held my breath.

He choked, smacked his lips, and snored with ragged breaths full of mucous.

I exhaled and tried to relax, but I kept my eyes on the stateroom door.

CHAPTER FIFTEEN

Halfway to the Andaman Sea, I swiveled in the navigation chair and plotted our position in the strait between Sumatra and Malaysia. In two days, we would turn to west into the Bay of Bengal and begin our long sail to the Maldives. It would be blue-water sailing, with no land within hundreds of miles. We would be on our own.

Unable to relax, I stood and climbed the stairs into the cockpit.

Brad manned the helm wearing white shorts and a white polo shirt. He was thirty-seven, and his first gray hair had recently appeared around his temples, which annoyed me, because instead of aging him, it made him hotter. Why did men age better than women? They had it so easy. With his dirty blonde hair, broad cheekbones, and arctic blue eyes, he bore a striking resemblance to Brad Pitt. Lanky and strong, he had defined muscles and six-pack abs.

"See any ships?" I asked.

"Not since yesterday."

I examined the sea. Nothing but curved blue horizon in all directions.

Brad closed his eyes and tilted his face to the sun. The wind ruffled his hair.

I had to admit Brad's rugged good looks had played a significant role in my decision to date him. And his dogged persistence. He had flirted relentlessly after he arrived at New England General Hospital, and when I left, the flowers and calls did not stop. His behavior had bordered on harassment, but I had been focused on my career, and with no social life, his attention had flattered me.

Men found me attractive, but I had not been searching and had no immediate options. I had only dated four men during my five-year residency at New England General Hospital and none of those relationships had lasted more than a few months. Men had trouble being second priority in a woman's life. I liked men, enjoyed sex, and had wanted to get married, but I had been on a mission. I had worked for years to become a pediatric surgeon, and I was close to achieving my dreams.

Eventually, my hormones had taken control, and I relented. Brad met me at the hospital with two dozen long-stemmed roses and the whitest smile I had ever seen. As a fellow surgeon, I had thought he would understand me better than the others. I had doubted the relationship would lead anywhere, but I needed the intimate touch of a man, the physical release after my long hours and intense surgeries. Brad had given me that. We were not soul mates, but he had satisfied my carnal appetite.

I sat on the bench and watched Brad at the helm. His appearance was his best feature—his defining quality—but what lay beneath troubled me. I had seen behind the curtain.

"Why can't we spot land?" I asked. "On the chart, the Strait of Malacca seems narrow."

"At some points, the strait is over one hundred and fifty miles wide, and we're only twelve feet above the surface, which means we can see less than four miles under perfect conditions."

I watched the swells roll past us. Miles and miles of seawater. "What marine life is out here?"

"There's another world below us. The Indian Ocean is over twelve thousand feet deep and conceals a mountain landscape like the Himalayas. They discover new species all the time."

"Anything dangerous," I asked.

"There are lots of dangerous animals out here—tiger sharks, bull sharks, white tips—but the most dangerous animal is man. We need to avoid the big ships out here."

"Don't forget the pirates."

"They're a threat, especially off the African coast, but we shouldn't have any problems between here and the Maldives."

"Why?"

"We'll be in the open ocean. Pirates target shipping lanes near choke points, like the Suez Canal. Our greatest danger will be our isolation. We will be alone."

"When did you become an expert on the Indian Ocean?" I asked.

"I've sailed my entire life, mostly in the Atlantic, but I've always wanted to sail Asian waters. I've read about it for years. If you don't hate this voyage too much, maybe we can try the South China Sea next year."

"You got me here . . . how, I'm not sure, but don't push your luck."

I set the table for dinner, some kind of white fish and salad, and Brad opened a bottle of Louis Jadot Pouilly-Fuisse.

I never drank much alcohol, probably because of my mother's raging alcoholism. I could not remember a night when she drank less than three or four glasses of wine. After the incident with my father, when I was ten, whatever self-control she had possessed completely disappeared. It had not taken long for her to fall into an uncontrollable skid. She drank every night, then every afternoon, then every morning. When I pictured her, I could still smell the whisky on her breath and the stale odor of sweat and desperation. Her liver failed halfway through my freshman year at Boston University.

I reclined on the bench and sipped the tangy wine, tasting hints of grapefruit and hazelnut. It soothed me, numbed me. It dulled my mind, clouded my memories, and took the edge off my pain.

"How are you feeling?" I asked.

"More nauseous, but the Tylenol lessened my headache and joint pain."

"Are you improving at all?"

"I'll be fine. Maybe it's something I ate on Bali."

"It's not food poisoning. I hope it's nothing serious, but you've been getting worse, not better, and I need you healthy enough to sail."

Brad nodded and gazed at the sea. "I needed this, Dags."

"What?"

"This. To get away from it all."

It may have been the motion of the boat or the wine, but I felt dizzy and a little tipsy after only two glasses.

Brad leaned across the couch and parted his lips to kiss me. It took me by surprise, and I turned my head away without thinking. His lips landed on my cheek. He looked sexy, but how did I feel about him as a person—his lack of empathy, his narcissism, hiding the lawsuit from me? His violence. My feelings were ill defined, but I did not desire him. Not now.

He paused and looked at me, not appearing to notice my lack of interest. He cupped my breast in his hand. It had been six months since we had had sex, six months since I had an orgasm, six months since I had touched myself. My nipple rose to his touch. He draped his muscular arm over my leg and slid his hand between my thighs.

"No, not now," I said. "It doesn't feel right."

Brad pulled away and glared, the fierceness returning to his eyes.

I tensed.

"Damn it, Dagny. When?"

"I don't know. Soon."

"I can't wait forever. I need sex."

"I will. I promise, but not right now.

"When?"

"I don't know."

Brad slid off the bench and clambered to his feet, bumping into the table and knocking over his glass of wine. The liquid sloshed onto the table.

"You're ruining both our lives."

"Brad, I—"

"Fuck this. Everything is so fucked up." His face reddened and the veins in his neck bulged.

"I'm sorry, really."

"The baby, the hospital . . . you. It's too fucking much."

"Why don't we—"

"How much of this can I take?" He balled his fists.

A flash of adrenaline hit my system. I sat up and placed my hands on the edge of the table, ready to move.

"Seriously, fucked up," Brad said.

He stomped through the cockpit and climbed below.

I did not blame him for being frustrated, not with the pressure of the lawsuit weighing on him, but his anger had boiled to the surface without warning. It happened fast, like a flash storm. He held a deep rage inside him, and it scared me. What if he became more violent? We were alone at sea, and I could not dial 9-1-1.

What would I do if Brad lost control?

CHAPTER SIXTEEN

The wind intensified and shifted, coming out of the north the moment we reached the end of Sumatra. I took a starboard tack, and the yacht heeled to port, the sails filling and stretching. My fingers tightened against the wheel and I glanced at my safety harness. The early morning sun hovered low above the sea. Brad slept, leaving me in charge. Captain Dagny. I bit my lip as my eyes darted between the sails and the horizon.

Brad popped out of the companionway a minute later. He inspected the sails, checked the radar, and smiled.

"Welcome to the Andaman Sea," he said.

"Are we heeling too far?

"Let me take the helm."

I unlatched my tether and Brad slipped behind the wheel. He was not wearing a harness, but if that concerned him, he did not show it. A lifetime of sailing in New England had endowed him with a confidence on the water I wished I possessed. I sat behind him and clipped onto a lifeline.

Brad clicked through the control screens, studied the chart, then turned off the autopilot. He plugged in a new course—due west.

"I'm glad the wind woke me up. We head west from here, across the Andaman Sea, the Bay of Bengal, and the Indian Ocean. Next stop, the Maldives."

"How are you feeling today?" I asked.

"Achy, jittery, sick to my stomach. I don't know."

"I'm getting concerned. Let's head to Sumatra and see a doctor."

"No."

"But you're getting worse," I said.

"It's only a stomach flu."

"It doesn't sound like a stomach flu. I can't sail this yacht without you, and this is our last chance to make port until we hit the Maldives."

"Turning to port," Brad said.

"Our discussion's over?"

Brad spun the wheel and the yacht responded. Wind poured over the transom, the sails tightened, and we heeled hard to port. I held onto the bench as the bow oscillated between large swells and our speed increased from five to twelve knots. My legs and arms tingled.

"Is this too fast? Is it safe?"

Brad smirked. He let out the main sail, and the yacht slowed. "This is perfect. The currents change from east to west in winter. We're in a transition phase, and by the end of our voyage, they'll be moving counterclockwise across the northern Indian Ocean."

"Can we use the autopilot at night?"

"For now, but the winds, currents, and weather change fast out here, faster closer to the equator. The Bay of Bengal is famous for its monsoons."

I stared at the horizon. "Great."

"Don't worry."

"The sea is much rougher."

"This is nothing," Brad said. "Wait until we hit some weather."

The bow bounced up and down, filling my stomach with butterflies and making me light-headed.

"I feel a little sick," I said.

"You'll get used to it. This is only the beginning. We're headed for the unknown, so get ready to take on everything nature can throw at us."

I went below to find the Dramamine.

CHAPTER SEVENTEEN

A wave crashed against the bow and woke me at sunrise. I held onto the mattress as the yacht pitched like a rollercoaster. Sunlight reflected off whitecaps, streamed through the stateroom windows, and danced around the room as if nature put on a light show. The sea and air sparkled with life.

Brad had taken the last shift and should be at the helm. I hoped. The AIS made our rotating shifts unnecessary, but I felt safer with one of us awake and on deck at all times, and taking shifts provided the added benefit of my not having to sleep in bed with Brad. He had not forced me to fend off any of his sexual advances in days, but my respite would not last. I had not fulfilled my physical obligations as a wife, and my chest tightened thinking about it.

The stateroom became hot and stuffy, and I stood on the mattress and opened the hatches. Warm air blew across my face, a sign this would be another scorcher. I peeled off my underwear and walked naked across the berth into the bathroom, or *head,* as Brad reminded me daily. Brad, the nautical jargon Nazi.

Natural light radiated through a large window over the sink, and I kept the lights off and soaked it in. Being at sea—away from the smog, the people, the traffic—recharged me. It made me feel human, part of nature. *Strong.* The head was modern and sleek, with a teak deck, ceramic sink, and other luxury appointments. I climbed into the shower stall, behind a clear plexiglass door, and turned on the rainfall shower head. I let the water flow though my hair and over my body. I turned it off, lathered, and turned it back on to rinse. Brad insisted we take "navy showers" to save our potable water. We would be in trouble if we finished it.

After, I slipped on a skimpy black bikini, something I had owned for years, but had seldom worn. I had never minded showing off my toned body but working eighty-hour weeks had limited my sunbathing time. I inspected myself in the mirror. The baby weight had disappeared, and my familiar shape reflected at me.

I grabbed a cup of coffee from the galley, climbed on deck, and smiled at Brad. It had been a long time since I had smiled without thinking about it. *An excellent sign.*

"Morning, beautiful," he said, rubbing his temples.

"Feeling any better?"

"Worse. Really shitty."

"Can I do anything for you?"

Brad shook his head.

Arguing with him about returning to port would make him dig in his heels, entrench his position. He never liked me to baby him, not when it came to his health. I sat beside him.

He held the wheel with both hands, his muscles rippling in his forearms, and a light layer of perspiration beaded his brow. The sun had bronzed his skin, and despite being ill, he looked strong. I leaned across him to put my coffee in the cup holder and my breast brushed his arm.

Brad smiled.

"Brad, listen . . . I'm sorry about last night. I wish I felt like myself. We're both under a lot of pressure and—"

"I'll try to be more patient."

"The past six months have been awful for both of us. I feel guilty about it."

"Let's try to start over, enjoy the trip."

"At least we have a pleasant day," I said.

"Not for long. Weather's headed our way."

I soaked in the blue sky and the thin stratocumulus clouds. "It's gorgeous."

"You're facing the wrong direction," Brad said, jerking his thumb over his shoulder.

I turned and stared over the transom. Giant clouds blanketed the horizon and dark towers climbed high into the sky, like fluffy mushrooms.

"Those look ominous."

"They're cumulonimbus clouds, formed by water vapor riding on strong air currents. See farther to the north, those high, fuzzy clouds are cirrostratus. They're frequently associated with monsoons."

"You're a meteorologist now?" I asked.

"I researched the monsoon threat before we left."

"Can we outrun it?"

"Not a chance, it's moving much faster than us. The forecast has it crossing the Bay of Bengal by this afternoon."

My shoulders tightened and my breathing grew shallow. "How bad?"

"It's a serious storm. Winds as high as fifty miles per hour, according to the forecast. It'll be sporting, but we can handle it."

"How can we sail in fifty-mile-per-hour winds?" I asked.

"I'll reef the sails by furling the genoa and lowering the mainsail halfway down. I think it is safest if I just steer us though the heavy swells. It's called running off."

Adrenaline passed through me, like a cool wind. "Won't the waves be too big?"

"It'll work. If the wind gets too strong, we can try lying ahull."

"What's that?"

"I drop the sails and batten the hatches, and then we hide below. I'll deploy a sea anchor to prevent us from turning sideways, but we will drift and if we turn broadside to the surges, we risk capsizing."

My stomach felt empty and my cheek twitched. "Capsizing?"

"It's not as dangerous as it sounds. If a rogue wave broadsided us, we'd roll over and the yacht would right itself, because the keel is heavy. It's designed to do that, which is why monohulls are safer than catamarans. When double-hulls go over, they stay over."

My skin chilled, despite the warm air. "Won't the cabin flood and sink us?" My voice sounded raspy.

"It's airtight. If we secure it, we may take on a little seawater, but we have pumps and we'll be fine. That's not the danger."

"Yeah, that doesn't sound dangerous at all," I said.

"The real danger from capsizing is damaging the mast. Dragging a ninety-foot mast through swirling currents causes tremendous pressure. It's not difficult to snap it off."

"You're scaring me again. How many ways are there to die out here?"

"Don't worry, this is an enormous yacht. We would only try that maneuver in hurricane-force winds. I'll stay on deck and steer us through the peaks. I can also turn into the wind and heave to, which means I backwind the genoa to counteract the main and keep us close to a standstill. I've done it before."

"You've sailed through a monsoon?"

"I've been in the Atlantic during some good blows. None of them as bad as this will be, but I've been in strong enough storms to know what I'm doing."

"Pirates and monsoons. You planned an interesting trip."

"Thanks." Brad rubbed his temples and grimaced.

"What's wrong?" I asked.

"I've never had migraines before this. I took four aspirin, but it's still brutal."

I stared at the clouds in the distance. They looked menacing, as if they possessed evil intent. I bit my nail and shuddered.

CHAPTER EIGHTEEN

The sea air—humid, salty, tangible—infused everything, as if the ocean wrapped us in its arms. Wispy clouds accumulated overhead. Cumulus masses, heavy with moisture, approached our stern, and monstrous cumulonimbus clouds filled the eastern horizon. The intensifying wind drove the swells high around us and the coming storm propelled the yacht across the surface at thirteen knots.

"The storm looks bad. I decided to heave to the yacht," Brad said.

"What do we do?"

"I'll lower the sails halfway, backwind the genoa, and use the sea anchor to slow us down and keep from being broadsided. I'll stay on deck and steer."

"Isn't that dangerous?"

"I'll wear a life vest and keep my safety harness on. We could hunker down inside, but I know you're scared. Don't worry. I'll get us through this."

"The size of this storm is amazing. It spans the entire horizon."

"Monsoons dominate life in this part of the world."

Brad and I donned yellow raincoats, foul weather pants, rubber boots, and safety harnesses. I felt cartoonish, like a child playing dress up, and I would have laughed, if not for my trembling. Brad wanted me to stay below when it hit, which was fine with me, but I also wanted to be ready in case he needed me. I hoped he would not.

The storm had seemed so far away, but it had moved in fast and was on top of us within two hours. The sky darkened, and the clouds fused into a thick gray blanket. The firmament lowered like it wanted to merge with the briny deep. The heavens opened and rain stung my face and hands. Lightning flashed in the distance, then closer, then all around us. Thick bolts of electricity exploded inside the black cloudscape, stabbing the ocean. Thunder boomed across the surface, loud and terrifying. How could the lightning miss our mast, the highest point for hundreds of miles?

"What happens if we're struck by lightning?"

"The chance of getting hit is less than one-tenth of one percent."

"Those are the odds of losing a baby to SUIDS, so you can understand why that doesn't soothe me."

Brad nodded. "The odds do increase when we're the only boat in sight."

"What if a thunderbolt hits us?"

"Lightning strikes the highest point. We have a lightning rod on top of the mast, which should direct the energy into the water, but a strike could ring our bell a bit."

"What's the worst case?"

"It could jump from the mast and hit us, stopping our hearts or creating other serious trauma. It could fry all of our electronics. Worst case, it could blow a hole in our hull."

I glared at Brad. *Was he kidding me with this?* The weather was not his fault, but he had not explained the dangers we would face. He had pitched this trip as a getaway from our troubles, but it seemed more perilous with each passing day.

"Is there anything we can do?" I asked.

"Go below and stay away from metal surfaces. Unplug all the electronics but keep the AIS alert system on. The storm will reduce visibility to a few yards and if there are any tankers nearby, I want them to see our radar signature."

"What if a thunderbolt destroys our radar?"

"We won't get hit by lightning."

I hurried downstairs and unplugged what I could, but they had built most of the electronics into the bulkheads and I could not disconnect them. The sea raged and our yacht bounced, yawing from side to side like a metronome. I swung from handhold to handhold, propelling myself through the cabin, checking everything. Bile rose in my throat, and I forced it back down.

I climbed on deck and connected my safety strap to the lifeline, my shaking fingers fumbling with the latch. Brad struggled with the wheel, turning us to port, then to starboard, always keeping our bow perpendicular to the waves. Whitecaps foamed atop the surges and we rode down them into deep troughs before climbing the following waves. Our yacht had become a carnival ride and my stomach flipped with every descent. The swells grew—giant hills rolling across the surface—and the rain came harder, pounding in my ears like an oncoming train.

"Hold on to something. I'm coming about to face the storm."

"I'm scared."

Brad nodded. He waited for the yacht to break over the next crest. Our bow dipped, and we increased speed as we skidded down the far side of the wave. When we hit the trough, Brad spun the wheel to port, and we came about. For a moment the swell we had just crossed caught us broadside, but our momentum spun us around and we rose to the crest as tons of saltwater passed beneath our hull. We rode down the other side, facing into the wind.

Brad turned until we were close-hauled, at a forty-five-degree angle to the wind and waves. He furled the mainsail until it was deep-reefed, and the yacht slowed. He reefed the genoa too, backwinded it, and canted the wheel to port to let the contrasting forces cancel each other. The genoa backfilled, arresting our forward momentum, and we hove to. Waves splashed over the bow.

Brad set the wheel and pulled a sea anchor from a bag. It was a submarine parachute and would keep our bow facing the wind. He took a knee and rubbed his forehead, as if he was in pain.

"Take the helm, but don't turn the wheel unless we drift. Keep us pointed into the waves."

"You're much sicker today," I said, but the wind carried my words away.

Brad stopped as if he would say something else, then shrugged and shuffled along the starboard gunwale. He carried the sea anchor in his left hand, using his right to clip his safety strap onto the lifelines. He had to unclip every five feet when the clasp hit a stanchion and then secure to the next section of line. The deck pitched and yawed as the bow plowed through the oncoming waves. Water splashed high over the sides, soaking him. He fell to his knees but staggered to his feet and pressed forward.

I could not take my eyes off him.

It took him almost five minutes to reach the bow where he hooked onto a lifeline near the bow sprit and spread his feet for balance. I could barely see him through sheets of driving rain. The bow pierced the crest of a wave and the yacht hovered for a moment, before canting forward and taking a frothy, avalanchine slide into the trough. My stomach turned, as if I was skydiving. The bow crashed into the next whitecap and Brad disappeared behind a cloud of frothy sea. My heart raced.

The mist cleared as we climbed the next liquid mountain. Brad stood there, facing the raging storm.

At the peak, he spun his body like an Olympian in the hammer toss and threw the sea anchor over the bow. It hit the surface and expanded. The yacht jerked as the sea anchor dragged against the force of the sea and we slowed. Brad gave me a thumbs up and made his way back to me.

"The anchor will keep our bow pointed in the right direction. Get below and batten the hatches and secure the compartments. I want to stay on deck in case anything happens. I've got the helm."

Brad sounded commanding and strong. He took charge and knew what to do. I had never seen him with this kind of confidence at home, or even in the hospital, but here, he was in his element. Had he been born two centuries too late? I worried about leaving him on deck, because if anything happened to him, I would be lost. I could never survive on the ocean alone. I squeezed his arm and retreated below, pulling the hatch closed behind me.

Rainwater poured off my rain suit onto the deck, and I shrugged it off. I walked around the chart table, salon, and galley, making sure I had unplugged every device. I confirmed the AIS broadcast our identification and position, and I flicked on the radar screen. We were alone.

The cabin deck continued to pitch, but with our speed reduced, the movement was less violent, and I used handholds to drag myself into the starboard berth. I sat on the bed and squinted through the porthole at Brad behind the helm then I laid back and held the sides of the mattress to keep from sliding. I tried not to cry.

If he meant for this trip to relax me, sailing through a deadly environment seemed an odd choice, but I had to admit, facing mortal danger had taken my mind off Emma. The fundamental striving for survival quitted my inner critic, silenced my meaningless worry, and focused my faculties. Sailing had literally and figuratively put me back in charge of my life. It made me conscious of my choices, forced me to act instead of wandering around in a daze.

I grabbed onto the bed frame, locking my fingers around it as if my hands were vices, and flexed the muscles in my arms to steady myself. My heart pounded in my ears from exertion and fear. Our precarious position reminded me that life was fragile, that I was alive, and that I wanted to stay that way.

Faced with death, I knew I wanted to live.

CHAPTER NINETEEN

I stood at the helm with my fingers wrapped around the wheel. The sky had cleared after the storm passed, but a powerful northeast wind continued to blow, and the yacht heeled hard to port. *What if a rogue wave hit us?* I shivered. Being on the ocean was like rock climbing without a rope. If anything went wrong, we had limited options and no one to save us. Facing genuine danger made the everyday irritants at home seem trivial.

Brad had been at the helm all night, valiantly steering us through cresting waves and gale-force winds. His sickness had weakened him, but somehow, he had persevered. The monsoon had pushed us over seventy-five miles further south than we had planned, but he plotted a fresh course toward the Maldives and set the autopilot before retiring. His health had worsened since Bali. He had only been asleep in the stateroom for an hour, so it would be cruel to rouse him.

We sailed on a beam reach, and the harder the wind raged, the more nervous I became. If we heeled too much, Brad had told me to either let out the sails or turn away from the wind. I knew I should make some sort of correction, but I worried about messing with the sails. One mistake and I could capsize us. I decided to turn southwest. I flipped to the autopilot on the control screen, switched it off, and rotated the wheel a few degrees. The yacht responded, and the compass spun as we veered to port.

Wind gusted over the transom and our deck leveled, but we slowed too much. The sail leech luffed, and the canvas flapped like bedsheets on a clothesline, and I worried about making an accidental jibe. I let the boom out and the sails filled again. Our speed increased as we ran away from the wind. I smiled, proud of my adjustments, and pictured my father watching me handle the tiller between buoys in Boston Harbor.

I manned the helm for hours, all by myself, my confidence growing. Brad slept all morning, and I checked on him after lunch. He looked unconscious, drooling on the pillow and snoring. He needed his rest, so I tiptoed out of the cabin.

At about four o'clock, he emerged from below, his hair tussled, and the shape of his pillow imprinted on his cheek.

"How long was I out?" he asked, his voice hoarse and groggy.

"Nine hours."

"Wow. I must have been drained. I can't seem to shake this flu. My entire body hurts."

"I'm concerned about you."

"Any problems sailing?"

"None. The wind intensified, and we were heeling too much, so I turned away from it and righted the boat."

"You changed course?" he asked.

"A little, to prevent us from capsizing."

Brad leaned over the instruments, bumping me with his body. I glared at him as he read the map.

"We're forty degrees off course," he said, his voice sharp and full of criticism.

"You told me to steer away from the wind to reduce our heel."

"When did you change course?"

"This morning."

"What time?"

"I don't know . . . around seven o'clock."

"Jesus Christ, Dagny," Brad said, his eyes searching the horizon. "You've been sailing forty degrees off course for eight hours."

"Don't yell at me."

"We're making twelve knots, which means you sailed over a hundred miles in the wrong direction."

"I was scared we'd capsize."

"We weren't going to capsize."

"This is supposed to be a vacation, and you said we weren't in a hurry, so what's the problem?"

"The problem is, we're too close to the equator."

I put my hands on my hips. He was challenging my decision, second guessing the actions I took while he slept. My confidence wavered.

"And?"

"The currents and the winds reverse at the equator. Things become unpredictable," he said.

"I didn't know. I was afraid."

Brad glowered, and the veins in his forehead bulged. He turned the yacht to starboard, trimmed the sails, and set the autopilot.

I was wrong and did not have a reason to be angry, but I resented him for leaving me in charge, and then criticizing my choices.

"I'm sorry, but you know I haven't sailed in decades. At least I kept us afloat and didn't run into anything, and that's as much as I should be required to do."

"Just don't change course without checking with me."

"If you're awake."

Brad stared straight ahead, ready to explode.

I cringed, but his anger remained hidden behind his mask. I descended into the salon, feeling his stare burn into my back. I plopped down on the couch and closed my eyes. Two more weeks to the Maldives.

Shit.

CHAPTER TWENTY

Brad's muscles rippled under his tee shirt as he held the wheel.

The storm had pushed us south, and my mistake had driven us farther off course. Now, we floated on the equator where the wind had disappeared. The ocean flattened like a parking lot, and we swayed on the surface as the current pushed us away from Malé. With no breeze, the relentless sun beat down on us and transformed the deck into a griddle.

I sipped coffee and ate our last banana, the end of our fresh fruit. I savored the final bite, brown and mushy. I threw the peel off the stern, and my eyes followed it as it flew through the air and landed in our foamy wake.

A large, gray dorsal fin broke the surface thirty feet behind us, and I jumped when my brain registered what my eyes had seen.

"What the hell is that?" I screamed.

Brad flinched and spilled his coffee. He jerked his head around. "That's a shark."

"No kidding. Why the hell is it following us?" I asked.

My fingernail found its way into my mouth.

"Maybe it's waiting for something to fall overboard or maybe it's just curious. Propeller sounds and electrical fields attract sharks."

"Electric fields?"

"All the electronics onboard emit some energy. Even the human body gives off bioelectric fields. I've heard stories about sharks attacking small electric engines."

"Is it dangerous?"

"Only if you're in the water. Relax, you're safe. A shark can't hurt you here."

"Didn't a great white eat the boat in the movie, *Jaws*?"

"That's happened for real. Sometimes sharks attack boats, usually after they're hooked on fishing lines or when people harass them, but we're on a yacht. Even Jaws couldn't sink us."

The dorsal fin turned to port and dipped below the surface. I jumped to my feet, ran to the side, and leaned over the gunwale. A black shadow, at least twenty feet long, swam alongside us. It stayed five or six feet below the surface and its image blurred in the refracted light. The tail moved in lazy strokes, outpacing us.

Brad put his hand on my shoulder, and I jumped.

"Don't get close to the edge. Sharks can launch themselves out of the water."

I gawked at him like he was nuts. "What kind is it?"

"I think it's a great white."

"Like *Jaws*. See, it's dangerous."

"That was a movie. Sharks don't feed on people, well . . . not often."

"I didn't know great white sharks inhabited the Indian Ocean."

"The most common man-eaters in the Indian Ocean are whitetips, but tigers, bulls, and great whites hunt these waters too. Western Australia has the highest concentration of great whites in the world, and it's not too far from here."

"You think it swam from Australia?"

"Great whites are predators. They move with the seasons and follow prey. Their migratory patterns usually keep them close to shore, but females sometimes go deep."

"Why?"

"I don't know, but I read somewhere that females are different. For the past decade we've had a great white problem off Cape Cod. Conservation laws caused the seal population to surge, and that brought the sharks. A great white killed a swimmer a few years ago."

A school of fish jumped into the air, twenty yards away. Long boney fish broke the surface as if they were trying to fly.

"What are those fish doing?" I asked.

"They're fleeing from a predator. The shark is somewhere behind them and headed their way. They're flying out of the water to avoid getting eaten."

The gray fin broke the surface ten yards off our port side. It slowed and matched our speed again.

"What the hell is it doing?"

"No clue."

"It makes me nervous."

"Just stay in the boat."

CHAPTER TWENTY-ONE

I manned the helm while Brad picked at his food in the cockpit. His appetite had diminished, and he had lost weight since Bali.

"So far, we've had a pirate scare, a monsoon, and a great white shark," I said. "You chose a unique way to draw me out of my depression."

Brad rubbed his forehead and closed his eyes. He seemed weaker and more agitated every day, but he would not let me examine him.

"I doubt those were pirates, and you performed well in the storm," Brad said. "The shark isn't a danger to us either. I hoped this trip would help you. I—"

"It is helping. I know you did this to snap me out of my funk and bring me back to life. Getting away from Boston, getting away from everything, has given me some perspective. I'm thankful."

"Good. I'm sorry, I haven't been as supportive as I could have been. This has been stressful for both of us. Losing Emma crushed me too."

My eyes widened with surprise. Brad never apologized for anything. He had been trying to be nicer to me on this trip. He had serious flaws, but at least he made an effort. I needed to try harder too—for him.

"I'm sure this year has been hell for you too. This trip was a clever idea, and I know you did it to help me recover."

Brad tried to smile but grimaced instead. "There's, uh, something . . ." He broke eye contact and stared at the horizon.

"What is it? I thought you'd be happy I came around to your plan."

Brad faced me. "There's something I have to tell you."

That did not sound good.

"What is it?"

"I didn't plan this trip just to help you. I wanted to leave Boston because the hospital suspended me."

"What?"

"I told you about the malpractice lawsuit, but it's worse than that. I'm suspended, pending an internal investigation."

"You only told me about the malpractice suit after I heard about it from a friend. Would you have told me if I hadn't found out on my own?"

"Of course, I—"

"Why didn't you mention the suspension then?" I asked.

"I don't know. It's embarrassing."

"You should be *more* embarrassed about hiding it from me."

"I know. I—"

"You *what*, Brad?"

"It's hard to . . . it's not good. I think they're planning to fire me."

"I'm sorry you're going through this, but I could have supported you if I'd known."

"Why are you mad?"

I stuck my hands on my hips, indignation building inside me, like steam inside a teapot. "You lied to me."

"I didn't lie, I just didn't tell you. It's not—"

"It's a lie by omission. We're supposed to be in this together. What else are you omitting?" I asked.

"What does *that* mean?"

"You know what it means. What else aren't you telling me?"

"Nothing. There's nothing else." he said.

"Nothing else? No one else?"

"What do you mean '*no one else?*' What are you saying?"

I pinched my lips. I could not accuse him of having an affair without a shred of evidence, but I sensed it. I knew it.

"Now's the time to come clean. I want to hear all of it."

Brad sat on the couch. "Okay, there's more."

I held my breath.

"I'm not having an affair, if that's what you're implying, but I didn't tell you about something else." He closed his eyes for a moment then looked away. "A patient sued me for malpractice in my previous position at Suffolk County Hospital. It's the reason I left and went to New England General Hospital. They, uh, they asked me to resign."

"When?"

"Right before General Hospital hired me."

A knot tightened in my stomach. The practice of medicine had become a litigious endeavor, and being sued for malpractice had grown more common, but if Suffolk County Hospital had asked Brad to resign, they must have found him at fault in the earlier lawsuit. Forcing him to leave was almost an admission of wrongdoing.

"Did Suffolk County lose the suit?

"They settled to make it go away."

I realized I was biting my nails and pulled my finger out of my mouth. "I'm surprised General Hospital hired you with a recent malpractice lawsuit on your record."

"This is hard for me to talk about," Brad said.

I crossed my arms over my chest. "Obviously."

"General Hospital hired me because of my parents."

Brad had not told me his family sat on the board of directors at New England General Hospital until after we were married. I had known they were wealthy and occupied many boards, but their interests ran to finance, not medicine. I never connected Brad's coming to New England General Hospital with his parents' influence, but I had not known about his spotty record.

"They asked the hospital administrator to hire you?"

Brad stared down the companionway and would not meet my eyes. "Yes."

I felt nothing but contempt for him. Committing malpractice was bad enough, but worse, he had used his parent's influence to secure a new position. His insecurity, his competition with me, his need to prove he was better—it all made sense now. Maybe I could forgive him for his weakness, but I would not tolerate his lies.

"This trip, this last minute getaway, was about you fleeing an unpleasant situation. It wasn't for me at all, was it? You wanted to escape—"

"That's not true. I thought this trip would help you."

"You should have told me about your suspension."

"I'm telling you now," Brad yelled. "I don't feel well, and I don't need this shit. Take the wheel." He stomped down the companionway and slammed the stateroom door.

I stood in the helm, unsure of what I was doing behind the wheel or in our marriage. Something caught my eye, and I turned. The shark's dorsal fin cut through the yacht's wake.

The great white stalked us.

CHAPTER TWENTY-TWO

Brad stayed below, complaining of increased nausea and weakness, leaving me to sail the yacht alone. I could fool myself into thinking it was a sign he trusted me, but he probably checked the instruments in the salon to make sure we stayed on course. Even if he did, I still sailed the boat by myself. *Me*—piloting a yacht at sea—something I had never imagined doing. Maybe immersion behavioral therapy worked.

My anger at Brad dissipated, not because I forgave him, but because his lying about his suspension did not surprise me. It was his nature. Would I get angry at a dog for eating a piece of food off the floor? Brad was scared, weak, flawed in many ways, and his efforts to hide his true character from me had failed in less than a year. I saw through him, saw his incompetence, saw his violence.

Brad, the rich, gorgeous, doctor—the surgeon everyone thought was perfect—was a deeply insecure man. Maybe his lack of confidence came from having his parents give him whatever he wanted, from toys as a child, to admission into college, to a job at New England General Hospital. Brad had never needed to fend for himself, to cut his teeth in the world, to survive by his own merit. Down deep, he knew it, and that knowledge had eaten away his confidence. It made him competitive, petty, and afraid. Brad pretended to be a successful surgeon and a powerful man, but he knew he was not. Now, I knew it too. No, I was not angry at Brad. His behavior reflected who he was, and he would not change. Not ever.

He had denied having an affair, but I still felt the toxic infection of suspicion. I did not have evidence, but did I need to prove it? My suspicion meant I did not trust him, and that was the death knell for our relationship. Maybe it was unfair to punish him for my insecurity, but my feelings were genuine and his flaws real. Did I have to remain loyal to him? To our marriage?

A faint breeze, thick and salty, blew out of the northeast and tousled my hair, but I did not tie it into a ponytail. I enjoyed the way nature touched me, caressed me. Being on the sea, away from everything and everyone, made me feel natural, forced me to search inward, allowed me to feel human again.

The yacht bobbed, almost stationary. The sails luffed and hung from the mast and I pulled in the boom to trim them, but nothing worked, and they fluttered, powerless. I became a child flying a kite on a windless day. I set the autopilot and wandered the deck.

The sun dipped low, an orange, shimmering ball hovering over the horizon. Rays of light glittered off the waves. The surface glistened, the air cooled, and the sea smelled stronger, fishier. I stood in the bow riding the swells above the submerged mountains of an aquatic wilderness, as millions of mariners had done before me. Evenings uncloaked a magical quality, hinted at the unknown world below, offered the promise of adventure.

I bobbed on the current, as if I rode atop the bloodstream of the earth itself, and I experienced something unexpected and transformative. For the first time, I understood the vastness of the universe and the smallness of man, but still cherished the significance of a single life. Man was nothing—and everything. My actions had little effect on the universe, yet I was part of it, connected to all beings, a small piece of something bigger. I had never been religious, but I opened myself to the existence of something greater than myself, a spiritual presence. I did not believe in God in the mythological sense, but the universe, galaxy, and the sea before me had all been created. I had been created. I was part of this, and I felt it deep in my cells. In my heart. In my soul.

I exhaled, and the stress left my body, a red cloud of anger, betrayal, and frustration streaming from me. I lifted my eyes to the heavens and saw the first stars sparkling in the nautical twilight. I sensed Emma with me. I pictured her, and instead of suffering the wrenching pain of grief, I warmed with her love.

I felt connected.

Did getting away from the daily stress of my life in Boston allow me to unwind? Did removing myself from the house where tragedy struck give me distance? Maybe escaping the constant sympathy and pity provided me with the space to see myself as whole. Sailing the yacht gave me a sense of accomplishment again, made me forget how my life had collapsed.

Maybe the visceral danger of sailing on blue water had put things into perspective. Out here, it was harder to generate anxiety about esoteric concepts or to drown in negative emotions. Being at sea and in constant peril made me focus on the present, on the world as it existed. Sailing while worrying about things I could not change was like running from a bear and stressing about my taxes. The sea brought life and death, and my ability to reason—not my emotions—was my tool to survive.

I lay on the deck and watched the stars grow brighter.

CHAPTER TWENTY-THREE

I stared across the table at Brad, both of us silent. We had not discussed his suspension again after our fight. I felt a little better for the first time in a long time, so why ruin my mood with a confrontation? The psychological contentment I experienced had massaged my soul and given me a moment of peace in the storm. I could not lose it. Not yet.

I ate my salad and smiled at him. I softened my expression, careful to keep any judgment or criticism off my face. I averted my eyes, like a polite stranger on the sidewalk. *I come in peace.*

Brad had slept for hours, his symptoms worsening. He seemed much weaker than yesterday, and his food lay untouched on his plate.

He leaned back and leered at my body. It had been hot all day, and I had shed my shorts and tee shirt in favor of my Brazilian bikini—a gift from Brad. My more modest swimsuit sat in the washing machine, and I wore this for the first time. My breasts bulged out of it and the thong left little to the imagination.

He stared at my chest without an ounce of self-consciousness. Apparently, he had forgotten our fight and did not care what I thought about him. Men were simple. His eyes glazed over from the wine. Almost nothing remained in the second bottle, and I had only consumed one glass. I had seen that look before. Brad was drunk and horny.

"You've got a sexy body, Dags."

"Thanks," I said, and covered my chest with my arms.

"I mean it. You make me hot."

I looked at the water.

"I want to fuck you," he said. Crass, brazen.

"Aren't you sick? How can you think about sex when you can barely hold your head upright?"

"I can't help it. I'm a man."

"Listen. I know it's been a long time, but—"

Brad lunged, grabbed me around the waist with one hand and squeezed my ass with the other. He dropped his head over my bikini top and wrapped his lips over the material.

"Brad, no."

I tried to push him off, but he pressed his body flush against me, and I felt his arousal against my leg. He was much stronger than me and I could not physically stop him if he was determined. Brad reached between my thighs and rubbed me over my bikini bottom. I grabbed his wrist and tried to pull his hand away. He slipped his fingers under the fabric and touched me.

"I said, no. Stop it right now."

Brad's paused but kept his hand inside my bikini. He scowled with the sour expression of a scolded child.

"It's been six months," he said, slurring. "I need sex."

"I don't feel sexual, I—"

"You're my wife. You have an obligation . . . we have an obligation to each other. Goddammit."

I wanted to lash out at him, to stomp my feet and yell. My sex drive had always been healthy and denying him his release was not like me, but he knew why I had lost interest. He knew what had happened. I opened my mouth to protest.

"Fine . . . okay," I said.

His eyes opened wide. "Really?"

I had surprised myself too. It had just slipped out. Maybe it was guilt, or maybe I wanted to get it over with, so he would stop asking. Maybe I wanted it too.

"Yes, but a quickie. Let's do it before I change my mind."

Brad smiled like he had won the lottery. My hesitation and lack of enthusiasm did not seem to diminish his libido. He reached around my thighs and pulled me towards him, sliding me onto my back. He hooked his thumbs under my bikini bottoms and pulled them past my knees, exposing me. The breeze tickled my skin, enhanced my nakedness.

"Here?"

"There isn't another person for hundreds of miles. I want to hurry, while I still have permission."

He slipped my bikini bottom over my feet and dropped it on the deck. He leaned close and pulled the drawstring of my top. It fell away, and I slipped it off. It may have been the sea breeze or six months of abstinence, but my body seemed ready, even if my mind was not. Brad stepped out of his swimsuit, erect, and his eyes flared with prurient desire. He mounted me without taking his shirt off.

I had little appetite for sex and my feelings about Brad were confused. I had committed to abstinence after Emma died, not as a conscious choice, but from a lack of interest. How could I feel pleasure while I grieved? How could I allow myself to have fun, to seek selfish gratification? My denial had gone on for so long, it seemed normal.

Brad guided himself inside me, and though I was wet and ready, it still hurt when he entered me. I had not touched myself in six months and this intrusion felt like the night I lost my virginity on the floor of my parent's living room. A pinch of pain followed by pleasure.

Brad groaned and moved in and out of me, his eyes locked on my nipples, like my body existed for his pleasure. He had not even kissed me. I gazed at the stars and cleared my mind of dark thoughts. I concentrated on the physical sensations and my body warmed and tensed. My anxiety faded behind the familiar tingle, the flow of blood, the building pressure. I arched my back and rubbed against him, rocking back and forth with his motion—faster, desirous, lustful. I throbbed and my mind grew fuzzy.

Brad thrust deep and stopped. He scrunched his face and groaned, swelling inside me, filling me with warmth. He supported himself with his arms and his body bucked once, twice, three times, then he collapsed onto my chest. I wanted to tell him I was close too, but I did not know if having an orgasm was something I should allow myself to do. Not yet.

Brad braced his hands against the cushion and lifted his weight off me. He stared into my eyes with a hazy, dreamy quality. The tart odor of wine hung on his breath.

"Thanks, Dags. I needed that."

I smiled, unsure of my feelings.

He rolled onto his knees and pulled out of me. He stood and slipped on his shorts, wobbling on unsteady legs.

"I need to crash. I'm wiped out," he said. "Will you take the helm for the first watch?"

I nodded. Silent.

Brad descended the stairs, leaving me alone to stare at the stars. He had been aggressive before I consented, another window into his violent tendencies, a glimpse into the beast within. Would he become more forceful?

I sat up. If I had not agreed to have sex, would he have stopped, or would he have raped me? Now that I had consented, would he expect our sex life to resume as normal and want sex again tomorrow? What would he do if I declined?

I shook my head. How could I even think like that? Brad was not capable of marital rape. He had his flaws, serious issues, but he would never violate my body. He would respect my decision, my right to refuse. I shrugged the thought away.

In my heart, I remained unsure.

CHAPTER TWENTY-FOUR

The sea stilled, and the surface turned opaque as the horizon changed from cobalt to coal. The earth darkened, and the sky transformed into a brilliant canvas of sparkling light. The water lapped against the hull, the sheets groaned, and the halyard shackles clanged against the mast. The yacht became a music box, gliding across the earth's surface.

After having sex with Brad, I remained naked on deck, a part of nature. Human. The smallness of mankind—my very existence—on display beneath the infinite space of the universe. I connected to the earth, to Emma, to God. Emotion bubbled inside me, like lava inside a volcano. My body convulsed with sobs as my grief poured out. I cried for a long time, then something happened.

I felt better.

There, sliding across the surface of the Indian Ocean, beneath the stars, at one with Mother Earth and under the eyes of God—I found peace. Losing Emma had almost destroyed me, but I was alive, and as long as I drew breath, I would fight to survive. I wanted to live again, be happy, embrace the gift of life.

The sails luffed and the black canvas flapped in the wind. I walked to the helm and turned on the instrument panel. I tightened the sheets until the boom swung close to the gunwale. The sails smoothed, and the boat heeled, almost imperceptibly, but I noticed. I had become one with the yacht, sensing its every movement. I was sailing. Me. The city girl from Boston—the woman with aquaphobia. I piloted a sailboat across the vast Indian Ocean, half a world away from home.

Had I given myself to Brad because of my guilt from denying him for so long? It had been a primal act, physical, not emotional. We had never kissed. It may have been obligation, but it had also brought carnal pleasure. Fast, but stimulating. I had denied my body any release since before Emma—a form of self-flagellation—and I needed it. I missed the physical pleasure, but not Brad. He had become incidental to my needs.

Had I ever loved him?

I had recognized lust and envy in the eyes of the nurses on the surgical floor when I had visited Brad at New England General Hospital. I remembered a young auburn-haired nurse—all blue eyes, red lips, and big tits—staring at Brad as he walked past. She had whispered something to another nurse, and they had giggled. Brad always had women eating out of his hand. His stunning features, great body, and wealth were all aphrodisiacs. How many times had he acted on it? Had he cheated when we dated? Had he done so after we were married?

How easy it was for men to have sex. They seemed willing to couple with almost anyone, simply for the physical release. Sex was probably better for men when it involved love, but emotion was not a prerequisite. Men and women differed in many ways, and Brad was the man every woman wanted. On paper.

I had dated Brad for fun but married him for Emma. I did not believe in abortion and marrying my baby's father had seemed natural and right. I had wanted her to have a father at home, and Brad had treated me with respect. And he wanted to be a father. How could I have resisted?

There had been sacrifices. Brad bought the house in Newton and yanked me away from the only home I had ever known. I had always pictured myself sitting before a roaring fire with a golden retriever, but Brad hated dogs, and I had abandoned my dream. Marriage involved compromise.

I had seen signs of trouble right away. Brad had made an offhand comment, saying New England General Hospital's top surgeons were all married, and now that he was engaged, he hoped they would accept him. I had tried to ignore it, but it laid the seeds of doubt. Had Brad wanted to marry me to increase his social standing and please his parents by settling down? If that was his goal, he should have picked a rich socialite, because his parents had never warmed to me.

My doubt had taken root the day Brad met me for lunch on Beacon Street. I had been enjoying our date until he pulled a document out of his briefcase and slapped it on the table. My memory of that moment remained crystal clear.

"What's that?" I asked.

"It's a prenup."

"Are you serious? You think I'm after your money?"

"Of course not, but my parents think—"

"What? That I got pregnant on purpose?"

Brad looked like he had eaten a lemon. "No one is saying that. They're just being protective."

"Of you?"

"Of their business. Our family has run Coolidge Financial Services for generations. Jacob Coolidge founded it in 1898 and it was one of Boston's largest banks in the early twentieth century. It's—"

"I get it. Your family has old money, and they want to protect it, but what does that have to do with us?"

"I'm an only child and I'll inherit all of it someday. They're concerned. That's all."

"I don't give a shit about your money."

Brad's wealth was nice, but I would never marry for money. Women who did acted exploitive, whorish. I enjoyed the money, the luxury car, expensive restaurants, jewelry on my birthday. Having financial freedom was not the most important thing, but it beat the alternative. I had been poor after my mother died, and I had milked the insurance money through my undergraduate and medical schools. I had finished the last of it when I started my general surgical residency, a job which paid little, but offered valuable experience. During that five-year period, the most I ever made was fifty thousand dollars—not much in Boston— but I scraped by, living frugally.

"I know you're not after my money, but they have to be cautious."

"What did your family do? Have me investigated?"

Brad looked away.

"Come on, Brad. Did they?"

"Maybe," he said.

"I'm a doctor, not a hobo, and my earning potential's high. I know my salary as a fellow is meager, and I have almost three hundred thousand in school loans, but—"

"They're protective about their money."

"Their money or your money?"

"It's all the same. They're worried."

"I make peanuts at Boston Pediatric, but after I become board certified, I'll make over two hundred thousand as an attending pediatric surgeon. I've developed powerful human capital and my financial future is bright."

"I know all that, and I told my parents, but . . ." Brad stared into the distance.

"But you can't defy them," I said.

"They hold the purse strings. Dagny, please, I—"

"Give it to me," I said.

I snatched the paper off the table and signed it. I did not need Brad's money.

"I'm sorry. I don't know what to say."

"What bothers me is that you *want* me to sign it. It shows a lack of commitment to our marriage, like you're planning its dissolution, before it even begins."

"They require it."

"If that's true, you don't possess the independence a thirty-seven-year-old man should have." I handed him the signed document and headed for the exit. "I'm going to my condo tonight. Alone."

I still remembered the look on his face. Another awful memory.

I walked along the deck to the bow where the rise and fall of the boat increased, and my gut flopped.

I grasped the halyard and leaned over the side. The ocean turned to ink at night, a curtain pulled over the world below. I did not observe the great white, but I had read somewhere that sharks were nocturnal feeders, and I sensed its presence. Somewhere close.

I stared into the darkness, sorting through my history with Brad. Money had not been the only issue. Brad's family had caused other problems. They had been in Boston for hundreds of years and were prominent figures in the community. Brad never missed an opportunity to comment about his blue-blooded ancestry. He wore his family's history like a crown.

Brad knew my mother had neglected me, and he acted like I had been an orphan he found on the street. He pushed me to take a genetic test and research my family's ancestry. I did and discovered my family arrived in Massachusetts in the 1606, more than a hundred years before Brad's ancestors. Learning my Steele family history interested me, but I judged myself based on my own accomplishments, unlike those who believed they could inherit success like the family silver. Brad had mentioned his own lineage far less after my discovery.

That was when I first noticed Brad's competition with me. It was a one-sided competition, because I believed couples should root for each other to succeed, not hope their spouses failed so they could feel superior. Brad seemed envious of my intellect and of my ability to make it on my own, without a family fortune. With his recent revelations about his botched surgeries, I understood why he was also jealous of my surgical skills. I was a rising star at Boston Pediatric Surgical Center— at least I was until my leave of absence—and Brad might lose his job.

When I examined our relationship, through the lens of his jealousy and competition, everything seemed different. Had he moved me to a suburban house because he knew I thrived in the city? Had it been a way to flaunt his wealth? Had he chosen to escape on a boat because of my aquaphobia? Was everything designed to make him feel better about himself?

I had an epiphany.

I had become a doctor because of my childhood tragedy. I had specialized in pediatric surgery because of my mother's neglect. I had married Brad because I wanted a secure home for my unborn child. I had always known these things, but thinking of them together, here at sea, with nothing to stand between my memories and my reason, led to one, inescapable fact.

I had lived my life for others.

Being a doctor made me happy, but I had to take charge of my life and follow my own path. Chart my destiny and find my happiness. And I had to do it without Brad.

Brad was handsome, wealthy, and had moments of kindness, but he was also narcissistic, childish, and spoiled. It had taken me ten months to agree to date him for a reason. He was not smart enough. He was not compassionate enough. He was not my soulmate, and I did not love him. I had never loved him. Maybe it had been the hormones or my genetic need to protect Emma, but whatever it had been, it had vanished. Staying with Brad would be as unfair to him as it was to me. When he awakened, I would tell him.

I wanted a divorce.

CHAPTER TWENTY-FIVE

I felt reborn.

The sun rose behind us, filling the world with color and light. I had stayed on deck all night, scared and excited, full of dread and hope. Today I would ask Brad for a divorce. Telling him while stuck on a boat was bad timing, but now that I had decided, hiding it would be dishonest. I had to tell him everything.

Today was the first day of the rest of my life.

I stood at the helm and fidgeted, too energized to sit. I sipped a coffee, more from habit than need. For the first time in many months, my mind cleared, and I knew what I had to do. I would return to Boston Pediatric Surgical Center and finish my fellowship. I would move back into my home in Boston and eventually my personal life—my love life— would right itself. I would continue to see the hospital psychiatrist and find a way to cope with my grief.

Brad's violence would only get worse the more comfortable he became with me. It was only a matter of time before he hit me. I had married Brad because of our baby and now our baby was gone. It was cliché to get divorced after losing a child, like so many couples unable to recover from the trauma, but my reasons for divorce were not about Emma. The marriage had been for Emma.

The divorce was for me.

I climbed below, tiptoed through the salon, and peeked into the stateroom. Brad lay sprawled on the bed with the sheets wrapped around him. He glistened with sweat, and his hair had matted into clumps. He looked pale, with dark circles under his eyes, and he snored like a grizzly bear. I backed away and closed the door behind me.

I needed to talk to someone, and my thoughts turned to Jessica. I reached for the satellite phone and dialed. The connection hissed and clicked.

Jessica answered, and I heard the clamor of the emergency room—monitors beeping, the murmur of voices, someone screaming. It sounded like home.

"Dagny?"

"Can you talk?"

"I always have time for you. Give me a second to walk into the hallway."

"Sure."

The ambient noise disappeared. "That's better. You okay, sweetie?"

"I'm good. I mean really good."

"Oh?" Jessica asked, her voice rising. "Let's hear the straight shit."

"I came to a decision, and I need you to tell me if I'm nuts."

"I'm listening," she said, hungry for gossip.

"I'm going to ask Brad for a divorce."

Static popped and crackled over the line.

"Jessica? Are you there? Did you hear me?"

"Oh, I'm here. I've been waiting for you to dump that asshole since the first day I met him."

"I'm not making a mistake?"

"Have I ever lied to you?" Jessica asked.

"Probably."

"I mean about important stuff," she said.

"No, you're always brutally honest."

"Believe me when I tell you, divorcing Brad will be the best thing you've ever done."

"You don't think I'm doing it, because of what Brad and I went through? It's not PTSD, is it?"

"Brad's a narcissistic prick who only cares how good you look on his arm. You're not dumping him because you experienced a tragedy. You only married him because you were pregnant."

I had never told Jessica that. I had always praised Brad in front of her. Anything else would have been disloyal. "It was that obvious?"

"Everyone knew why you married him. He's a goddamned sexy piece of ass, but he does not deserve you. I mean, you're gorgeous too, but he can't possibly challenge you intellectually."

"Marrying him seemed like the right thing to do. It—"

"Oops, they need me. Someone's coding. I have to go. You're doing the right thing."

"Thanks, I needed the reality check," I said, but she had already disconnected.

I tiptoed to the stateroom and listened to Brad's snoring, thick and spasmodic. I would wait. I climbed back onto the deck.

Divorcing Brad was the right call. We had never melded, and I had never become part of his family. Brad and I had visited his parents at their waterfront home in Rockport, on Massachusetts's North Shore. I had sipped tea and shifted my weight on a stiff Victorian chair in their living room, while I stared through their floor-to-ceiling windows at the Atlantic Ocean. They had set the thermostat to seventy degrees, but it had seemed much cooler. I could still picture the expressions on their faces.

"I think you're making a mistake," Mrs. Coolidge said. "You barely know each other."

"Dagny's perfect for me," Brad said. "I love her."

"She's not our people, no offense dear, but we come from different worlds," Mrs. Coolidge said.

There it was—the elitism. I wanted to remind her my family had arrived in Boston first. Instead, I set my tea on the table and tried to make nice.

"Mr. and Mrs. Coolidge, you make a valid point. I agree Brad and I have moved fast, but we're thinking about the baby."

Mrs. Coolidge cast a frosty stare. "There are procedures to remove *that* problem."

I opened my mouth, but nothing came out. I turned to Brad. "I'm done here. Take me home."

That was the last time I had seen his parents. They did not attend our wedding.

Brad had been raised Protestant, and I had grown up Catholic, but neither of us were religious, and I had agreed to a civil ceremony. Brad paid fifty dollars for a marriage license and one month later, we arrived at Room 601 in Boston City Hall—an antiseptic office in a concrete monstrosity. My wedding day.

"Are you sure this is okay with you?" Brad asked. "We can reserve the club and do it next month. I have a hundred people who would come and none of them would care you're pregnant."

Brad had dozens of acquaintances, people he called friends, but he was not close to any of them. The thought of rallying a group of virtual strangers around us to celebrate something so intimate, seemed wrong.

"I don't have any family left and only one close friend. If your parents and family won't attend, it seems weird to have a big wedding. All I need is you." I put on a brave face.

At three o'clock on a Friday afternoon, Brad and I waited for our turn to be married. I wore a stylish white dress, not a wedding gown, because my stomach bulged and the thought of wearing a gown in my state of pregnancy seemed desperate, sad. Our no-nonsense wedding was nothing like I had imagined as a child. The dress, the ceremony— the man. It all felt wrong, joyless. What would my father have thought about a ceremony like this? What would he have thought about Brad? No one could equal the man my father had been. I knew I idolized him and only remembered the good stuff, and I was certain there were things about him I had not liked, but I could not think of any of them. I simply could not.

Jessica and her husband stood beside us. Jimmy seemed to like Brad, or at least he acted like he did. Jessica held my hand and smiled, the kind of look you gave your daughter before she received a vaccination. It said, "be brave and it will be over soon." When it was our turn, I handed my bouquet to Jessica, and stood between two potted plants in front of a justice of the peace.

Jessica leaned in and whispered in my ear. "Are you sure you don't want to run for it? It's not too late."

Jessica had never kept her thoughts to herself, which was one of the things I loved about her.

"I'm sure," I lied.

The judge made a few perfunctory remarks, the minimum to make the ceremony binding, and Brad and I said our vows. That was it. We were married, wed in a government building before a room full of bureaucrats. I felt like the judge had sentenced me.

I shrugged away the memory and sipped my coffee as the ocean rolled past.

I slipped my hand into my sweatshirt pocket and grasped the plastic medicine bottle containing my Xanax. I pulled it out and shook it. Enough pills to keep me medicated until we reached home. I had used them as a lifeline, but now, they did not seem to hold the same power. I wanted to feel like myself again, so I hefted the bottle in my hand and threw it over the stern. It plopped on the surface and floated away.

I would do this myself.

I needed to tell Brad I wanted a divorce, and I needed to do it now.

CHAPTER TWENTY-SIX

Doubt and fear spread inside me like a fungus. If I waited another minute, I would lose my nerve. I went below and knocked on the stateroom door.

No answer.

I knocked louder and Brad stirred. I opened the door and leaned inside.

"Are you awake?" I asked.

"What time is it?"

"Almost one o'clock. Are you okay?"

Brad leaned on his elbows and groaned. "I feel like shit."

"You drank almost two bottles of wine."

"This isn't a hangover. I'm sick."

Hearing that triggered my best impulses as a doctor and I crossed the room and sat on the bed beside him. Despite my decision to leave Brad, I cared for him and wanted him to be healthy and happy. I pressed the back of my hand against his forehead. His skin simmered.

"You're feverish. Does the medical kit have a thermometer?"

"I need aspirin."

"What are your symptoms?"

"Don't baby me."

"Come on. What hurts?"

"Splitting headache, fatigue, aches. I'm hot and my mind is fuzzy. I feel awful."

"Stay in bed and rest. I'll take care of you."

"I can take care of myself, but I'll need you to sail until I feel better. One of us needs to keep watch."

I hesitated. Manning the helm during a windless night was one thing, but what if the wind picked up? What would I do in a storm? I swallowed and tried to sound strong. "I'll stay awake until you're healthy enough to help. I can set my watch alarm and take twenty-minute catnaps on deck."

"Damn it. It's too dangerous to sleep. If you don't wake up, we could hit something and die," he said.

"There's not much of a chance we'll hit anything now. The wind died, and we're only making one knot."

"Tankers don't use the wind, Dagny. Container ships, and other commercial shipping are all over this part of the ocean. I think we're south of the shipping lanes, but we still have to be alert. I've explained this to you at least ten times."

"I told you I'll take the watch," I said.

"Trim the sails when you see them luff and milk the most out of whatever wind we have."

"I'll get the med kit."

I retrieved the medical bag and opened it beside the bed. I pulled a thermometer from the first module and took his temperature. Brad scowled at me while we waited. He did not enjoy being treated like a patient, because of his competitiveness or some macho thing, but I could not help myself. Every instinct I had made me want to care for him.

He looked flushed and diaphoretic. He fidgeted and seemed anxious. I removed the thermometer and read it. "One-oh-one. Not too bad. I'll get you a cold washcloth and a bottle of water to take Tylenol."

"I don't feel well."

I returned and gave him his medicine, then heated a can of soup for him. I held the bowl in front of him.

He pushed it away. "I'm nauseous."

"Fine, but you have to eat. Let me know when you think you can stomach it."

"You need to get on deck. What did I tell you? We could get rammed and sink."

"I'll take care of it. Shout if you need anything."

Brad reclined and closed his eyes. He looked sick. Really sick.

I left and closed the door without a sound. I took my place at the helm and scanned 360 degrees of blue ocean. The wind had disappeared, and the sails drooped from the rigging. If it did not pick up, I would have to turn on the engine and use our limited fuel.

It would be cruel to discuss divorce with Brad while he suffered. Despite his faults, Brad could be a decent person. He had married me and cared for Emma. He had dragged me, kicking and screaming to the Indian Ocean, and had allowed me to break free of my grief—not completely, but enough to clear my mind, and I could finally see a way through my pain. I would always be grateful to him for that.

I could wait one more day to talk to him about our future.

CHAPTER TWENTY-SEVEN

I shook myself awake after falling asleep at the helm. The sun beat on my face, which meant I had slept for more than an hour. I stood and searched for ships, but the horizon remained clear. We were alone.

I would have to be more careful. Brad had been right—not having someone on watch was dangerous and I could not rely on the AIS alarm. I had been awake all night thinking about my future, and I had taken care of Brad all day, so I was not surprised I had fallen asleep. If Brad did not improve today, I would set my alarm and take brief naps.

On our second day without wind, the sea flattened like a lake, and the sails hung like towels on a hook. I checked the GPS and our position had not changed. I stretched and went below to check on Brad.

I tapped on the stateroom door. No answer. I opened the door and slipped inside. The bed was empty. A flicker of panic shot through me.

Brad retched inside the head, and vomit splashed in the toilet.

This is not good.

"Brad?" I knocked on the door.

"Leave me alone."

"Can I get you anything?"

"I'm sick, damn it. Leave me alone."

I stared at the closed door. He must not have slept well. "Okay. Let me know if you need anything."

"Get out."

I retreated to the galley, made coffee, and climbed on deck. The cloudless day caused the temperature to rise. Our yacht bobbed on a current pushing us west, away from the Maldives. I walked around the deck and stretched my legs. Something splashed off the starboard side, and I whirled around with my heart pounding. A large fin cut through the water.

The great white shark had returned.

I moved away from the gunwale out of reflex and tripped over the cabin coaming. I stumbled and threw up my hands to catch myself but hit the deck hard and fell against the lifelines. The back of my neck tingled, and I peered over the side. The black shape swam just below the surface then dove under the yacht.

I walked to the port side, taking more care this time, and combed the surface with my eyes. I did not spot the shark. Why did it scare me? The beast was huge, but we sailed a massive yacht, and I did not plan to go swimming.

I had spilled the coffee on my shorts, so I went below to change and get another cup. Brad tossed and turned in bed. I sat next to him and put my hand on his forehead, which felt damp and warm. At my touch, his eyes swiveled toward me, bloodshot and yellow.

"How do you feel?"

He blinked, like he was trying to focus. "Bad."

"You're hotter. When did you take Tylenol?"

"What?"

"How long since you took anything?" I asked.

"I . . . I don't know."

"I gave you 650 milligrams at eleven o'clock last night. Did you take anything this morning?"

"My head hurts."

"We need to lower your fever," I said.

I retrieved the medical bag and shook two Tylenol out of the bottle. I raised them to his mouth, but he turned away from me. I leaned over to insert the thermometer, and he snatched it out of my hand.

"Come on, Brad. I need to know how high your temperature is. You know I do."

He glared at me and stuck the thermometer in his mouth.

I took it out after it beeped.

"Shit. Now, it's one-oh-two."

Brad dragged himself into a seated position and shook the sheet off, agitated, restless. I got him another cold washcloth and a drink from the refrigerator. He took them and leaned back in bed.

"Lay down and rest," I said.

"I know what to do. I'm a goddamned surgeon too, or did you forget?"

I stood. Doctors were the worst patients. "What can I get you?"

"Leave me alone and let me sleep."

Brad scratched his head furiously, wrapped himself in the sheet, and turned away. He seemed angry and confused.

Fevers could do that.

CHAPTER TWENTY-EIGHT

Perspiration coated my skin in the sweltering heat. The wind had vanished, and the yacht lay motionless on the flat surface. I removed my tee shirt and used the soft fabric to wipe the sweat off my forehead. I dropped the damp shirt on the cushion beside me. Even in a bikini, the still air clawed at my skin.

The wind had been absent for days, and with a limited amount of diesel fuel, we were at its mercy. The breeze would increase eventually, but I did not want to think about having to sail without Brad. I had checked on him every hour, hoping he would get better. I needed him to deliver us to the Maldives.

The ocean sparkled, a rich blue—cool and inviting—but the thought of going in the water still terrified me. I had not swum since I was ten years old and there were thousands of feet of saltwater beneath us. My fear was genuine, and that was before I had seen the shark. The image of a jagged-toothed monster stalking the depths below—unseen and hungry—sent a cold jolt through my stomach.

Splashing water over my face and body would feel refreshing but jumping into the shower would disturb Brad. I opened the instrument panel and flipped to the screen controlling the swimming platform. It appeared simple enough, with buttons to raise and lower it. A drop of sweat dripped off my forehead onto the screen. I pressed the button, and the stern opened with an electrical hum. The platform unfolded outward and descended on its hydraulics until it extended parallel with the surface. The teak deck hovered a few inches over the water.

I searched for the shark before I descended the wooden steps. My eyes swept the surface one last time, and I stepped onto the sturdy deck. The ocean remained flat, with no wind or noticeable current, and the platform felt stable. I relaxed and knelt along the edge of the dock. I stared into the depths, but my face reflected off the glassy surface.

I leaned over, cupped my hands in the water and splashed my face. It was not as cold as I had hoped, but still cooler than the air.

The ocean did not scare me as long as my feet remained on solid ground, and spending weeks on the yacht had dulled my fear. I should have done this years ago. I dunked my hands again and splashed a handful of saltwater over my chest. It dribbled down my torso and onto my legs, cooling me.

The shark broke the surface ten feet in front of me, its gray nose sticking out of the water.

I threw my body back from the edge and fell onto the center of the dock.

The shark rolled its head over and stared at me with a black eye—the face of a devil.

I leapt to my feet and scrambled up the steps. My heart raced, and my head spun. I took shallow, rapid breaths but continued to tremble.

I crept to the stern as the beast's head lifted again, flashing rows of white teeth. Its jaws smacked open and shut, and its head submerged. The shark stroked its giant caudal fin and slid past the dock, in no apparent hurry. The sun gleamed on its dorsal fins as it swam along the port side of the yacht and disappeared beneath the surface.

I pushed the lift button, and the dock retracted against the stern. Maybe the electric currents had drawn the shark. Whatever it had been, I would never do that again.

CHAPTER TWENTY-NINE

I spent the afternoon scanning the ocean and did not see the shark again, but I sensed it lurking nearby, staying close, waiting for something. The fine hair lifted off my arms.

At twilight, I went below and listened at the stateroom door. Nothing. Brad needed sleep more than anything, so I crept in without knocking.

He snored and smacked his lips like he was thirsty. He tossed and turned in a hyperactive sleep. He scratched the top of his head, rolled over, and scratched it again with his other hand, obviously uncomfortable.

I poured a glass of water and set it beside him. I touched my wrist to his forehead, careful not to wake him. His skin simmered.

He swatted my hand away in his sleep and scratched again. When he pulled his fingers away, blood dripped off his fingernails.

I leaned over and examined him. Dried blood matted the hair on the crown of his head. Had he scratched himself hard enough to break the skin?

Brad's filmy eyes opened and grew large, filling with rage. He jerked his head off the pillow and grabbed my shoulders.

"Get the fuck off me," he yelled.

I opened my mouth in a silent scream.

His fingers dug into my flesh, sending shooting pains down my arms. He pushed me and I stumbled off the platform and crashed against the wall. Surprise spread across his face and he gawked at his hands, as if

121

they were controlled by another person and had acted without his permission.

"What the hell?" I asked. "You hurt me."

"I'm sorry. You startled me. I, uh, I must have been dreaming."

He seemed contrite, but my shoulders ached, and my hands shook. I hugged myself, more unnerved than injured.

"That hurt."

"What the hell were you doing to me?" he asked, his tone sharpening.

I took a half-step backward. "I saw you scratching. You're bleeding."

Brad's eyes softened again, and he rubbed his scalp. He removed his hand and stared at his fingertips, which were stained red.

My feet had rooted to the deck. "What is it? Why are you bleeding?"

"Something must have bitten me. I don't know. The bat, maybe."

My blood chilled. "The bat? You told me it didn't bite you."

"I didn't think so."

"Did it?" My throat had constricted, making my voice high, panicky.

"It bounced off me, but I never felt a bite."

"Bats carry all kinds of diseases. You should have let me examine you. I could have taken you to a doctor in Bali."

"I said I didn't know it bit me. It's not my fault. I'm a doctor too, you know. Don't tell me what to do."

"Let me examine it."

"I'm fine. Leave me alone."

"You're not fine. You still have a fever."

"Get away from me . . . please."

I glared at him. He would not allow me to examine his head and insisting would only infuriate him.

Should I worry about Brad or fear him?

CHAPTER THIRTY

Brad attacked Emma in her grave. His hands tightened around her throat, crushing her trachea, and she choked and squirmed, struggling to breathe. Her face turned blue and her eyes rolled white. I reached for her, but I could not move my arms. I tried to scream, but nothing came out.

I jolted awake to the beeping of my watch alarm. My muscles ached and my head pounded. I leaned forward on the deck lounger, my eyes darting around. Stars filled the sky and empty ocean surrounded us. We had not moved or seen another ship for days. Brad's condition, the lack of wind, the shark—all left me with an impending sense of doom.

I could not fall back to sleep after those horrible dreams, so I opened my Mac Air to do some research, which always calmed me. It had worked when my mother stumbled around the house drunk and when med school had seemed impossible. It would work now. The infected wound on Brad's head must have come from the bat in the temple cave. What else could have done it?

I opened a browser and queried bats indigenous to Indonesia. Over eleven million hits popped up, and I scrolled through the results. Indonesia was home to hundreds of species of bats, a fact I did not remember reading in their tourism ads. I searched for the Pura Goa Lawah temple, opened Wikipedia, and read. Nectar bats infested the cave at the temple site, so next, I typed in "nectar bat Bali" and found several ecology websites.

The cave nectar bat seemed like the likely culprit. They were brown or black, with heads shaped like dogs, furry bodies, and pointed ears. They were not carnivores and fed on the nectar of plants. One picture showed a cave nectar bat sticking its long pink tongue into a flower.

Did it even have teeth? Optimism filled me.

I searched further and found an animal website which claimed all bats had canines. My hope deflated. That cave nectar bat had fangs and could have bitten Brad. Carnivorous bats seldom bit humans and usually feasted on bugs or other tiny prey. Small fangs did not always cause pain, which meant Brad could have felt the bat strike him, but not its bite.

But if nectar bats were herbivores, why had it bitten him? I read more.

Sometimes bats attacked humans, because they carried rabies—a neurological disease, which drove the bats into madness. Less than one percent of all bats carried the rabies virus, according to a website about animals, but another website claimed six percent of bats had it. How could those numbers be accurate? There had been thousands of bats in that cave on Bali, and if one percent had rabies and started biting the others, the percentage of carriers would surge.

I researched the symptoms of rabies and most sites urged prevention through rabies vaccinations. According to the Center for Disease Control, over fifty-nine thousand people died each year from rabies, mostly in Africa and Asia. The disease had almost been eradicated in the United States, with only one or two people succumbing to it annually. Rabies vaccines proved effective, and even if a bat bit an unvaccinated patient, a doctor could administer post-exposure prophylaxis. The incubation period for the virus was anywhere from five days to ten years, with an average of about three weeks.

Unfortunately, once a patient displayed symptoms, it was too late to get treatment. It seldom happened in the United States, unless patients awakened in a room with a bat but did not know it had bitten them. Because of that possibility, the medical protocol required administering treatment if a patient had been asleep in proximity to a bat.

We should have gone to a doctor.

I read further and gasped. The mortality rate for patients exhibiting symptoms was almost one hundred percent. There had only been seven recorded cases of patients surviving after symptoms became visible. I slammed my laptop shut.

Brad does not have rabies.

But if he did and these were the first symptoms, he would die. I could not handle his death. Not now. Not after Emma. He did not have rabies, and that was that.

I climbed on deck and stared at the water. I checked the instruments. I inspected the sails. I paced the length of the yacht. I rubbed my neck and ran my fingers through my hair.

"Damn it."

I was a doctor. Burying my head in the sand may be easier than facing the possibility Brad had contracted rabies, but it was not a rational response. Understandable, but not rational. I needed to consider the worst-case scenario and allow myself time to plan. Brad probably had the flu, but if it was something more serious—if it was rabies—I would have to use my mind to solve the problem. Reason had always been my refuge, and I would think my way through this.

I opened my laptop and scrolled through the symptoms again. After the incubation period, infected patients displayed flu-like symptoms for two to ten days. Patients presented headaches, weakness, nausea, anxiety, and hyperactivity. Rabies attacked the neurological system and caused confusion and cerebral dysfunction. Brad had displayed all of those symptoms, but the flu could also explain it.

Except his bloody head.

In the acute phase, the trademark behavior of patients infected with rabies included excessive salivation—drooling like a dog—difficulty swallowing, and hydrophobia. Patients had exhibited extreme fear of water for as long as there had been records of rabies infections.

People contracted the disease from wild animals. Dog bites caused a rabies epidemic in Bali in 2008, but the disease was under control now. Most people in the United States contracted the virus from bats, but any animal could carry it. After furious rabies burned itself through the brain, patients experienced paralysis, coma, and death. It was a savage virus and a horrible way to die.

I clicked on a video of an African man strapped to a hospital bed, with an oxygen mask covering his mouth. He jerked in bed, growling and barking while a doctor documented his symptoms—two weeks post dog bite. The patient's eye flared like a wild beast.

Can this be real?

My eyes darted to the companionway.

I opened another black and white video showing Persian villagers taken to the Pasteur Institute after being bitten by a wolf. One man had legions on his face. According to the narrator, a patient developed hydrophobia on his third symptomatic day. An agitated man tossed and turned in bed. In another clip, he spit water after trying to drink, coughing and gasping. By day five they had tied him to a bed, where he lay soaked in sweat and frothing at the mouth. His eyes rolled in his head. He became paralyzed, sank into a coma, and died.

I glanced at the companionway again. Had I heard something?

I closed the video and opened another, from Bhopal, India. A group of people stood in the street watching a man on his hands and knees, eating food off a plate like an animal. A woman tried to give him a sip from a jug and the man lunged at her, snapping his teeth like a rabid dog.

Tears filled my eyes. "Oh my God."

If Brad had rabies, there was nothing I could do. He could be dead in as few as eight days. I seethed with anger. Brad's ego had prevented me from examining his head on Bali. If I had seen blood on his scalp, I would have known the bat had bitten him and he could have visited a doctor before departing. Now, it was too late. All we had was a medical kit. And me.

What will I do if he dies?

CHAPTER THIRTY-ONE

Brad had been asleep for hours, and I paced around the deck to calm myself. I had suggested calling for help, but he had refused, and I had seen no point in arguing. If he had rabies, there was no medical cure at this stage, but at least I could get him palliative care to make his last days less painful. We needed to find a port.

I sat in the cockpit with my laptop and checked the wind and weather forecasts. I found nothing specific for our location, but they forecast no storms for the northern Indian Ocean. I Googled "no wind in the Indian ocean" and a dozen articles about the doldrums popped up.

"Shit."

The doldrums described a windless vacuum, occurring within five degrees of the equator, especially north of it, where we now floated. The doldrums lay between the East and West trade winds, on both sides of the equator, where the sun's radiation heated the air and forced it straight up. Windless conditions could persist for weeks and flash storms were possible.

We have to get out of here.

I climbed into the cabin, laid a chart of the Indian Ocean over the navigation table, and compared it to the computer screen showing our GPS location. It was fifteen hundred miles from Banda Aceh, at the tip of Indonesia, to the Maldives. We had been averaging eight knots, before the storm pushed us close to the equator. Crossing the Indian Ocean should have taken us seven or eight days, and we were almost halfway there, so if we had a consistent wind, we could make it in about four days. Unfortunately, the wind had died three days ago, and the current carried us in the wrong direction.

I estimated we had eight hundred fifty miles left to go. If some wind returned and we could increase our speed to three knots, it would still take eleven days to reach the Maldives. If the bat had infected Brad, he did not have long. I could burn our limited fuel, but we did not have enough to make it. Turning on the engine could get us closer, but it could also attract the shark.

A shiver passed through me, and I decided not to worry about irrational fears in the face of a genuine crisis.

I checked the fuel gauge, which showed 260 gallons of diesel fuel remaining from the 264 we loaded in Bali. I opened the Beneteau manual and confirmed we would burn three gallons of fuel per hour, at 2,000 RPMs, which should give us a speed of 8.5 knots. At that rate we could motor for 86 hours. I read the reference chart. One knot equaled 1.15 mph, making 8 knots 9.2 mph. I scribbled some quick calculations on the edge of the chart. We could cover 791 miles before the fuel ran dry, but I would need to save some fuel—at least three gallons—to navigate through a channel and dock. We could motor at 8 knots for 85 hours and get within 7.5 hours of the Maldives.

I could also motor due north and try to catch the trade winds, but that would take me in the wrong direction, and I may not find them, which could waste fuel for nothing. Motoring against the current would slow us, and if the wind increased, I could use the sails too, but those were unknown variables.

Brad may not have rabies, but I had to assume the worst and get him to a hospital. If I used the motor, and he did not have rabies, I would only have wasted our fuel.

I read the motoring instructions, climbed the stairs, and started the engine. The vibration rumbled through the bare soles of my feet as I throttled the engine. The sails flapped wildly, and I furled them. I confirmed the autopilot had us on a western heading—straight for the Maldives—and went below to see how Brad was doing.

He sat upright in bed with his head cocked, listening to the motor.

"What is that?" He asked. "What's that noise?"

I hesitated for a moment. Did he not recognize the sound of our engine?

"I'm using the motor to escape the doldrums."

"What? We don't have enough fuel. You're wasting our diesel." He shook his head back and forth in a feverish tantrum. "Don't do it."

"Brad, listen to me. You're sick and I need to get you to port. I'm heading for the Maldives. We can admit you to a hospital there."

"Hospital? I don't need a doctor. I have the flu."

Should I tell him I suspected rabies? He would probably know it was incurable at this stage. It seemed cruel to worry him, but as a doctor, I believed a patient always had the right to hear the truth. It was not my decision to protect a patient from facts about his health, even when the patient was my husband. I sat on the bed next to him.

"Honey, I don't want to frighten you, but there's a chance you contracted rabies from that bat."

"Rabies? Impossible."

"I could be wrong, and I don't want you to stress out. It's only a possibility, but the wound on your head isn't healing, which indicates a rabid bite."

"I scratched it. I'm bleeding, because I scratched it in my sleep. I have the flu."

"You may be right."

Hope swelled my chest. Maybe he had the flu and had scratched off a scab. Even if the bat had bitten him, maybe it did not carry the virus.

"If I'm showing symptoms of rabies, I'm dead," he said, his voice cracking.

"Don't think about it. Try to stay hydrated and get some rest. If this is the flu, you'll recover in a few days. Let me plan for the worst."

"Who's on watch?" he said, panic flashing in his eyes.

"What do you mean? I'm here with you. There's no one else."

"Who's on watch?" Brad yelled.

"Brad, try to focus. There's nobody else onboard."

"We need to watch for tankers. I'm going on deck," he said, and slipped his leg off the bed.

I put my hand on his knee to stop him. "I'll go. I'll take the watch. Get some rest."

"I have insomnia. I tried to sleep, but I can't. My throat hurts."

More symptoms of rabies.

CHAPTER THIRTY-TWO

It had been almost two weeks since Brad first displayed flu-like symptoms and he had experienced two days of acute symptoms. If my diagnosis was correct, he could be dead within a week. I could not believe it. Sure, I wanted to divorce him, but I did not want him to die. This trip had been hard, and what should have been a transformative experience had turned into a nightmare.

Poor, poor Brad.

I went below to check on him and paused outside the stateroom door to listen for his snoring. It sounded like he was talking to someone. I cracked open the door and leaned into the berth. He slept, facing away from me.

"I'm sorry, Emma," he said.

I froze when I heard him utter our daughter's name. He was dreaming. I had experienced my share of those nightmares myself, and I wanted to wake him, but I hesitated because he needed to sleep.

"I know, you're dead," he said.

Icy fingers stroked my spine. I stood in the doorway with one foot in the passageway. I did not wish to wake him, but I hated to see him suffer, and I could not listen to his dream about Emma.

"I did not murder you," he said. "No, I didn't mean to kill you."

What did he say? Did he think he killed Emma? My mouth parched, and the room spun.

"An accident . . . yes," he said. "What? Don't say that. You're mean."

I could not take it anymore. I had to wake him. I walked around the bed and stopped cold—Brad's eyes were wide open.

"Look Emma, Dagny's here too," Brad said, looking directly at me. "Say hello to Emma, Dags."

I covered my mouth with my hands and stepped backward. He was delirious, hallucinating.

"Wake up Brad, you're dreaming."

"I can't sleep. I'm talking to Emma."

"Emma's not here."

"She's standing right beside you."

My chest tightened and tears filled my eyes.

"You're scaring me. Stop it."

"I have a little secret," Brad said, grinning like a madman. "Want to hear it?

"No, Brad. I don't want to hear anything. Go to sleep."

"She's a little bitch."

"Who's a bitch?"

"Emma. She's a lying bitch."

"Stop it, Brad. Stop it. Don't talk about our dead daughter like that. How dare you!"

"I told her not to tell, but that little bitch wants to blame me." Spit flew from his mouth. "I'm not sorry. I'm not."

I opened my mouth, and a sob escaped my lips. I could not catch my breath. What was he saying? Had he done something to Emma? My pulse thumped in my ears.

"You're hallucinating," I said. "Emma's not here. You didn't do anything."

"Poor little Dags. Always the good one. Always so sad. You don't know what it means to be sad."

Brad sat upright, his eyes red and full of hate. The beast had returned.

I willed my body to move and exited the berth, shutting the door behind me. My hands shook and tears flowed. He could never hurt Emma. He was hallucinating. It was the fever talking. That's all.

Just the flu.

CHAPTER THIRTY-THREE

We were in trouble. Big trouble.

Brad's condition worsened, and if he had contracted rabies from that bat, it was a death sentence. I studied the empty horizon. Under diesel, we made eight knots, but it would take three or four days to reach port, maybe more.

Last night, I had slept on deck for hours, unable to cope with Brad's delirium. He scared me. The sleep had helped, but mental and physical exhaustion consumed me. His hallucination had terrified me, and I could not bring myself to consider whether he had killed Emma, a possibility too horrible to contemplate. I could not entertain it. Not here.

I needed advice; confirmation I was doing everything possible. I slipped down the companionway into the salon and listened. Faint snoring drifted out of the stateroom. I plopped into the captain's chair and powered up my laptop.

Who should I call? I could contact Boston Pediatric Surgical Center, but if Brad did not have rabies, I would sound like an alarmist and the staff already seemed concerned about my mental well-being. But I could not ignore the obvious diagnosis because it was too nightmarish to accept. Who could help me?

Eric.

When Jessica and I had seen Dr. Eric Franklin outside the hospital, he had said to call if I needed anything, and he had seemed sincere. Eric had the expertise I needed, and I could count on his discretion. Hearing a friendly voice would help too.

I checked my watch. We floated off the coast of India, ten and a half hours ahead of Boston, which made it eight o'clock at night there. I found Eric's home number in my email contacts and typed it into Skype. The call went right to voice mail. He had an iPhone too, so I tried him on FaceTime.

The screen changed and Eric's face appeared. Seeing him, I almost burst into tears. He appeared confused for a moment, then his face brightened with recognition.

"Dagny, it's good to hear from you. How are you?"

Seeing Eric—someone I trusted and cared about—overwhelmed me. I smiled, but a tear ran down my cheek. "Hi Eric. I'm glad you answered."

His forehead wrinkled. "Are you okay? What's wrong?"

"I have a problem, and I need your advice. Can you talk?"

"Always. Is this about you or a patient?"

"It's my husband, Brad."

Eric nodded, seeming less happy than a moment ago. "What can I do for you?"

"I'll probably sound a little paranoid, but I need a second opinion."

"Go on."

"When Brad and I visited Bali, a bat flew out of a cave and hit him on the head. It's possible it bit him, but he—"

"Did he begin treatment?"

"He didn't notice the bite, but two days ago, I found a minor puncture on his head and it's still bleeding. Do you—"

"Is he symptomatic?"

"Flu-like symptoms. He's diaphoretic, low fever, headaches, nausea, weakness . . ."

"Has he manifested any neurological anomalies?" Eric asked.

"Delirium. I don't know. It could be the fever. Flu does that."

"How long since his first symptom?"

"He's been sick for a couple days, but his flu-like symptoms started over a week ago."

"And how long since the bat bite, er, the potential bite?"

"Nine days. Let me ask you, if it was a bite and if the bat was rabid, could he exhibit symptoms this fast?"

"The incubation period averages about thirty days, but I have known symptoms to appear in as few as five days. Outcomes depend on the strength of the virus strain, the health of the patient, and many other confounding variables. Predicting the disease's behavior can be difficult, which is why treatment needs to start immediately post-exposure."

"He could be symptomatic already?" I asked.

"Yes. We don't know which toxin or virus he picked up, but rabies attacks the nervous system, and symptoms occur when the virus reaches the brain. If the bat bit his head, the onset would be rapid."

I realized I had been chewing on a nail and pulled it from my mouth. "I researched rabies online, and I've seen the outcomes. If he has it, what can I do?"

"Are you alone right now? Is he there with you?"

"He's sleeping."

Eric cleared his throat. "Rabies is treatable before the patient is symptomatic, but once the patient exhibits neurological damage, there's no cure. Dagny, I'll give it to you straight. If the virus has reached his brain and is causing visible symptoms, the disease has almost a one hundred percent mortality rate. I'm very sorry."

I took another breath. "How long?"

"It's impossible to say, but if the behavior you described is rabies, then it's rapid onset. I would guess he would last less than ten days after the first acute symptom."

"Is there anything I can do?"

"Only palliative care to make him more comfortable, ease his pain. I'm sorry. I know this is difficult to hear after all you've been through this year."

"Yes."

Something bumped in the stateroom, and I glanced at the alcove. Brad's snoring continued.

"Based on your description, my diagnosis is Brad contracted rabies, but I haven't examined him, and it's possible you're seeing symptoms of another illness. If there's no hydrophobia, your husband may have contracted something else. My advice is to get him to a hospital as soon as possible."

"That's what I'm doing, but it's easier said than done."

"How can I help?"

"Tell me what to expect." I said.

"Flu-like symptoms for about one week and acute symptoms for roughly ten more. That's followed by paralysis, coma, and death. Some patients experience periods of lucidity as their impending death looms near."

My eyes misted, and I teetered on the verge of losing it. This wasn't another patient; it was my husband and the only person onboard who knew how to sail.

"Why didn't we see the wound bleeding before this?" I asked.

"It's probably a tiny puncture. When rabies become symptomatic, old wounds bleed again. Maybe it itched, and he scratched it open."

"What a horrific disease," I said.

"I have to ask you something, but I want to be delicate. Rabies is a highly contagious virus. The primary factor limiting the number of epidemics is the rapid progression of the virus and the high mortality rate. Have you been exposed?"

I pictured Brad on top of me, filling me with semen the day before his symptoms worsened. I had worried about him and had not considered my vulnerability. My stomach knotted.

"Brad and I were intimate, once. It's spread through bodily fluids, right?" I held my breath.

"Rabies spreads through saliva, or through direct contact with blood or spinal fluid. You can't get it from sexual contact alone, but an open-mouthed kiss would be an exposure."

My mind raced to remember that night on deck. "I, uh, I think I'm fine. I haven't kissed Brad at all. We had intercourse, but we didn't kiss." I blushed, wondering what Eric thought about sex without kissing.

He exhaled and sounded relieved. "You're probably fine, but I recommend you get tested and receive treatment, just to be safe. If you've had an exposure, the clock is ticking for you too."

"I will, whenever we get to land."

"Good. I care about you."

How should I respond to that? "To be clear, Brad's life depends on whether these symptoms are rabies?"

"Yes. Watch for abnormal behavior, hallucinations, aggression."

"Aggression?"

"Rabies affects people in two ways. The virus can cause paralysis, coma, and death—known as paralytic rabies—or patients can develop furious rabies."

A lump caught in my throat and I swallowed. "That doesn't sound pleasant."

"It's not. With furious rabies, patients become hyperactive, agitated, and confused. They can't sleep and often hallucinate. The classic symptoms are excessive salivation, difficulty swallowing, and hydrophobia. The pathological aversion to water is a unique sign. Some patients experience priapism, involuntary erections and orgasms, often dozens of times per day. Certain strains of rabies make people more violent than others."

I stopped biting my fingernail. "That's not good news."

"Where are you now?" Brad asked.

"We're in the middle of the Indian Ocean."

"Can you get to port?"

"I'm trying, but the wind . . ."

"I don't want to scare you Dagny, but this is serious. In the acute neurological period, patients become hyperaggressive. They foam at the mouth and make high pitched groans, which sound like barks. Patients have attacked people . . . even bitten them. There's a reason mythology surrounds the disease."

I rocked back and forth on the bench with a sour taste in my mouth.

"You're saying if he has rabies, he could become dangerous?"

"Extremely."

I thanked Eric and ended the call. I stared at the bulkhead leading to the stateroom. Brad had rabies and would die. He had been sick, exhibiting prodrome symptoms for a week. His violence and hallucinations over the past two days were acute symptoms, which meant he had eight days left, maybe less. He was dangerous, and I had no one to help me.

I faced this crucible alone.

CHAPTER THIRTY-FOUR

I sat behind the helm, blinking to keep my eyes open. I had not slept more than four hours in the past three days and my arms and legs felt leaden, useless. I closed my eyes to rest for a second.

I awoke to a rumble, blissfully unaware for a moment, before I remembered my circumstances and adrenaline surged through my veins. How long had I been asleep? I stood, and pain stabbed my neck and shoulders from sleeping on the bench.

Something felt wrong.

A breeze blew in from the south and the sky darkened beneath thick, black clouds. I picked up the binoculars and scoped the ocean to port. A flash backlit the clouds.

Lightning.

Despite being stuck in the doldrums, a storm had appeared out of nowhere and headed directly toward us. I inhaled deeply to subdue my growing panic. I did not possess the skills to get us through a storm. Brad had reefed the sails and used the sea anchor to keep our bow into the wind, but I would have trouble doing it. He had also explained something about lowering the sails and riding out a storm below but warned we could capsize. My hands shook.

I had about twenty minutes to prepare. I jumped online, searched for sailing techniques, and found a website listing my options. I could reef the sails, use storms sails to navigate, heave to, or lie ahull. Gusts blew harder, and the storm came fast. I had to act.

Since I had already lowered the sails, I decided to ride out the storm below, where I could take care of Brad. I turned the ignition off, and the motors stopped. I dug out the sea anchor and threw it off the bow to keep us pointed into the wind and surging sea. It took less effort than Brad had needed during the last storm, because the weather was not yet on top of us.

I sealed the companionway behind me and ran through the yacht battening the hatches and stowing everything loose in the cabin. I carried two plastic bottles of Evian into our stateroom and monitored Brad.

He mumbled as he slept, and his skin beaded with perspiration. His eyes opened, and he shouted as if he was delirious or having a nightmare.

The yacht pitched as the waves grew. The patter of rain hitting the deck increased in frequency and volume. I had first seen the storm thirty minutes ago, and it had already arrived. Maybe its speed meant it would blow through fast. The doldrums were known for weather extremes.

I wrapped my arms around Brad as the boat tossed us. He opened his eyes and looked up but did not seem to recognize me. Drool dripped out of his mouth and onto his tee shirt. A low groan slipped from his throat, almost a growl. I hugged him close, avoiding his saliva, and shut my eyes.

The hair on my body rose, as if I had become weightless. Energy radiated around me, and my skin tingled, then a deafening crack filled my eardrums. I bolted upright.

Lightning strike.

The charred odor of an electrical fire tickled my nostrils. Light gray smoke curled through the air above us. I jumped off the bed and ran into the salon. Black smoke poured off the instrument panel above the chart table. Flames flickered inside it.

I retrieved the fire extinguisher from under the sink and yanked the safety pin free as I shuffled to the chart table. The wall ignited and heat warmed my face.

I aimed at the center of the control panel and doused it with dry chemical foam. The flames resisted for a few seconds, but the foam suffocated them, and the fire retreated. I emptied the extinguisher, and the fire died. The panel smoked, then stopped.

I panted from the exertion and sweat glistened on my skin.

The storm surged outside, and the cabin bucked like a wild horse. My heart beat out of my chest. I checked the rest of the cabin, but nothing else burned, and we did not appear to be taking on water. The thunderbolt must have hit the lightning rod, which directed the bulk of the charge into the ocean. I used handholds to reach the chart table and threw myself into the captain's chair. The cabin reeked of burned wires, and I gagged.

The fire had charred the instruments like a toasted marshmallow. I pushed the power button. Nothing. I hit several of the buttons. Nothing worked. The storm had fried the electronics, which meant no internet, no radar, no maps, and no AIS alert system. No Skype.

If I could not navigate or call for help, we were dead. I picked up the satellite phone and heard a familiar beep. The phone still worked.

Thank God.

I leaned on the chart table, put my face on my forearm, and wept.

The boat rocked less as the thunder moved past us, and the storm quieted. I climbed the stairs and opened the hatch. The showers had reduced to sprinkles, and the inky clouds moved behind us, dumping curtains of rain in the distance. The sky cleared to the south, and I exhaled.

I donned my harness and made my way to the bow to retrieve the sea anchor. I pulled on the line and dragged the anchor toward me. It weighed a ton, and the taut line cut into my hands. My muscles ached and my skin burned, but the anchor drew closer. I hauled the anchor until it floated under the bow, but I could not lift it.

I leaned over the lifeline and strained with my legs and back. The anchor broke the surface and seawater poured out, dumping its weight, and it flew toward me.

I lost my balance and stumbled, waving my arms in the air. The lifeline caught the hollow of my knees, and I tumbled into space. I reached for the edge of the boat, but missed, and plummeted through the air.

My feet splashed into the water as my safety harness tightened and dug into my shoulders and waist. The tether strained against the lifeline, and I swung like a pendulum back toward the hull.

I threw up my hands and slapped them against the side to protect my head from striking the hull. I panicked, flailing for a handhold. My body ached from the impact.

"Oh, God, no," I screamed. "Help me. Brad, help me."

I squeezed my eyes shut. My throat tightened, and I had trouble catching my breath. I started to hyperventilate.

I'll die if I don't pull myself together.

I opened my eyes. Swells rocked the boat, and I placed my open palms against the fiberglass to steady myself.

I looked at the edge of the gunwale above. I grabbed the tether with both hands, and the polyester strap dug into my skin as I rotated on the line. I climbed.

I reached for the gunwale, seven feet above the waterline, but it remained out of reach. My muscles fatigued, and I slipped back into the ocean.

If my tether snapped, I would be lost at sea. I would float for a day or two and drown. My worst nightmare. Then I remembered something more frightening.

The shark.

I pressed my body against the hull and watched the surface but saw nothing. I had viewed YouTube videos of great white shark attacks, their rows of razor-sharp teeth tearing into the flesh of sea lions. They attacked from below.

I stuck my face in the water with my eyes wide open, and the salt burned them. Sunlight streamed into the deep and disappeared into the blackness.

Get out of the water.

I faced the yacht, leaned back, and planted my bare feet against the hull. I pulled myself higher, hand over hand, stopped, and shuffled my feet under me. My breath came harder as I climbed again. The bow bobbed against the sea and my feet struggled to cling to the slippery hull. I splayed my toes wide. One misstep and I would fall.

Three feet to go.

I pulled again with my arms. My strength dissipated. I had nothing left.

When my head was parallel with the deck, I slid my foot higher, pushed off, and lunged for the deck with both hands. My arm slipped between the lifelines and I hooked the lower line with my elbow. I grabbed the gunwale with my other hand and pulled myself up. I lifted my knee onto the deck and hugged the lifelines.

I stood on shaky legs, my entire body quivering. I held on with both hands as I stepped over the lines and onto the deck. I fell to my knees and rolled onto my back.

Safe.

I held my face in my hands and cried.

When my breathing returned to normal, I made my way to the cockpit, using my lifeline, despite the calm sea.

I took the helm. The control panel was black, destroyed by the lightning. The Maldives lay due west, which meant I could follow the sun and worry about more precise navigation later. I would hit land eventually. I needed to get us moving. I gripped the ignition key and turned it.

The engine did not start.

CHAPTER THIRTY-FIVE

The storm disappeared as rapidly as it had come, and it took the wind with it. I raised the sails, but they hung from the rigging like old bath towels. The doldrums persisted. The ocean seemed indifferent, infinite.

I had let the engine rest overnight, which exhausted my knowledge of engine mechanics. I tried the ignition key again and a clicking sound emanated from the compartment below deck. The engine coughed once, twice, then rumbled to life.

I exhaled and smiled.

I pushed the throttle forward and motored west. Without wind, the ocean had flattened, and the bow pushed through long shallow swells. I had lost the autopilot when lightning destroyed the electronics, and I had to tie a line to each side of the wheel to maintain our course. Not a perfect solution, but forward motion, any movement, exhilarated me. We may not be on the right course, but at least we were no longer adrift.

Eric's medical opinion had been hard to hear, but I trusted it. I trusted him. He reaffirmed my suspicion of rabies and my decision to head to the closest port to admit Brad into a hospital.

The bite wound lay near Brad's brain, so if the bat had transmitted the rabies virus to him, his neurological degeneration would be accelerated. It had been three days since his acute symptoms began, which meant I would learn his fate soon. What would happen if he died and left me alone on this boat? Too many things could go wrong—too many ways to die.

One crisis at a time.

I went below, tiptoed across the deck, and opened the stateroom door. I peeked around the corner. The bed was empty. I stepped into the room. I knocked on the head door.

"Brad, are you in there?"

No answer.

"Honey?"

Nothing. I tried the handle, and it turned. I cracked the door open and leaned in. Empty. A chill tickled my spine, and my heart raced. I ran into the salon.

Nothing.

"Brad?" I yelled, panic rising in my throat.

I hurried aft and opened the door to the starboard berth.

Vacant.

Had he fallen overboard in his delirium? I sprinted to the port berth, my heart pounding in my ears. I flung open the door and screamed.

Brad stood there staring at me.

"My God, Brad. You scared me. What are you doing out of bed? Why didn't you answer me?"

"Grrrp, aaah," he mumbled, drool spilling over his lip.

"Jesus, Honey. What's wrong? Are you in pain?"

"Head hurts," he said, squeezing his forehead with both hands.

"Of course, it does. Let's get you to bed," I said, and took his arm.

Drool dripped off his chin, and I remembered what Eric had said about rabies being transmitted through saliva. I stepped to the side and guided him into the stateroom. I helped him into bed, dug three Tylenol out of the bag, and handed them to him. I had to avoid touching his mouth.

"Here, Brad. These will help with the pain and keep your fever low. Swallow them, and I'll get you something to drink."

I went to the galley and returned with a glass of Evian. Brad held the Tylenol in his open palm, appearing confused.

"You have to take the pills, honey. Trust me."

I raised his hand to his mouth and tilted it until he dropped the pills on his tongue.

"Good. Now take a sip and swallow them," I said.

I lifted the glass to his lips. "Drink this."

"Nnnngh."

The water flowed into his mouth, and he tried to swallow but gagged. His head bobbed forward like a chicken. Water dribbled over his lips and out of the corners of his mouth. It dripped off his chin. I pulled the glass away and stepped back to avoid his slobber.

I set the glass on the floor and dug in the medical bag for latex gloves. I had been in denial for too long. He had rabies, and I needed to follow the medical protocol and protect myself. I donned gloves, lifted the glass and tried again.

"You need to hydrate and take these pills. I know you're delirious, but you have to do this if you want to feel better."

I sounded more optimistic than I felt. I pressed the glass against his lips. Brad slammed his mouth shut and shook his head, like a baby avoiding food.

"Come on, Brad. Drink this."

"Nooo."

"Come on."

I tilted the glass and poured it into his mouth. He seemed unable to swallow, choking and spitting it out. His eyes widened—angry, wild. He slapped the glass out of my hand, and it shattered against the bulkhead.

I fell backward, my hand stinging from the blow. He had been so fast.

Brad pounded the bed with his hands. He wiped the back of his arm across his mouth.

"No," he yelled, and swung his legs over the side of the bed.

The muscles in his thighs and calves contracted in spasms, and he grabbed them, grimacing.

I stepped back, afraid, unsure. Pain shot through my foot and up my leg.

I lifted my foot off the ground and bent my knee to examine it. A large shard of glass protruded from the sole of my foot.

"Dammit," I yelled.

Brad gawked at me.

I stripped off my gloves and threw them into the corner. I yanked the shard out of my foot, and blood dripped onto the deck. I hopped into the head, pulled a wad of tissues out of their holder and applied pressure to the wound. I turned to Brad.

He stared at the pool of blood on the floor.

"Don't move. Let me clean it up. I don't want you to cut yourself."

He raised his gaze, meeting my stare, and I saw intelligence behind his eyes. "Sorry. I'm sorry," he said, lucid again.

I exhaled, and my stress poured out. "It's okay, honey."

I hopped to the medical bag and cleaned my wound with alcohol. It looked deep, and I needed stitches, but I was too worried about getting the glass off the floor to deal with it now. I applied a sterile dressing and wrapped my foot in a bandage.

I tested it on the deck, stepping on my forefoot. The wound burned, but I could walk. I swept the glass up, under Brad's watchful gaze.

"Try to sleep," I said.

I closed the door behind me and climbed on deck.

Brad's anger and strength scared me. He always had a violent side, but this was different. Primal anger. Feral. He was not acting like himself. He exhibited neurological impairment and something else. I had never seen it before, but I had no doubt.

Brad had hydrophobia.

CHAPTER THIRTY-SIX

Brad had rabies. I was certain of it. I clamped down my panic and tried to analyze the situation. I used this skill often as a doctor when I had to look into the innocent eyes of a dying child and make sound decisions without crying. Empathizing with patients led to emotional responses, and those interfered with my ability to do what the situation required.

I had to think clinically.

I wanted the Wi-Fi more than ever. It was a miracle the satellite phone had survived when the lightning destroyed the main electronics board. Luckily, the phone sat in a separate panel and relied on its own communications pod on the mast. I needed to get Brad off the yacht, either by reaching port or by requesting a medical evacuation.

I dialed Eric, and he answered with a groggy voice. It was late in Boston and he had been asleep. I apologized and got to the point.

"Brad has hydrophobia."

"I'm sorry, Dagny."

"His behavior is erratic, and he's in discomfort. I'm worried about him, but also about my safety."

"Of course."

"I need to ask a hospital in the Maldives or India to send a boat or a helicopter. I would find the information myself, but I lost the Wi-Fi connection when lightning struck our boat. I—"

"Lightning? Jesus. Are you okay?"

"I'm at least a three-day sail away from being okay. Can you find a number for a hospital and patch me through?"

"I met an Indian doctor at an infectious disease conference a few months ago. Let me find his number. Stay on the line and I'll conference you in."

I waited on hold, listening to echoes and pops. After an eternity, Eric's voice came through the speaker.

"Dagny, I have Dr. Arjun Singh on the line with us. He is a senior researcher with India's Ministry of Health and Family Welfare, in New Delhi. I briefed him on your situation and your husband's diagnosis."

"Thank you, Eric. Dr. Singh, I need to get my husband to a hospital. If my diagnosis is correct, and it's rabies, he needs palliative care."

"Where are you, Dr. Steele?"

"That's the problem. We lost our navigation system in an electrical storm, but based on our last position, I estimate we are five hundred miles south of Sri Lanka, close to the equator. I'm using the motor to head for the Maldives."

"Dr. Steele, I fear you have two problems. First, if you cannot provide an exact position, there's no way for a ship to intercept you. Eric told me you're on a satellite phone, which could be tracked to determine your coordinates, but there's a second and superior problem. Even if we knew your exact position, I'm afraid the Government of India would deny you entry."

"Did I hear you right? India won't give my husband a visa to enter the country?"

"I'm afraid not. Your husband is a likely carrier of rabies, an infectious disease. To be blunt, you are also a suspect carrier at this point."

"Your government will deny medical care to Americans at sea? How can that be? What about your Hippocratic oath? Don't you—"

"Dagny, it's out of Dr. Singh's hands," Eric said. "This isn't his decision."

"I'm afraid Dr. Franklin is correct," Dr. Singh said. "Rabies is an infectious disease and India has an extensive history of outbreaks. We suffer twenty thousand deaths from rabies every year, and our Ministry has to consider the health and welfare of our own people first."

I knew I was being unfair. Eric was right—this was not Dr. Singh's call. Brad groaned inside the stateroom.

"What can I do, Dr. Singh?"

"Even if India were to accept your husband, there's nothing to do except hydrate him intravenously, use analgesics to reduce his pain, and sedate him to prevent him from hurting himself or others."

"I want to do that. Help me stop his suffering. Where can I take him?"

"I suggest you contact a private medical evacuation company to take both you and your husband to a country willing to grant you entry," Dr. Singh said.

"Which country will let us in?" I asked.

"I'm afraid I don't know. The Maldives will probably respond the same way as India. Most countries in Africa and Asia battle rabies. People do not vaccinate their dogs, which has prevented us from eradicating the disease."

"Dagny, let me interrupt," Eric said. "Do you know who to call for an evacuation?"

"The boat has a service on contract. I don't know how it works, but I'll call them."

"Good luck, Dr. Steele," Dr. Singh said.

"Thank you. I'll need it."

CHAPTER THIRTY-SEVEN

Brad looked bad. He lay in bed with his hair soaked in sweat and stared at me with unfocused eyes.

"You're very sick, Brad. I have to issue a mayday and evacuate you to a hospital."

"What? Why?"

His voice sounded tight and high-pitched, probably from a swollen throat. Brad would die—I was almost certain—but telling him would not help. He was already difficult to handle, and I did not need him to panic.

"You contracted something from that bat, and you need to get tested in a hospital. I don't have prescription analgesics or anything to sedate you."

"Watch for tankers," he said.

"Brad, pay attention. I'm calling for help. We need to get to shore now."

"No."

The rabies had become acute and his cognitive ability muddled. I could not save him, but I could get him to a hospital where they could ease his pain. I would call the medic service under contract with the yacht and hope they could trace our satellite phone and pinpoint our location. Maybe they could send a ship or a float plane.

"You rest, and I'll get help," I said.

"No . . . the tankers."

I closed the door to the berth and walked to the navigation center. I found the telephone number for Medevac Worldwide Rescue on the first page of the yacht's reference book.

I dialed, and an operator directed me to their emergency liaison. I explained my husband may have rabies and India would probably deny us entry. I told him we motored for the Maldives, but our fuel would not last. Worse, we had lost all the navigation equipment.

"I have your information here," the man said. "I'll contact your satellite company and see if they can give us your location. If we ping your phone with three or more satellites, we can use trilateration to pinpoint your location."

"Trilateration?"

"It's a more exact method than triangulation."

"How accurate is it?" I asked.

"Theoretically, we can calculate your position within fifteen meters."

I breathed a little easier. "What's next? What's the process?"

"Once we know where you are, we must figure out which country will accept you then determine how to evacuate you to a receiving facility."

"My husband's in pain. How can we expedite this process?"

"Stay on the line and we'll trace your call. This will take some time."

"Please hurry."

A glass shattered behind me, and I whirled around.

Brad stared at me from the galley. His ice-blue eyes swam in bloodshot sclera, and heavy eyelids hung above dilated pupils.

"You startled me." I said. "Are you in pain?"

Brad stared and leaned against the galley where he had knocked a glass to the floor. Perspiration beaded on his forehead and drool dribbled off his chin.

"No," he said, his voice thick, as if he had a mouth full of honey.

"The lightning destroyed our electronics. They have to trace our call."

"No."

He trembled and swayed.

I knew he did not understand our situation, but anger boiled inside me. "You need a hospital. I'm getting help."

Brad growled and moved across the deck with his fists balled. I held my hands in front of my face to defend myself, and he snatched the phone away from me.

"Brad, stop it. They're triangulating our position."

Brad stared at the phone in his hand, then he raised his gaze and met my eyes. He bared his teeth and ripped the cord out of the wall.

I gawked at the torn cord dangling in his hand and my tears flowed. I steadied myself on the chart table.

"How could you? You're going to die and there's nothing I can do about it."

I pushed past him then stopped at the starboard berth and looked back. He stood there with the phone in his hand.

"Now, we're all alone," I said. "You may have killed me too."

CHAPTER THIRTY-EIGHT

I awoke in the starboard berth on day four of Brad's acute symptoms. How long had I been out? I had not slept more than a few hours since he fell ill, and when he destroyed our last link to the outside world, it had been too much for me. My worry about him, my fear of the ocean, the lack of wind, the shark—it had been more than I could handle.

I peered through the porthole. The sun had set, which meant I had been asleep for at least four hours.

I slipped off the bed and winced when I put weight on my injured foot, now swollen and painful. I balanced on the ball of my foot and exited the berth into the dark salon. I climbed the stairs to the deck and gazed at miles of black sea. The engine hummed as we motored west through the windless night.

Brad had been violent and scary, but I needed to check on him. I owed him that as a doctor. And as his wife. I tried not to think about his imminent death.

I climbed below and entered to the dark stateroom. Brad lay atop the sheets and breathed through thick mucus. His leg twitched, like a sleeping dog, probably from muscle spasms. I watched him for a few minutes, then inspected my body. I had not bathed in two days, and I felt tired, dirty, and out of ideas. I needed to shower, drink a pot of coffee, and develop a plan to reach shore.

I stepped into the head and inched the door shut. I stood in front of the mirror and stripped off my bikini. Underneath, my white skin contrasted with my bronze tan. I had not realized how dark I had become since we had taken to sea. Lines of salt crisscrossed my skin where sweat had dried.

I examined my reflection in the mirror. I looked ten years older than I had on land. I pulled the dressing off my foot, and it bled. I would need to give myself stitches and take an antibiotic or risk infection. I reapplied the dressing to avoid staining the deck any more than I already had.

I opened the shower stall, stepped inside, and closed the plexiglass door. I turned on the faucet and stepped under the large, rain-forest showerhead. Warm water beat against my breasts, like a thousand fingers massaging my stress away.

I dipped my head under the flow and let it embrace me. I reached for the shampoo and lathered my hair while the water ran. I had no intention of taking a navy shower. I needed this.

I rinsed the shampoo out of my hair, slipped a washcloth off the rack behind me, and lathered it with a bar of soap. I scrubbed my face, upper body, and legs. The warm water felt like the fountain of youth. I spread my feet and rubbed the cloth between my thighs. The soft cloth felt good. I lathered again, turned away from the shower head, and cleaned my posterior. I let the soap wash down my legs. I could stay in there all day.

I turned around and screamed.

Brad stood inches from the plexiglass door. He stared at me with dilated pupils and perspiration beading on his forehead. His eyes drifted between my legs.

I covered myself with my hands.

He did not move. His erection pushed against his boxer shorts, and his eyes locked on me with the same leer I had seen in the eyes of middle-aged men when I jogged on Commonwealth Avenue in my skin-tight leggings. Brad's expression looked prurient, hungry, dangerous.

He pulled his boxers off and let them drop to the deck. He grabbed the stall handle and pushed the door open.

I threw myself against the glass, slamming it shut.

"Stop it Brad. What are you doing?"

"Grrrgh." Drool dripped off his teeth.

"Get out. I'm in the shower."

He opened the door again.

I leaned my weight into it again, and my feet slid until they bumped against the bulkhead. I used it for leverage and pushed. The door clicked shut.

"Brad, you're scaring me. Stop it right now."

"Fuck," he said, and pointed between my legs.

"Get out. I mean it."

What kind of neurological horror is this?

Brad's eyes rolled up in his head and he placed one hand against the stall. He grabbed himself with his other hand and orgasmed. Creamy ropes of semen splashed against the stall door. I watched. Horrified. Shaking. His ejaculate slid down the door leaving long soapy streaks. I had never seen Brad touch himself, not even during sex. What the hell was this?

I cried. This thing was not my husband.

Brad opened his eyes and gaped at his erection and the mess on the stall door. He wrinkled his forehead, confused. He raised his eyes to mine, as if asking a question, and cocked his head.

"Head hurts," he said.

I glared at him, silent.

He turned and walked away, dripping his seed on the floor.

I realized I had been holding my breath and gasped.

He groaned as the mattress settled under his weight. What should I do? If I had not closed the door, would he have raped me? Did he know what he was doing?

I'm trapped.

I pressed my face against the glass and cried.

Brad's snoring echoed through the cabin, more gurgling than breathing. I stepped out of the stall and peeked through the open door. He lay in bed, his feet twitching with muscle spasms. I had to get away from him.

I slid the door open more, and it creaked.

Brad stopped snoring.

I froze. I held my breath until his respirations resumed. I stepped over the mess he had left on the teak floor and stayed on my toes.

Brad's eyes were closed, and he smacked his lips, as if desiccated. When had he last been able to drink anything?

I had stored my clothes in the wardrobe on the other side of the bed. I slipped into the stateroom, three feet from the foot of the bed.

Brad snorted and bared his teeth, still asleep. Probably.

I stepped toward the bureau, and a hunk of glass pushed against my dressing. I stopped and lifted my foot before it pierced my skin. Tiny shards still littered the deck in front of the bureau.

I eyed Brad, who was getting another erection. This virus was demonic.

Brad grabbed himself, and his snoring stopped.

I had to move.

I swung the medical kit over my shoulder, tiptoed across the cabin, and shut the door behind me.

Brad groaned.

I made it, but what now? Where could I go? Would he try to hurt me?

Brad grunted, and the mattress squeaked.

I stared across the salon at the stern berths.

Brad's feet thudded onto the deck.

I sprinted aft for the starboard berth, as the latch on the stateroom door clicked open behind me. I slipped into the cabin and looked back across the salon.

My bloody footprints stained the deck and led right to me.

CHAPTER THIRTY-NINE

I perched on the edge of the bed with my eyes fixed on the inside of the door and listened to Brad stagger around the salon. He grunted like an ape as he opened and shut cabinets. What the hell was he doing? An image of him bursting through the door ran through my mind on a continual loop. My breath came faster.

The rabies virus had incubated in two days, and the acute phase had started after only one week of the flu-like symptoms. I had never seen a case of furious rabies and its terrifying neurological symptoms. The virus attacked the nervous system and manifested in unique ways as it destroyed people's brains. For thousands of years people had conflated rabies with myths about people metamorphosed into vampires, zombies, and animals. Monsters may not exist, but furious rabies transformed people into savage beasts.

Brad had punched his ex-wife and been physical with me, but he had not attacked me. Not yet. When he tried to force himself into the shower, he had seemed more horny and confused than angry. I tried to calm down. He had not attempted to hurt me. He would never do that.

I'm lying.

Brad had anger issues, and now that the virus had ravaged his mind, he could not moderate his behavior.

He will hurt me.

Brad's footfalls grew louder as he approached my berth. The sounds stopped close to my door. His labored breath came in thick, raspy grunts. Had he seen my bloody footprints? What was he doing?

The door handle jiggled.

"Dagny?" His voice sounded strange, unnatural. Alien.

The fine hair on my neck tickled, and I hugged myself. I said nothing. I had locked the door, but it would not be difficult for him to break it down. I examined the portholes along the wall. They allowed light and air inside but were too small for me to climb through.

What was I thinking? Brad was my husband. My sick husband. He was in pain and I was a doctor. He needed me. I could not let my fear prevent me from helping him. He was dying, but I could ease his suffering. I stood and reached for the door. I wrapped my fingers around the lock but did not open it.

I listened. Brad's throaty breathing sounded like an animal. A sick animal. People should avoid rabid animals, right? Still, I had vowed to love him in sickness and in health. I had also sworn an oath to help patients in need. I had to overcome my fear and act like a doctor.

I turned the silver knob on the lock halfway—hesitant, unsure.

Am I making a mistake?

Brad slammed against the door with a bang, and I jumped. It sounded like he had slapped the door with his palms. He pounded again. The door shook, and the knob jiggled, slipping the bolt into the open position. Unlocked.

I lunged for the latch and jammed it home.

That thing is not my husband.

Brad's footsteps faded away into the salon. I exhaled and plopped onto the bed. I needed a plan. I closed my eyes and assessed the situation. I had to treat this the same way I diagnosed a patient—observing and articulating the problems and thinking of ways to mitigate each of them.

Brad's mental condition had deteriorated to a point where he would not recover. I had to accept it. I had to sail to land, and I could not do that hiding in the cabin. I knew enough to operate the engine and sails and keep the yacht moving, but with our navigational systems gone, finding the Maldives would be difficult. We had been on the right course when the lightning struck, so if I followed the setting sun, we should hit the Maldives, or if we missed them—Africa.

Lightning had destroyed the entire electronics board, so the AIS was offline, which created a second problem. Ships would not see us, unless they manned their radars, and I would not get a proximity alarm if we were on a collision course with another vessel. If one rammed us, we would die.

My third problem was the lack of wind. We had been in the doldrums for days and it could last for weeks. Our gas would last for a couple more days, and I would not have to use the sails until we were close to the Maldives. I could deal with sailing problems later.

The weather still threatened us. The last lightning storm had moved in fast, and if another one hammered us, we may not survive. I did not have the skills for rough seas, and if a wave broadsided us, we would capsize. If the weather worsened, I would need to cut the engine, deploy the sea anchor, and batten down the boat. To prepare for a storm, I would have to leave the cabin.

The virus addling Brad's brain was my most immediate problem. He was in the acute stages of furious rabies—aggressive and violent. Brad seemed capable of hurting me, and in his diminished cognitive state, I could not count on him to have any self-control. His behavior in the shower confirmed it. My safety had to come first. He was in pain and dying, but I could not render aid while he raged. Even if he calmed down, I could not do much for him, other than administer Tylenol and provide emotional support.

If Medevac Worldwide Rescue had traced our location before Brad destroyed the phone, they may have dispatched a rescue ship. But if they had not triangulated us, they would not send help, because the ocean was too expansive to locate a lone sailboat. Eric knew I was in trouble, and he had feelings for me, so maybe he would send help.

I stopped daydreaming. No one would find us. I was alone on a ship with a rabid animal and nobody was coming to my rescue. I dropped my face into my hands and wept.

Brad stomped up the companionway and climbed on deck.

Was he looking for me in his confused state? What if he fell overboard? I should lead him into his cabin, but I could not move. He scared me and though I did not wish to acknowledge my feelings, it was true. I had become a castaway on a yacht, adrift in an oceanic wilderness with a man suffering from a neurological deficit—a madman.

I shuddered and hugged myself.

Sunlight filtered into the cabin from small portholes high on the wall, and I peered into the cockpit.

Brad trudged past, dragging his feet like he had coordination problems. The virus had devoured his nerve endings. He mumbled to himself, alternately angry and defensive, but I could not understand his words.

He paced in circles around the deck, his rants punctuated with high-pitched yelps—almost a dog's bark. He walked toward the starboard side and disappeared from my view. He stopped talking and I could not hear anything.

What's he doing?

The engine stopped.

CHAPTER FORTY

The yacht drifted to a standstill on the flat, saltwater lake created by the doldrums. We rocked side to side in the current, which pushed us away from our destination. If a storm hit now, we would capsize. The problems mounted and my situation seemed impossible. I laid on the bed and closed my eyes.

I awoke confused. I remembered lying in bed and nothing else. I blinked my eyes and my dire situation flooded into my consciousness, like receiving a death notice. Through the porthole, the sun hung low in the sky. I must have slept for hours, and I felt stronger, rested, which was something.

Brad yelled from somewhere on deck. I looked through the porthole at his feet near the helm, facing the sea.

"Fuck you, fuck you, fuck you," he yelled.

Was he talking to me?

He turned and stumbled into the cockpit. There was something primal about him now. He cocked his head to the side like a wolf searching for a scent on the wind. He extended his fingers—rigid, like claws. Maybe his hands had cramped. He drooled onto his shirt and growled.

I gasped.

He looked up, as if he had heard, but that was not possible. He curled his lips away from his teeth. Another spasm? He bit at the air, three times in succession, hunched over, and leered at me.

I ducked away from the porthole. Had he seen me? My eyes darted around the small berth, desperate to escape. The bed almost filled the room. Opposite a bench at the foot of the bed lay the en suite head, a bathroom much smaller than the one in our stateroom. Above the bench was a long cabinet, and two portholes opened high on the walls on each side of the berth. One faced the cockpit and the other the sea—both too small to climb through. A long rectangular window paralleled the bed, about five feet over the waterline, but it did not open.

Behind the bed, a raised platform extended to the stern, and a hatch opened in the transom. The hatches did not function as exits. Across from the head, two large cupboards hung from the interior bulkhead. One looked like a wardrobe, and the other was oddly shaped and only extended a few feet off the deck. The room felt like a prison—a prison with an insane guard patrolling the perimeter.

Brad walked out of my view, and I strained to listen. I stood on the bed and looked through the interior porthole. I saw the cockpit and the steering wheel, but not Brad. I turned toward the starboard wall and shrieked.

Brad pressed his face against the porthole and glared at me.

He knelt and hunched his back. Saliva dripped off his mouth. Matted hair hung over wide eyes, and his stare bore into me. I had seen that look before.

The beast had returned.

CHAPTER FORTY-ONE

Brad watched me through the window, like a lion preparing to savage an elk. Long strands of thick saliva hung off his lower lip.

I crawled across the bed and pressed my back against the interior bulkhead. I wanted to appear brave, pretend nothing was wrong, but my hands shook, and my lips quivered.

He seemed to recognize the fear on my face. He bared his teeth.

If he came for me, I could stay in the room and hope I had the strength to stop him from opening the door. Or I could run from the cabin and hide. But where?

Brad cocked his head and bit the air, sending saliva flying. He pounced at the porthole and his lip exploded from the impact. Blood flecked the glass. He seemed not to notice. He retreated, bumped into the safety lines, and moved toward the cockpit.

He's coming.

I had thirty seconds to decide what to do. I swung the medical bag over my shoulder and jumped off the bed. I ran across the cabin and grabbed the door handle. I heard Brad's feet slap against the deck as he landed in the cockpit. I studied the recessed latches on the cabinets beside the door, which differed from the wardrobe handles in our stateroom.

I dropped to my knees and pressed the buttons near the top of the cabinet. The latch popped, and the door fell open, revealing the engine compartment, a tight space between the stern berths and under the companionway. The engine lay before me, and heat radiated off it.

I stuck my head inside and looked aft. Beside the engine, hoses wound out of a white box, and other machinery hummed near it, probably the generator, water filter, heater, and air conditioner. The compartment extended ten feet to the stern, tapering near the end, and the ceiling angled down beneath the tender garage.

There's room.

I shut the small cupboard and opened the larger door, which also accessed the compartment. I peered into the unlit space again. Above me, the steps creaked as Brad stepped onto them. I did not have a choice.

I lowered the medical kit into the engine space and ducked inside. I hesitated before closing the cabinet. I had locked the cabin door from the inside and there was no other egress, so even in his impaired condition, Brad may figure out where I had hidden. I stepped back into the cabin, climbed onto the platform behind the bed, and opened the hatch over the transom. Maybe Brad would see it and think I had climbed out and fallen overboard.

Something slammed against the cabin door. Brad.

I scampered across the bed, trying not to make noise. He growled and slammed into the door again. Wood splintered near the hinge.

I climbed into the compartment, but when I tried to close it, there was no interior handle, because it had not been designed as a living space. I gripped the ends of the door with my fingertips and waited for Brad to make noise again. My fingers ached, but I had to time it perfectly. Brad slammed against the cabin door and wood splintered. I pulled the cabinet, and it clicked shut as the door burst open and fell to the floor.

Had he seen me?

I held my breath.

Brad stomped into the room, huffing and puffing. He banged into something on the ground, probably the broken door, and the head door slammed open. He yelped.

A moment later, he growled from the opposite side of the bulkhead. He banged against the compartment door, and I covered my mouth and shut my eyes. If he opened it, I was dead. The mattress springs creaked, and I heard him crawl across the platform behind the bed.

The engine compartment had plunged into darkness when I had closed the door, and I could not see a light switch. A few slivers of light flickered around the edges of the cabinets, but I could only make out dark shapes. The space reeked of diesel fumes and heated electrical wiring, and the back of my throat tickled. I could not cough. Not now. I swallowed to moisten my throat.

The mattress springs groaned again, and he landed on the deck, the broken door crackling under his weight. Brad stormed out of the cabin into the salon, and then pounded up the steps to the deck. I could not hear him anymore.

I crawled as deep into the compartment as I could and balled into a fetal position. The space felt warm and dry, and the sound of the generator made it difficult to hear anything, both a tactical problem and a psychological blessing. Brad's grunting and growling had pushed me to the edge of panic. Unfortunately, I would not hear him if he returned.

I nibbled my fingernail and waited.

CHAPTER FORTY-TWO

I could not see anything. Some light had leaked into the compartment when I first hid inside, but not anymore, which meant night had fallen. The humming of the generator filled my ears and my foot throbbed.

I ran my fingers over the bottom of my foot, and they came away slick with blood. I needed to find the medical bag and stop the bleeding. I braced myself against the sloped ceiling to avoid banging my head and leaned forward, swinging my arms across the deck like a blind woman. My fingers connected with the canvas bag, and I dragged it to me.

I unzipped the kit, dug through the first modules, and touched the familiar shape of a flashlight. I turned it in my hand and pressed the plunger. The light illuminated the cabin, blinding me, and I covered it with my palm. It was nighttime and probably dark inside the yacht, and if the beam leaked out of the compartment, Brad could discover my sanctuary.

I parted my fingers, letting a sliver of light escape, and maneuvered it around the engine compartment to reorient myself. A second door opened into the port berth. I had not seen it before, because the generator had blocked my view.

My foot had painted the floor with blood. I shined the light on my sole. The wound had clotted, but my movement had restarted the flow, and I needed to suture it. In the bag, I found hydrogen peroxide to sterilize my instruments, and a bottle of Betadine, a povidone-iodine for disinfecting the tissue. I collected suture needles, surgical scissors, nonabsorbable suture material, syringes, and a scalpel. I laid dressings and bandages beside me and ripped the corners of the packaging to allow quick access when needed.

This is going to hurt.

I popped three Tylenol in my mouth, ground them between my teeth, and swallowed the bitter powder. I wrapped a latex glove over the end of the flashlight to cloak the beam, and it glowed like a light bulb. I held the flashlight in my mouth to free my hands. I often joked that I had done so many surgeries, I could operate with my eyes closed, and I would almost have to do that now.

Now or never.

I laid a sheet of gauze on the deck and donned gloves to prevent the bacteria on my hands from contaminating my wound. I did not want to think about the myriad of pathogens inside the engine compartment. If my wound became infected, I would have a serious problem. I bent my leg and laid my foot on the gauze with the laceration facing me. I wanted to soak the instruments to disinfect them, but without a container, I had to pour the hydrogen peroxide over them and set them on the pad. I palpated the wound and confirmed I had removed all the glass.

It's time.

I soaked a dressing in Betadine, sucked in a breath around the flashlight, and dug the sterile pad into my laceration. Pain exploded through my foot and traveled up my leg, as if it had burst into flames. I jammed my eyes shut and saw colors.

I rubbed the gauze inside the wound to clear away any debris, using circular motions to push contaminants away from the site. Blood flowed, and I irrigated the area, dousing it with saline.

The glass had cut a jagged laceration through my sole and left an uneven flap of skin, which would be difficult to stitch. I pulled the loose skin with my left hand and sliced it off with the scalpel, biting hard on the flashlight. Stars flashed in my vision.

I dropped the severed flesh on the gauze and took deep breaths. I used the surgical scissors to even the ends of the skin, and my foot throbbed as if I had slammed it in a car door.

I squished the edges of the wound together, and blood bubbled between my fingers. The compartment filled with the sweet, pungent odor of iron, as if I had prepared a roast for the oven. I grasped the pre-threaded needle and placed it against my skin at the distal end of the wound. I tensed and inserted the needle. My eyes teared, and I stifled a groan.

I angled the needle at ninety degrees, pierced my skin on the other side. The inflamed area bled and burned. I pinched the shaft on the opposite side of the wound and pulled it until the suture tightened. It hurt like hell but concentrating on my craft—my life's calling—brought me peace.

I stuck the needle into my flesh near the first suture and did it again. And again. The laceration was four inches long, and it took twenty stitches to close. A thick sheen of sweat coated my body. My heart pounded and my respirations increased almost to the point of hyperventilation. I tried to take the pain without screaming or crying, but my tears flowed.

I poured Betadine over the closed wound to kill any remaining bacteria and patted it dry. I covered it with a thick trauma dressing, without unrolling it, to give myself added padding to help me walk. I wrapped the dressing in gauze and covered it with an Ace bandage.

Done.

I stretched out my leg, laid down on the deck, and closed my eyes. My breathing slowed and the burning pain reduced to a dull throb. I let myself fall asleep.

I awoke to a thumping noise. Brad. He ran through the yacht, hunting for me.

Ambient light filtered into the cabin and I reached for the flashlight. The bulb glowed orange, dim. I had left it on, and the battery was almost dead. I cursed myself for forgetting to turn it off. My foot ached, but no blood had seeped through the bandage, indicating the stitches and dressing had been effective.

It had been six or seven hours since I had hidden in the compartment and my bladder felt like it would explode. I wanted to sneak into the head, but if Brad found me, I would have nowhere to flee. That left one alternative.

I slid to the side of the compartment where the floor slanted toward the stern and moved forward until the roof was high enough to allow me to crouch. I squatted and urinated on the floor. The fluid hit the deck and echoed as if I peed inside a drum. I lowered myself closer to the floor to minimize the noise, and my urine ran between the machinery. The odor filled the room, but I did not care—the release was worth it. I only hoped the smell did not permeate the bulkhead.

I crawled to the center of the compartment and leaned against the generator, letting it warm my naked body. I was thirsty, hungry, and scared. I was out of ideas, but I could not stay there forever.

How could this get any worse?

The flashlight flickered, and the compartment plunged into darkness.

CHAPTER FORTY-THREE

My skin shriveled from dehydration, becoming aged and wrinkled, and salt stains ran down my arms like ant trails. The pain from stitching my foot had soaked me in sweat and drained my fluids. I wobbled in the dark, dizzy, and held my head in my hands. I had to drink something before I lost consciousness.

The wine cooler lay a few feet from the cabin door, but the refrigerator with the nonalcoholic drinks sat above the washing machine at the far end of the galley, adjacent to the stateroom. The last time I checked, it had contained a few cans of Diet Coke and a bottle of Perrier. The rest of the bottled drinks were in the hold beneath the floor. It would be too noisy to open the hold, but I might make it to the refrigerator without alerting Brad, assuming he was on deck or asleep.

A dehydration headache pounded in my temples. I had no choice.

I crawled through the blackened compartment and ran my fingertips across the wall unit I located the latch. I put my ear against the cool fireproofing lining the inside of the door and listened to the sounds of the yacht, but I could only hear the low hum of the generator and the beating of my heart. I slipped my finger around the latch, held my breath, and pushed it open.

The moon glowed through the cabin portholes, illuminating the engine compartment. I poked my head into the berth.

Empty.

I held the cabinet door and slipped into the cabin. Pain radiated through my foot, and I expelled a long stream of air to keep from screaming.

The cabin door lay shattered on the floor where Brad had broken it down. I peered through the doorway into the galley and enough moonlight filtered in to confirm it was unoccupied. Brad could be on deck or in the other berth or stateroom. I had no way to know. He could also be hiding in the salon, just out of view, waiting for me to show myself.

I shook my fear away.

I closed the cabinet behind me, and the clasp clicked into place.

Too loud.

I froze and waited. Brad did not come running.

I took a step and wood crunched under my foot. I stopped and examined the splintered wood and pieces of the locking mechanism spread across the floor, then placed my hand on the wall for balance and tiptoed through the rubble. The stitches in my foot pulled with every movement, and I bit my lip to smother the pain.

I poked my head out of the cabin. To my left, the companionway, navigation station, and salon were empty. In front of me, padded rails ran along the galley appliances and the back of the salon couch. I moved into the galley and braced my hands against both rails—using them as crutches—and limped forward on my swollen foot. I tiptoed to minimize the sound of my footfalls, but the stitches twitched, and my skin burned.

I stopped, halfway through the galley. I needed to arm myself. I opened a cabinet and removed a steak knife. It seemed small and impotent at the end of my thin arm. I replaced it and grabbed the butcher knife we had used to cut meat. I balanced the blade in my hand and the weight gave me a momentary sense of power, then my cheeks warmed, and I felt ridiculous. Could I use it to defend myself? Could I kill Brad?

At least having the knife was better than nothing—it gave me a chance.

The ocean lapped against the hull and the sound intensified my thirst. I glanced at the faucet over the sink, but I could not risk the noise I would make retrieving a glass and running the faucet. I shuffled past, without slowing.

I paused at the end of the galley and leaned around the corner. The stateroom door stood a few inches ajar. I listened. No sound. I stepped into the alcove and opened the cabinet containing the refrigerator, a quarter-sized unit, like the one I had kept in my college dorm.

I pulled the handle, and the seal popped. I opened the door, jiggling cans on the plastic rack inside. I held my breath and listened to the soft lapping of the sea against the hull. A plastic bottle of Perrier and two cans of Diet Coke sat on the shelves. I lifted the Perrier, careful not to shake the rack.

Behind me, something thumped on the deck in the stateroom.

He's coming.

I moved out of the alcove and looked at the berth. Too far. I would never make it.

Another thump on the floor. Louder, closer.

I slipped between the salon couches and ducked under the dining table.

Brad exited the stateroom and stood in the alcove. I only saw him from the knees down, and his calve muscles rippled with spasms.

I squeezed the bottle in one hand and the knife in my other, remaining motionless on my hands and knees. Brad stood still, facing starboard. What was he doing?

I peeked between the couches.

Brad stared at the open refrigerator which I had forgotten to close. He cocked his head like a dog trying to solve a math problem.

"Glompf, nnngh, where are you?" he yelled, turning toward the companionway.

The tabletop concealed me from his view. For now.

What was he thinking?

He stepped aft then stopped. His drool dripped on the deck in front of me.

An itch tickled my parched throat, and I had to cough. I pushed my tongue against the roof of my mouth and tried to squeeze moisture out of it, but I had nothing left. I ground my teeth to suppress the urge and took shallow breaths.

Brad moved forward to the companionway and climbed the stairs. If he turned, he would spot me under the table. I watched him ascend the steps and disappear on deck.

I coughed. I had to move now.

I crawled out from under the table and slipped around the couch. I backed against the railing and hurried toward the starboard cabin. I kept my eyes riveted on the top of the companionway. Brad remained out of sight.

I turned to step into the cabin and stopped.

Beyond the companionway and over the navigation table, the severed satellite telephone cord dangled from the instrument panel where Brad had ripped the phone from the wall. The frayed ends of wires protruded out of their plastic sheath. If I found the phone and spliced the wires, maybe I could call Medevac Worldwide Rescue and they could triangulate our position.

Something thumped on deck near the helm.

I had to hide. I climbed into the engine compartment, set the bottle and knife at my feet, and pulled the cover closed behind me. The room plunged into darkness.

I groped for my bottle and guzzled the Perrier. The liquid revived me as it coursed through my veins. I moved away from the doorway and sat on the floor. I could no longer hear anything outside the compartment. I was a prisoner in a hole, on a boat surrounded by thousands of miles of ocean, with a madman hunting me.

If I stayed there, I would die.

CHAPTER FORTY-FOUR

I sat in darkness with my eyes burning and my throat constricting. Despair boiled inside me, spreading from my heart through my chest until it consumed all of me. Tears rolled down my cheeks, and my chest heaved. My body spasmed. I pressed my hands over my mouth.

How did I end up on a boat?

After my childhood trauma, I had sworn I would never go near the water again. It happened twenty-one long years ago, but it felt like yesterday—the memory burned into my mind by scalding tragedy.

It had been a Saturday in July, warm and sunny, the kind of day New Englanders dreamed about all winter long. My father had woken me with a radiant smile.

"How about we spend the day together?" he asked.

"Really, Daddy? You don't have to work?"

"I do, but I'd rather go swimming with you, Princess."

I leapt out of bed, threw on a swimsuit, and an hour later, we arrived at the Roosevelt Center—a massive, Olympic-sized pool, with five diving boards and an expansive shallow end for kids. Parents and children splashed in the cool water, filling the air with giggles, screams, and joy. My father gave me ten dollars for snacks, and I skipped to the food truck to buy an ice cream cone.

Fifteen minutes later, I returned and found two dozen people huddled together, staring at something on the ground. I called for my father but did not see him. The pinched expressions of the people—now quiet and solemn—pulled me toward them like the gravity of a black hole.

I parted the crowd and saw my father laying on the cement, pale and still.

A lifeguard, a boy no older than eighteen, blew air into my father's lungs. Even then, I knew it was a poor attempt at CPR. I watched as my father's lips turned blue, and the color left his body. He died before the ambulance arrived.

I stood there and watched with ice cream dripping between my fingers and tears streaming down my face.

Later, I learned my father had hit his head and been underwater just long enough for liquid to seep into his lungs. The lifeguard had failed to roll him over and expel the fluid from his airway before starting CPR, and his efforts blew chlorinated water further into my father's bronchi, deep into his lower lobes. The lack of air caused a cardiac arrest, but the lifeguard never did chest compressions, depriving my father's brain of oxygen.

I had watched the life leave my father's body, all because nobody knew how to administer CPR. If they had, my father would have survived, but instead, he died. Needlessly. The person I had cared about most had been ripped from my life, lost, because no one had proper medical training. It had been the defining moment of my life, the reason I became a doctor, the reason I never swam again.

Yet here I was on a boat. A nightmare cruise.

Was I smart enough to think my way out of this? Was there a solution to the puzzle?

I could confront Brad and try to overpower him—end it right now—but that would result in my gruesome death. Or I could give up and accept defeat. It would be easy to slip off the stern, sink below the surface, take a final breath of saltwater.

I wiped my eyes. No, I would never give up. I had to take responsibility for my decisions and deal with my situation. Win or lose, I would fight to the end.

I needed to fix the satellite phone.

CHAPTER FORTY-FIVE

I did not hear Brad. I heard nothing. I was taking a huge chance, but if I fixed the phone, I could direct rescuers to us. I had to risk it.

I unlatched the compartment door and cracked it open. The berth remained empty. I stepped into the cabin and closed the portal behind me, because I could not allow Brad to discover my hiding place, my only sanctuary onboard. I tiptoed through the debris and peered into the salon.

No Brad.

I had not seen what he had done with the phone after he ripped it out of the wall, but if he had thrown it overboard, I was dead. I hoped it lay somewhere in the main cabin. It had to be there.

I stepped through the doorway and surveyed the furniture and tabletops. No phone. I squatted beside the companionway and squinted through the shadows on the floor.

There!

The satellite phone lay under the couch against the port wall. I squinted past the companionway into the night. No sign of Brad.

I limped through the galley, to avoid walking in front of the steps, and slid between the couches. I ducked under the dining table and crawled toward the port wall. I placed my cheek against the deck and stretched my arm under the couch. My fingers touched something plastic, but it squirted out of my reach. I stretched my fingers wide, pulling the muscles in my arm and back, and touched it again. I hooked the phone with my fingernails and dragged it to me.

I examined the satellite phone receiver in the dim light. Shaped like a walkie-talkie, it had a video screen, dial pad, and buttons for preset channels and scrolling. The power button was larger than the others, positioned on top. Wires hung from the bottom, like roots dangling from a vegetable freshly pulled from the earth. Four bundles of copper wires stuck out of the ripped black casing. Each bundle had a distinct color—red, black, green, white—and while I did not understand their individual functions, it did not matter, because color coding negated my lack of technical knowledge. I only had to connect the wires from the headset to the same colored bundles in the other half of the cord.

The satellite phone cradle hung beside the charred navigation panel on the aft wall, just above the captain's chair. The chart table lay only a few feet away, but to reach it, I had to cross in open view, within feet of the steps.

A shadow flittered across the floor, and I glanced through the companionway hatch. Brad walked through the cockpit. He extended his arms with his elbows locked and his fingers curled, as if he suffered from cramps or some kind of neurological impairment. He cocked his head and stared over the gunwale at the horizon, with his back to me.

What was he doing?

The smart move would be for me to retreat through the galley and hide in the engine compartment again, but I had the phone, and I was so close.

I can do this.

I crawled from under the dining table and moved across the deck on my hands and knees. I squeezed past the captain's chair, turning it until it faced the companionway. I crouched behind it. The sky was visible through the hatch, but not Brad.

I steadied my breathing and counted to ten. Still no sign of him.

I set the knife on the floor, stood behind the chair, and inspected the satellite panel. If Brad were to come below, I would see his legs as he mounted the steps, which would give me the opportunity to duck. In theory.

I grasped the other end of the telephone cord, with the same four colored bundles of copper wire flopping out of it. I knew nothing about the internal machinations of electronic equipment, but it seemed obvious I only had to splice the copper wires together to fix the damage.

Brad's footsteps thumped across the deck, somewhere near the helm. I stopped and focused on the hatch.

Nothing.

I pawed at the ripped cord and tried to expose the copper wires recessed inside colored casings, but I could not get hold of them. I clawed at the rubber with my nails, but it was too thick. I lifted the knife and stuck the tip into the wire casing, but the blade was too big to fit, and it cut the copper wire.

I placed the knife on the desk and used my teeth to bite the rubber. That worked, and I pulled the coating away, exposing half an inch of wire. I nibbled at the ends of three remaining colored bundles until all the wire was visible and my mouth filled with a metallic taste.

With the cord in the wall prepared, I turned my attention to the other half dangling from the satellite phone. I had to expose those wires too.

Something bumped on the wall behind me. Brad's footsteps clomped across the port deck. I leaned over the chart table and looked through the portholes, as Brad trudged past. I ducked and continued gnawing at the rubber. I had to hurry.

I exposed three of the wires, but the copper in the white casing had fused to the rubber and as I pulled it away, two of the four strands of copper wire broke. Would it matter? There were four bundles of four wires each, so would two broken wires on one bundle be a problem? I could not risk it.

Brad tramped past the portholes above the galley. He was heading back to the helm. Would he come below?

I retrieved the knife and cut two inches off the white casing. I used my teeth to open the end and exposed the wire, preparing all four bundles on both ends of the severed cord.

Brad entered the cockpit and bumped into something. He was coming. I had to stall him.

I turned to the electronics panel, charred black from the fire. Beside it was a manual switch for the navigation lights. The instruments were destroyed, but the redundant switches for the mast lights may still function.

Brad's footsteps landed on the deck and he bumped into the cockpit table.

I flicked the switch.

Brad's footfalls stopped. I peeked around the corner. He stood still in the companionway hatch. Had the mast lights come on? Brad turned and walked out of sight.

I lay the phone on the desk and went to work. I grabbed the copper wires from the white housing on each end of ripped cord and twirled them together. They held. I spliced the second, third, and fourth bundles together with trembling fingers.

Something banged near the main mast and Brad's footsteps pounded along the port side, returning to the helm.

I twisted the last bundle together. Done.

Brad landed in the cockpit.

I hit the power button on the satellite phone. The screen did not illuminate. I tried the other buttons. Nothing worked. Something else must have broken inside when Brad had ripped it from the wall. I deflated, my energy and hope draining away.

Brad climbed onto the first step.

I set the phone down and ducked under the chart table, swiveling the chair to conceal myself. I pressed my fingers against the soft leather to prevent it from moving. My lips trembled.

Brad stomped down the steps and stood in the salon. His breathing came in raspy snorts, full of mucus.

"Aargh," he shouted, his voice high and strained.

The knife.

I had forgotten the knife on the desk next to the phone. If Brad saw it and came to retrieve it, he would see me.

He walked closer, now only three feet away, and I smelled his rotten breath. He turned toward the port berth and crashed through the cabin door.

My heart raced. My body shook. The chair wobbled in front of me, but I did not dare release it for fear it would rotate and reveal me. I leaned around the chair.

Brad stood in the berth doorway, his fists balled, and his hair matted with sweat. He stared into the empty cabin and cocked his head, as if he sensed me nearby.

I glanced across the salon to the starboard berth. I would have to pass Brad to get there.

I lifted one hand off the chair and reached above, probing the desk for the knife. I touched the handle and plucked at it with my fingernails.

I slid it closer until I could grab the handle. I pulled the knife down behind the chair as Brad walked back into the salon.

I tightened my grip on the handle and held my breath.

Brad rambled across the salon and into the stateroom.

Was it a trick? Was he baiting me to show myself?

I stood and hesitated. I willed myself to move. I tiptoed through the salon to the starboard berth, keeping my eyes on the stateroom door. I expected him to burst through the door and catch me, but he did not.

I entered the berth and closed myself inside the engine compartment with a loud click.

Now what?

CHAPTER FORTY-SIX

I awoke from a nightmare, straining to scream, but unable to make a sound. How long had I slept? By the lack of light inside the compartment, it had to be night. The engines had been off for close to twelve hours, though it was impossible to judge the passage of time in the darkened hold. If we still floated close to the equator, the current pushed us away from the Maldives. The yacht rolled more, which meant the wind had returned. A storm could be coming. If the wind intensified, I needed to take the helm before we capsized.

It was day seven of acute symptoms, and Brad would probably only live for another three or four days. I could not survive that long without drinking water, which made waiting him out inside the engine compartment impossible. I had to control the boat to reach land. Eric had said paralysis and coma were the final stages of furious rabies. I would have a chance if I could wait until Brad became incapacitated, but how long would he last, and how would I know when it happened?

I heard nothing outside the compartment which meant Brad could be dead already.

My God, Brad . . . dead.

Sorrow brushed my fear aside, and tears filled my eyes. Brad had not been a wonderful husband, but he did not deserve to die, not like this. No one did.

Dr. Singh had said India experienced over twenty thousand deaths from rabies each year, and I had read there were more than fifty thousand annual deaths worldwide. If I survived this, I would combat this horrible disease. The challenge motivated me to keep fighting.

My swollen tongue stuck to my mouth and my head pounded. I needed to get water and food then wait for Brad to die. To survive, I had to sneak back into the galley, but fear riveted my feet to the deck.

Maybe tomorrow.

I grit my teeth and shook my head. I could not wait. I strained to hear Brad. If he was on deck, I could make it to the refrigerator and sneak back to my sanctuary. I had to try.

I would have to crawl to minimize noises, so I put my hands on the generator to orient myself and stretched my legs behind me. My foot struck the flashlight, and it skittered across the deck and fell into a trough between machinery with a deafening clank—the loudest sound in the world.

I froze. Beads of sweat formed on my forehead. Had Brad heard? Maybe he was on deck where the ocean would mask the sound, or maybe he was asleep.

"Aargh," Brad growled from the starboard berth, just a few feet away. It was low and guttural, like a bear defending a cub, a dog protecting a bone—a monster hunting me on a sailboat. He knew where I hid, and he had been waiting for me to show myself. Brad clawed at the compartment door, coming for me.

I reached for the knife, but I could not locate it. It had to be close.

Brad banged on the door again.

I abandoned my search for the knife and slid away from the sound toward the port berth. The exit panel was flush against the bulkhead, but I could not see it.

I shuffled to my left, and my leg pressed against a scalding hot pipe. I yelped and bit my tongue to stop from screaming.

Brad pounded on the door, clawing and scratching, grunting with bloodlust.

I rushed forward, feeling my way through the machinery. A thick plastic tube hung across my path. I climbed over it and fell, banging my mouth against a sharp corner. I tasted blood.

The latch clicked behind me. Brad had solved the puzzle. I moved faster and my head collided with the bulkhead. I slid my hands across it, searching for the door. The panel opened behind me, flooding the compartment with light.

I whirled around as Brad stuck his head through the opening and glared at me with bloodshot eyes caked with mucus. His skin had turned beet red from either fever or the sun, and his face and chest twitched with spasms. He no longer seemed human. He bared his teeth and saliva foamed over his lips.

He crawled into the compartment.

I turned toward the bulkhead where light illuminated the panel latch. I dug my fingers into it and the cabinet swung open into the port cabin. I glanced over my shoulder.

Brad hunched on all fours behind me. He leaned over the generator and reached for me with blood-stained fingers.

I kicked at his hand, but missed, and my heel connected with his chest. The force of the blow knocked him off balance, and he tumbled between the generator and the air conditioner. I turned, grabbed the edges of the opening, and pulled myself through. My knees struck the bottom lip of the compartment as I dove into the cabin, and I rolled onto my back.

Brad moved toward me—a malevolent shadow.

I knelt, slipped my fingers under the cabinet door, and slammed it shut. The latch clicked as Brad's hands thwacked against the wood.

I sprinted from the cabin, around the companionway, and into the starboard berth.

Brad crawled toward me bathed in shadows, his face a mask of rage. I slammed the panel shut.

Brad wailed like an animal trapped in the dark. The virus had not weakened him, as I had hoped. He was strong, violent, and savage. A nightmare. He slammed against the door. It would not hold for long.

I had to hide. But where?

CHAPTER FORTY-SEVEN

I fled through the salon into the galley and snatched a steak knife out of a drawer. It was better than nothing. I raced into the stateroom and slammed the door behind me. I threw the bolt, locking it, but that would not stop Brad either.

I examined the head, with its flimsy door. If I hid in there and he found me, the hatches were too small to climb through and I would be trapped. I eyed the hatches above the bed. Those I could get through, but what would I do next? I scooped my bikini off the floor and put it on. Somehow, being dressed made me feel less vulnerable.

Brad's pounding resounded inside the engine compartment, as he tried to punch his way through the panel. If he used his legs, he would break the wood in seconds.

I had to defend myself, but I did not possess any fighting skills. I had never punched anyone, never been in a fight, not even as a young girl. I had jogged six days per week and toned my body, but I did not lift weights and possessed little upper-body strength. I was no match for a muscular man.

To survive, I had to use my mind as a weapon.

Brad pounded on the door, his growls reverberating behind the companionway, as if the ship itself was growling. Wood splintered.

I climbed onto the bed and stood on my toes, my stitches pulling against my wound. I lifted my leg and balanced on my good foot. I grabbed the plastic hatch handle, pressed the release button, and turned it counterclockwise to break the seal. I pushed the plexiglass hatch open and salty air blew in my face. Brad would break free from the engine compartment at any moment.

I held onto the hatch and waited.

Wood splintered in the stern and Brad's feet pounded on the deck. He had escaped. A door slammed open, probably the head inside the berth, then his footsteps thumped across the salon. He banged into the stateroom door, kicking and punching it, as if blinded by rage.

I tossed my knife through the open hatch onto the deck. I pushed off the bed and pulled myself through. It took all of my effort to get my weight over the lip of the hatch. I squeezed myself through the small opening and climbed on deck. I closed the hatch behind me.

I grabbed the knife and stared through the plexiglass. The stateroom door burst open and Brad ran into the room—a feral predator in search of prey. He slobbered like a dog, spraying saliva and turning the yacht into a biohazard. His eyes darted around the room—wild, inhuman. He kicked open the bathroom door and dove inside. He crashed against the sink, knocking the soap and toothbrushes onto the floor.

Brad bounded out of the bathroom and across the room. He yelped when he stepped on broken shards of glass, but the pain did not slow him. He threw open the cabinet doors and whirled around looking confused. Brad turned and stared at the bed.

The wind whistled through the unsealed hatch. Brad lifted his gaze toward the sound and his eyes met mine. A grin spread against his face and he bit the air between us.

He jumped on the bed and reached for me, but his hands slammed against the plexiglass and he fell back on the bed. He scurried to his feet and jumped again, grabbing the lip and pulling himself up into the hatch.

I ran as fast as I could along the gunwale to the stern. I hesitated at the cockpit to make sure he was coming. His upper body slid through the hatch opening and he staggered to his knees on the deck. I jumped into the cockpit and hurried down the stairs. I missed the last step and landed hard on the lower deck, twisting my ankle. I crashed to the ground in pain and the knife slid across the deck.

I clambered to my feet. My laceration burned and my ankle throbbed. I hobbled across the floor, grabbed the knife, and limped into the stateroom.

Brad's footsteps pounded overhead as he ran the length of the deck.

I climbed onto the bed and tossed my weapon through the hatch, and it clattered on the deck. I jumped for the hatch but missed and fell back onto the bed. My legs had weakened. Behind me, Brad banged down the companionway. He would be on me in seconds, and I was injured and unarmed.

I bent my knees and catapulted myself into the air. I caught the lip of the hatch and pulled with all my strength. My waist cleared the hatch and my upper body lurched onto the deck, but my legs dangled inside the stateroom.

Brad dove for me and his hand collided with my thigh. I twisted my body, and he sailed by.

I pulled myself through the hatch and watched. Brad picked himself off the floor and climbed onto the bed. I gasped for air, my heart pounded, and my foot and ankle screamed for relief. My body craved nourishment and my strength waned. I could not keep this game of cat-and-mouse going for long. He would catch me this time for sure.

I slammed the hatch shut as Brad dove for it, and his hands banged against the plexiglass. He howled in pain.

I hefted the knife, but it would not be enough. He was stronger, wild, unstoppable. I had to evade him. It was my only hope. My eyes darted around, desperate for escape. I could jump into the sea, but that meant certain death. My eyes scanned the deck for something I could use against him.

Brad jumped and shoved the hatch open, knocking me off balance.

I fell to the deck.

His hands came through the hatch.

I stomped on the glass and knocked him back down. Any minute he would realize he could use the stairs to come on deck and finish me. I could drop into the cabin, but I would not have the power to climb back up. The end drew near.

Brad pushed the hatch open again. I slashed his hand with the knife, and he screamed and fell into the cabin. Blood dripped off the blade's edge. I had to get away, but where could I hide on a yacht? I looked over my shoulder at the bow. The bow line was coiled near the bowsprit.

That's it.

The best place to hide on a sailboat was not on the sailboat at all. I sprinted for the bow.

CHAPTER FORTY-EIGHT

I stuck the knife handle in my mouth, snatched the coiled line off the deck, and shook the end loose. I formed a two-foot-long loop and double-knotted it, the way I tied my running shoes. I yanked eight feet of line free of the coil, wrapped it around a metal cleat, and pulled it tight.

The hatch crashed open behind me and Brad's hands clawed at the deck.

I tossed the line off the bow and peered over the side. The loop hung two feet over the surface and slapped against the hull. An image flashed in my mind—the sun glinting off the blue water in the pool, behind my father's lifeless body. I grabbed the line with both hands and stepped over the lifelines. My heart pounded, and I squeezed the line to stop the tremors in my hands. I broke into a cold sweat.

I glanced at the hatch as Brad's head poked out of it, and he pulled himself on deck facing aft. I had to hurry before he turned and saw me.

I leaned against the line to make sure it stayed taut and stepped onto the side of the hull. I pushed away from the yacht, transferring my weight onto my feet. I descended, hand over hand, walking my feet down the hull toward the water.

I peeked over the gunwale one last time. Brad stood and flexed the muscles in his arms. He turned around, and I ducked. The line burned the skin off my palms, and I spread my toes to improve my tenuous purchase on the hull. I stopped halfway and bent my knees until my body lay against the hull. I dangled my healthy foot beneath me and used my toes to locate the loop. I slipped my foot into it, and the knot tightened around me. I shifted my weight onto my leg and took the strain off my arms. I loosened my grip on the rope.

Above, Brad growled and ran around the deck hunting me. The virus had devastated his mind, and his synapses failed to connect as the damage spread. His brain had become a neurological fireworks show. I doubted he would think to check over the side, which meant I was safe.

For now.

CHAPTER FORTY-NINE

I dangled from the bow, gripping the line—holding onto life. Above, Brad growled and scampered around the deck, like a wolf stalking a wounded doe. A moment later, the muffled sounds of breaking glass emanated from the galley. He seemed furious.

The wind increased, and the sails ruffled, heeling the yacht and providing some forward momentum. The sea undulated around me.

If I lost my grip and fell into the water, I could not climb back onboard without the line. Even where the stern sat lowest in the water, the deck remained far above the waterline. Unreachable. My foot pulsated where my stitches stretched. Blood dripped off my toes. I followed a drop as it plunged through the air and splashed into the ocean. A pink haze formed on the surface below me.

The shark.

Fear jolted me—an electric shock arcing across my nerves. How had I forgotten about the shark? I had read sharks could detect a drop of blood in the water from miles away, and Brad had told me they could leap out of the water after prey. I dangled two feet over the surface, like a worm on a hook.

My eyes flickered across the surface, frantic. The line creaked from my shifting weight and rubbed against gunwale. If the line snapped, I would not have to worry about drowning. The shark would devour me.

I closed my eyes. I had not been to church since my father's funeral, but I bowed my head and prayed. I did not ask for God to intervene and save me—that was too much for me to believe. Instead, I prayed I would be smart enough to find my way out of this predicament, to think my way to safety. But if a solution existed, I could not see it.

"Shit."

I shook my head. I had a madman above me and a shark somewhere below. The wind had increased, and no one manned the helm. Brad would only live for a few more days, so if I could outlast him, I had a chance to survive.

My good leg tired and the line dug into the sole of my foot. My teeth clenched around the knife handle and my jaw quivered with a spasm. My position was unsustainable and soon, I would be too tired to climb up the line. I needed to find a better hiding spot, somewhere safe to make a plan.

Blood soaked my bandage, and a red stream trickled across my foot and beaded on the tips of my toes. I watched droplets grow then break free and fall into the water. I balanced on my right leg, bent over, and wiped off the blood. I dried my fingers on my bikini bottom. A long bloody trail hung in the water as the yacht drifted eastward, and I waited for the wound to clot.

Below me, a black fuzzy shape skirted the port side, swimming ten feet underwater. The great white had returned. I became a cat toy hanging at the end of a string. I had no choice but to climb up on deck.

A dorsal fin broke the surface of the water forty feet off the starboard side and turned toward me. The shark followed the blood trail, which led to me.

I hoisted myself and braced my feet on either side of the bow for balance. I followed the fin with my eyes and waited. I would have to be quick.

Its nose broke the surface fifteen feet away. Its mouth opened as if it were tasting the blood in the water. The shark stared at me with its black eyes, flicked its powerful tail, and submerged.

I bent my right knee, shifting my weight onto it, and rotated to the port side of the hull.

The shark broke the surface, its jaws open and its eyes rolled back in its head. It snapped its teeth and banged against the bow, where I had just been hanging. It splashed back into the water and disappeared below the surface as quickly as it had attacked.

My body shook, and I hyperventilated. I did not care if Brad was rabid. I had to escape the shark. I lifted my left foot and swung my weight across the bow until I straddled it. I pulled myself higher as I walked with one foot on each side of the hull. My arms were weaker than I had realized. My strength and energy almost gone.

When I was a few feet from the deck, I reached for the gunwale and wrapped the fingers around its lip. I kept my right hand on the rope, because falling into the water would bring a fast and ghastly death. I lifted my head level with the deck.

I locked eyes with Brad.

He crouched on his hands and knees and snarled at me from three feet away. He must have heard the shark strike the bow. He growled and reached for me.

I ducked below the deck and my injured foot slipped on the bloody surface of the hull. I slammed against the bow. I grunted in pain, twirling in the air as I dangled from the line. The polypropylene cut into my palms. My muscles ached and my grip slipped.

Brad glowered over the side at me, his mouth foaming and his eyes afire.

I eased my grip and slid toward the water, burning more skin off my hands. I squeezed hard to stop my descent but continued to slide. I swung my feet and touched the loop with my foot, but it bounced away and I slid past it and into the water. I jabbed at the loop with my injured foot and hooked it. My weight landed on my laceration and I screamed.

I stood on the rope and lifted my other leg out of the water. I pulled myself upright. My skinned palms reddened the line, and blood dripped off my foot into the ocean. I jerked my head around searching the water for the shark but saw nothing but blue water.

Brad growled above me, and I stared back with a hatred mirroring his own. Brad pulled on the line with both hands, and I rose a few feet in the air.

He's so strong.

I pressed my foot against the hull and yanked the line away from him. I fell two feet and bounced against the yacht. The impact knocked the wind from my lungs and the knife fell. It disappeared into the ocean.

My only weapon—gone.

Brad growled and paced, radiating pure aggression. The neurological nightmare had consumed his mind. At least his hydrophobia would prevent him from getting close to the water. He would not follow me down the line.

That's it! Brad's hydrophobia.

I could use his rabies-induced, pathological hydrophobia as a weapon against him.

The hair on my neck rose, and I glanced over my shoulder. The dorsal fin headed for me. I gripped the rope and straddled the bow. I had to be ready.

This time, the shark advanced from the port side and dove below the surface.

I rappelled to the other side of the hull as the shark burst out of the ocean. It snapped at the port side, exactly where I had been.

I had pushed too hard off the boat and the tension on the line swung me back across the bow. My momentum carried me towards the shark.

Oh God, I can't stop.

The shark shook its head as I slid toward it.

I raised my legs to avoid its open mouth and kicked its nose, pushing off the beast. I smacked against the hull and braced my feet against the fiberglass.

The shark thrashed, searching for food, but came up empty and disappeared below.

It's now or never.

I pulled my bikini top off with one hand, leaned over, and dragged it through the water. If the shark appeared now, it would bite me in half. I held the soaking-wet bikini top in my teeth and climbed like a mountaineer, my fear giving me a surge of strength. Brad clung to the bow sprit and hung over the edge—waiting for me. I stopped, a few feet out of his reach, and took the bikini out of my mouth.

"Want some water, Brad?"

He cocked his head as if trying to process my words.

"Don't forget to hydrate," I yelled.

I threw the bikini, heavy with saltwater, and it struck him square in the face, dousing him. He yelped and fell away, out of sight.

I climbed hand over hand until I reached the top. I could not go back, or the shark would have me, and with my strength depleted, I did not have the stamina to climb the line again. I had to confront Brad now. I grabbed the gunwale and hauled myself up and over. My bikini top lay in a puddle on the deck.

Brad had vanished.

CHAPTER FIFTY

The water had frightened Brad away—for the moment. I did not understand what was happening in his virus-addled mind, but he would return to hunt me down, and he would do it soon. With my energy exhausted, I functioned on adrenaline alone. I had to find another place to hide.

The entrance to the foresail locker lay in front of me. I opened the hatch, climbed halfway down the ladder, and shut the hatch behind me. The stifling cabin had been closed since we left, and the pungent odor of fiberglass tickled my nose. I rubbed my face to avoid sneezing. I locked the hatch, but only a thin piece of plastic held it closed. If Brad found me, he would breach it, and I would have nowhere to run.

A minute later, Brad ran across the deck toward the bow. He shook his head, frothing with rage.

I had barely made it. I let go of the handle and descended the ladder on my toes. I pressed against the wall in the cramped compartment, as far away from the hatch as possible.

Brad stomped on the deck and banged his hands against the lifelines. The stanchions creaked under his furious rage. He had realized I escaped, but did he think I had fallen in the ocean and the shark had taken me? He howled in a frenzy.

I wanted to scream, to cry, to make it stop, but I could not make a sound. I hugged myself and whimpered, too dehydrated for tears.

Brad stepped on the hatch and it creaked beneath his weight. He scanned the deck, and saliva dripped onto the plexiglass. He grunted and moved aft, out of view.

I was not safe here. I opened a cabinet and found two bottles of Evian. I twisted the caps open, smudging the plastic with blood, and guzzled them, one after the other. My body soaked in the liquid like a plant in the desert. I did not see any food.

I moved toward the ladder to locate Brad and stubbed my toe on a canvas bag.

The mast ascender.

It could work, if I had the courage. I slung the bag over my shoulder and climbed the ladder. The sun reflected off the glass, and I could only see a few feet in any direction. I gripped the handle. I had no choice. I unlocked the hatch and opened it halfway. I poked my head up and viewed the empty deck.

Time to go.

I bounded up the ladder onto deck, and tiptoed toward the mast, careful to avoid the stateroom hatches. I crouched low, in case Brad watched from the cockpit.

I made it to the mast. I untied a sheet from a cleat at the base and retied it to a cleat along the gunwale. I set the bag on the deck and dug out the harness. I clipped the ascenders to the sheet, as I had seen Brad do in the Java Sea—a lifetime ago.

Something crashed in the cabin below.

Had he heard me? I had to hurry.

I stepped into the harness and through the loops in the bottom ascender. I stood and pushed the top ascender over my head. I sat in the bosun's chair and took my weight off my feet. I reached below, raised the lower ascender, stood in the straps, and repeated the process. I had climbed four feet off the deck when Brad craned his head out of the cockpit.

"Yaaa," he yelled.

"Shit, shit, shit."

I pushed the ascender above me and sat back into the seat.

Brad came for me.

I grabbed the lower ascender, but I pulled it too fast and it did not move. I used both hands and slid it higher.

Fifteen feet.

I stood in the stirrups and raised the top ascender.

Brad lunged for my leg.

I sat back in the chair and lifted my feet.

He swiped at air as he sailed past, his fingers inches from my ankles. He toppled onto the deck and rolled.

I lifted the lower ascender and stood, pushing the top ascender with me.

Brad sprinted across the deck and jumped again.

I sat and lifted my legs in the stirrups. He missed me by two feet. I climbed until I hung twenty feet off the deck, beyond his range.

I gasped for air and my heart beat as if I had suffered a heart attack. I managed a breath and gazed upward. Sunlight glinted off the communications pod, seventy feet above. I did not intend to go higher. Blood dripped off my foot onto the deck, and my raw hands darkened the ascender. Sweat poured off me, and fatigue wore away my resolve. I had to rest.

The bosons chair swung side to side. I looked below. Brad held the line in his hands.

He started to climb.

CHAPTER FIFTY-ONE

Brad hauled himself, hand over hand, climbing the taut line toward me. His weight rocked my boson's chair, and I held on as it whipped back and forth. I had to keep going. I stood, raised the upper ascender, sat in the elevated seat, and pulled the lower ascender after me. I repeated the process and did not look down. I did not rush and moved as fluidly as possible. One mistake and he would catch me.

"Smooth is fast, smooth is fast," I repeated.

My technique improved, and I raised the seat eight times before I stopped to catch my breath. I peered between my legs. Brad had stopped climbing. He hung from the sheet, twenty feet off the deck. He arched his neck and stared at me. The muscles in his arms twitched with spasms. He lowered himself.

He lost his grip and fell.

Brad struck the deck with a snap and lay still on the deck. My head swooned, and I shut my eyes. I had never been suspended in air. Heights terrified me, but I had been too scared to notice until now—my desire to live overcoming my fear.

Brad groaned.

I opened my eyes.

He shook his head, dripping saliva everywhere. He rolled onto his knees, stood, and squealed. Brad collapsed on the deck holding his lower leg. The cracking sound had been his fibula or tibia fracturing. Or both.

Brad stood, balanced on one leg, and glared at me. He bit the air. He limped away and disappeared into the cockpit.

Had my inability to recover from Emma's death begun a chain of events that led to this nightmare? Was I responsible for Brad's infection? Had my weakness doomed him? Doomed me? I shook my head. I could not go down that path. Not now. Not ever.

"This is not my fault," I screamed.

I swayed in the seat, sixty feet above sea level. From my perch, I could see eight or nine miles, and I explored the horizon in all directions. No land. No ships. Nothing but ocean. Off the port side, the great white's dorsal fin broke the surface and cut circles around our yacht. I hung from the mast, trapped above a great white shark and a madman who wanted to kill me.

What the hell was I going to do now?

CHAPTER FIFTY-TWO

My tongue swelled in my desiccated mouth and my parched lips cracked. I needed more water, and I wished I had grabbed my bikini top off the deck, because my chest glowed bright red. My entire body stung from sunburn, and fatigue hung on me like a heavy coat. Brad stayed somewhere below, in the shade, probably sleeping in bed while I clung to the mast.

I hated him.

That was not fair. He was sick, and the virus had turned him into a monster, but I could not shake the feeling his neurological damage had unleashed a propensity for violence which had already existed. If Brad had been able to control his temper when he had been healthy, maybe the disease would not have presented like this. It had turned him into a flesh-eating monster. A rabid dog. A zombie.

The air cooled as the sun sank low on the horizon, bringing relief. The sails flapped in gusts of light wind. I had locked the wheel on a westerly course, which was the correct direction, but if the wind blew too hard and I did not make adjustments, we could capsize. Having the sails deployed with an unmanned helm would be catastrophic in a strong breeze.

I hung from the seat, halfway up the mast. What would I do when the sun set? If I fell asleep, I could fall. I needed to secure myself to the mast, but to do that, I would have to reach the top, ninety feet above the deck. My fingers and toes tingled, just imagining it. If I was going climb up there, I needed to move before dark, because it would be too easy to slip free of the stirrups once the sun set. I lifted the lower ascender and straightened. I moved the upper ascender and climbed higher.

"Don't look down. Don't look down. Don't look down." I repeated it like a mantra.

I locked my eyes on the top of the mast—far, far away. My stomach fluttered and my arms tingled. My fine motor skills grew sluggish and my vision dimmed. This terrified me more than the shark. Well, maybe not. I repeated the process again and again, and the summit drew near.

Five minutes later, I reached the satellite and communications pods, charred black from the lightning strike. If another thunderstorm hit, I would have to get below. I put my hand on the largest pod and used it for balance. I climbed over it, reached the crest, and wrapped my arms around the mast. I was strapped into the ascender, but I had to secure my upper body to the mast, because if I nodded off, I could topple out of the harness and fall to my death.

What could I use?

I untied my bikini bottom and held the mast as I slipped it off. I pulled my body flush with the mast with my left hand and draped the bikini over my arm. I used my right hand and teeth to tie it to the mast. I tugged on it. It would not hold my weight, but it would tighten against my hand if I fell asleep and leaned away from the mast, and that should wake me. In theory.

I hugged the mast and pressed my cheek against the smooth surface. I wanted to close my eyes, fall asleep, and awaken back on Commonwealth Avenue to discover the past year had been a dream, a horrible nightmare. I craved the safety of my childhood bed but hiding from reality would not help me. Not now.

I stared at the horizon. A few days ago, I had been terrified pirates would attack us. Now I prayed for thugs to board our yacht. How fast circumstances and perspectives changed. Rays of sun pierced the surface around the yacht, illuminating twenty feet below, like a swimming pool. A dark object swam thirty yards off the port side. It had to be the shark. I followed it with my eyes for a long time, then the sun set and turned the surface opaque, hiding the denizens of the deep.

Looking at the deck made me dizzy but focusing on the horizon mitigated my fear. A fall would kill me but staring at the horizon tricked my primitive lizard brain. From ninety feet in the air, I could see eleven or twelve miles. Something caught my eye on the southern horizon. What was that? I strained my eyes and leaned forward. A light flickered.

A sailboat!

The mast light blinked on the horizon as the sailboat bobbed on swells, then it vanished. The sky became a canvas of colors, and my vision dimmed and blurred in the low light, but I did not take my eyes off the spot where I had seen it. Darkness fell, and I strained to see the sailboat again. I needed the light to be there, needed another person on the ocean with me, needed to know I was not alone.

My eyelids grew heavy and my body begged for rest. My head jerked once, twice, three times. My eyes shut and I could not open them. My breathing deepened, and I pictured Emma smiling at me. Warmth radiated through me, and my pain disappeared.

CHAPTER FIFTY-THREE

I awoke in a panic and flung my arm into space.

"Help," I screamed.

I jerked in the swing and remembered where I was and what had happened. I clung to the mast and wrapped my feet around the satellite array. My heart raced, as if I had awoken during a skydive.

Day eight of acute symptoms.

The sun had risen above the horizon and the wind had strengthened, filling our sails and heeling the yacht a few degrees to starboard. Waves splashed against the hull as our speed increased. We had escaped the doldrums. From the sun's position, the yacht had drifted during the night and now pointed to the northwest. I oriented myself to find the other sailboat's light but saw nothing. I scanned 360 degrees of horizon.

The other sailboat had disappeared.

Adrenaline coursed through my veins and I balanced on the edge of panic. I tried to calm myself. I had made it this far, and all I had to do was outlive Brad. Once paralysis set in, or he slipped into a coma, I could take control of the helm and make for port. He had broken his leg and would not last much longer. I just had to hold on.

I peeled my tongue off the roof of my mouth. I needed water and food, and my bladder ached for release. My foot had stopped bleeding, but had swollen like a balloon, and my raw palms burned.

I untied my bikini bottom from the mast and draped it over my shoulder. I held the mast with my hands, arched my back to tilt the bosun's seat, and released my bladder. The urine pooled in my seat and leaked over the side, running over my legs, but I did not care. I needed relief. The urine dissipated in the light wind and rained on the deck. Two days ago, peeing off the mast would have been humiliating, degrading. Now, it was a logical step for survival. Circumstances changed perceptions and prioritized needs. I had seen the same phenomenon in the surgical waiting room, but now I understood it.

I smelled the pungent urine, a sign of dehydration. How much longer could I last without water? I trained my eyes to the south. Where had the sailboat gone? Something drew my attention, and I blinked to focus.

A faint light flickered on the horizon. My old friend had returned. Maybe it was wishful thinking or my imagination, but the light appeared larger. The light had a greenish hue which could be a visual trick caused by reflections off the surface, but if it was green, it would mean it sat atop the starboard side of the mast. Mast lights on cruisers were green to starboard, red to port, and white from behind. Green would indicate the sailboat headed in a westerly direction, and I could still see the light, which suggested the sailboat charted a parallel course within twelve miles of us.

I did not know if I could survive without help. Even if the virus incapacitated or killed Brad, I would still have to get to port alone. My sailing skills were novice, and I had no equipment to navigate, not even a compass. I needed to contact the sailboat. But how?

I could see the distant mast light, because I was high above the surface, but the other crew could not spot us from their deck. If they noticed our radar signature, the normal response would be to give us a wide berth, not close the gap. I had to send an SOS, and with our radio fried, it would have to be a visual signal.

The flare gun.

When I toured the yacht in Bali, Brad had mentioned he stored a flare gun in the foresail locker. I cursed myself for not thinking of it when I had hidden in there, but I had been trying to escape and not contemplating rescue. The flare gun was my only tool to signal the boat. I had to retrieve it.

I swiveled in my chair and looked down. My head spun and nausea crept into my throat. I closed my eyes, held onto the mast, and breathed.

I opened one eye and peeked again. The deck and cockpit appeared vacant.

Where was he?

Was Brad able to walk on his broken leg? Had the virus paralyzed him? Was he dead? Not seeing Brad—not knowing what he was doing—frightened me more than watching him sitting beneath the mast.

I stretched my arms and legs to get the blood moving again. My foot hurt. I leaned over to touch the bandage and my bikini bottom fell off my shoulder. I reached for it, lost my balance, and grabbed the mast to steady myself. My bikini flapped in the wind and fell over the side and into the ocean. Now, I could not tie myself to the mast. I needed to get the flare gun and signal the other boat, because I may not see another one for days or weeks. Or ever.

I had to try.

The process for descent was the reverse of ascending. I transferred my weight off the seat and lowered the device. I sat back, lifted my feet out of the stirrups and lowered them. It took four repetitions before I found my rhythm.

I stopped twenty feet above the deck and inspected the yacht from bow to stern. I tried to see through the stateroom hatches, but the sky and clouds reflected off the glass. I craned my neck toward the cockpit, but the Bimini top hid half of it from view. Brad could be there, lying in wait, or he could be below, but it did not matter. I had no viable alternative.

Butterflies fluttered in my belly, but I had faced fear before. I had made it through the loss of my father and the subsequent neglect by my alcoholic mother. Cutting into my first patient had taken incredible courage. I had survived Emma's death. This voyage had forced me to face my worst fears, and I had survived. I could do this. If Brad was waiting for me, I would fight him. I would not die like a sheep, afraid to fail.

"I love you, Emma. If I don't make it, I'll find you."

I grabbed the ascender and lowered myself. I stepped out of the harness and onto the deck. Pain shot from my foot, through my spine, and into my brain. My hamstrings had tightened in the harness, and I had trouble straightening my legs. I took one tentative step. And another.

I glanced at the cockpit. If Brad rounded the corner now, there was no way I could climb the mast or outrun him. I shuffled across the deck toward the bow without making a noise. I knelt beside the foresail locker and looked aft. Nothing. I lifted the hatch and climbed the ladder. I had to place the heel of my wounded foot on each wrung to avoid popping the stitches. I paused halfway and closed the hatch behind me.

I dropped to the floor and moved to a cabinet. I removed a bottle of Evian and drank it all. I downed a second bottle. And a third. My stomach bulged under the strain and the liquid flowed through me, rejuvenating my body and restoring my strength. I opened a storage compartment and dug through the supplies. I found a white tee shirt with the yacht's name, "KARNA," printed in gold on the front. I slipped it on, and it hung mid-thigh and melted away my goose bumps. I delved farther into the container and located a Swiss army knife. I clipped it to my shirt.

In the far corner of the compartment I discovered a black box, made from heavy plastic. I set it on the bed and popped it open. The flare gun rested inside. It had a French name and looked like a revolver with an oversized barrel. I drew the heavy gun, pressed a lever, and snapped the barrel open at the breach. Three flares wrapped in plastic were wedged inside the box. I ripped one open, and inspected the flare, which resembled a shotgun shell, only wider and longer. I slipped the flare and gun back into the box.

I could not carry the gun and use the ascenders at the same time. I searched the cabin for line or a strap but found nothing. I thought for a moment then pulled the sheet off the bunk. I cut it with the knife and tore off a long strip of fabric. I looped the strip through the case handles and tied it over my shoulder like a bandolier. I removed the last two bottles from the refrigerator, drinking one and saving the other for later. It would get hot during the day. I rummaged through the cabin, careful not to make noise, but found nothing else.

Time to go.

I climbed the ladder, cracked the hatch, and peeked over the brink. Brad stood on the starboard side of the cockpit staring at the mast. He knew I had come down.

CHAPTER FIFTY-FOUR

I slipped down the ladder and backed away from the hatch. The other sailboat could disappear from view at any moment, and every second I waited could mean losing my chance. Besides, there were only a few places to hide on a yacht, and even Brad's damaged brain would eventually consider checking the foresail locker. I had to ascend the mast, but I would never make it with him standing there.

The thought of leaving the compartment weakened my knees, and I leaned against the bulkhead for support. I pictured Emma's face. I had faced my darkest days and come so far. I could do this.

I had an idea.

I opened the storage compartment again and searched for something heavy and easy to handle. I found a fishing rod holder under the bed and hefted it in my hand. It was the right weight, but too long. There was nothing else. I squeezed the bottle in my hand. I would want it later, but if I never made it up the mast, water would not matter. I had to use it.

I climbed the ladder and looked through the plexiglass. I could not see Brad. I unlocked the latch and raised it a few inches. Brad stood near the mast facing the bosun's seat with his head cocked. He turned and looked at the cockpit, trying to solve the problem. I had to hurry before he figured it out.

I raised the hatch, praying he would not turn around, and eased my upper body through the opening. I twisted my torso, cocked my arm, and threw the bottle high into the air with all my strength. It sailed over the Bimini top and landed with a clunk near the helm. Brad whipped his head toward the sound. Had he seen the bottle? He limped aft, the bones in his leg crunching under his weight. The sound sickened me.

I climbed through the hatch as he loped toward the cockpit. If he turned, he would have me. I tiptoed, trying to be quiet, and the bloody bandage squished between my toes. Flames radiated through my leg, and I grit my teeth.

A wave smacked into the bow and the deck swayed and pitched. I lost my balance and fell hard on my side, sprawling on the deck. I twisted and glanced at the stern. Brad had fallen too. He hung across the safety lines, facing away from me then stood and swatted the lines with an open hand.

I clambered to my feet and hobbled to the mast. I slipped into the harnesses and tightened the belt around my waist. I watched Brad stumble into the cockpit. He tilted his head toward the sky and snarled. I raised the ascender, sat in the seat and stood in the stirrups. I elevated the seat and repeated the process, faster than before. The gun case banged against my hip, each time I stood.

"Yaaa," Brad yelled.

I looked over my shoulder, and he glowered at me from the stern. He raised his hands over his head and curled his fingers. He snarled and climbed onto the deck.

I hung only ten feet in the air. I turned away from him and focused on speed. Raise ascender . . . sit . . . raise stirrups . . . stand. Brad trudged across the deck toward me, thumping his leg as he moved. The noise grew louder, closer.

He neared, but I did not turn to check. Any wasted motion would slow me.

"Aargh," Brad screamed below me.

I looked down. Brad jumped and slapped the line with his hands, missing me by inches. The chair swung in the air, and I clung to the harness to avoid falling. He crashed to the deck and screamed in pain. I continued to climb.

I reached the top and rested.

That had been close. My life had come within seconds of ending, and now that the danger had passed, my hands shook. I hugged the mast to steady myself. Cumulus clouds crawled across the blue sky. I breathed in the salty air, fresh and thick. The yacht bobbed in the ocean as the wind blew harder and the sea surged. The mast swayed, exacerbated by my weight. I had almost died, but I survived. My body tingled with exhilaration, stronger than ever before. Fighting for my life and using my wits against my enemy, against nature, had empowered me. I had turned my mind into a weapon and won—not the war, but a minor battle.

Hope existed.

I leaned back in the seat, which dangled as high as before, but this time, I felt safer, more secure. I examined the horizon to the southwest. It took a minute, but I caught flickering sunlight reflected off the other boat's mast. I had three flares. A flare may not be visible during daylight, but if I waited until night and the sailboat disappeared, I would regret missing my chance.

I swung the case under my arm, rested it against my waist, and hooked the mast with my feet. I would not drop the flare gun after I had almost died retrieving it. I drew the gun, opened the breach, and set it inside the case. I pulled a flare from the opened package and loaded it into the gun. I snapped the breach closed and held the gun in my hand.

The wind carried Brad's high-pitched screams to my ears. He balanced on his injured leg and swatted the mast with his hand, sending vibrations into my legs. I ignored him and swiveled in my seat to face the distant light.

I raised the flare gun over my head. I had never fired any kind of firearm before, and my heart raced, either from fear of the gun or the possibility my signal would go unnoticed.

I inhaled, held it, and squeezed the trigger. The metal dug into my raw finger, but the gun did not fire. Hunger and dehydration had weakened my grip, and I could not pull the trigger all the way back. I wrapped my left hand over my right and used two fingers. The trigger inched back.

The hammer snapped forward, and the gun exploded. A red flare rocketed from the barrel, high into the air at the tip of a fiery red tail.

The flare rose higher and higher. It exploded in a starburst, a thousand phosphorous fragments burning through the sky—the Fourth of July in the Indian Ocean.

My eyes followed the flare as it plummeted and disappeared into the brine, leaving a trail of white smoke behind. I searched for the green light but saw nothing. I waited for a full minute. And another. My eyes burned and my throat tightened. A tear ran down my cheek.

The ship had vanished.

CHAPTER FIFTY-FIVE

The afternoon sun burned my skin, turning it cherry red. I hung in the seat with the gun case secured against my hip. Brad had paced the deck for hours after I fired the flare, incensed by either the explosion or my escape. Maybe the rabies made him sensitive to loud noises, but his own incessant shrieking did not seem to bother him. For me, it was another story. His manic growling tore at my nerves and chilled my bones.

He wanted to tear the flesh from my body.

Brad stayed on the deck and monitored me. He did not appear to have anything human left inside him, but he knew enough not to leave me alone again. His primitive brain recognized he had cornered me, treed his prey. He knew I had to come down, and when I did, he would slaughter me.

He bared his teeth like a grizzly and scratched his nails across the deck.

I looked away. I pulled my tee shirt off and fashioned a turban to shade my eyes from the sun. My tongue swelled, but I continued to sweat—a positive sign—because once I stopped perspiring, heat exhaustion came next, followed by heatstroke and death. My stomach rumbled from hunger. I had not eaten in days and my strength waned.

The halyards clanked rhythmically against the mast, calming me, and I drifted at the edge of sleep, fighting to stay awake. I could not lash myself to the mast, unless I untied the gun case and used the strip of bed sheet, but I would risk losing the flare gun. I forced myself awake.

My thoughts drifted to Eric. Shy Eric. Kind Eric. Brilliant Eric. He exuded an inner peace, a quality Brad pretended to have, but never did.

I had doubted Brad's suitability from the beginning, but once I had married him, I committed. I never cheated on him, never flirted, never entertained romantic thoughts about another man. Loyalty meant everything to me, but somehow, Brad's raging below—waiting to kill me—had freed my mind to think about Eric and an alternate future. If I made it through this, I would tell Eric what his friendship meant to me. The fantasy kept me going.

I spotted the sailboat again, catching glimpses of its mast in the distance, at least ten miles away. If I saw it after dark, I would try another flare. Either it would work, or it would not.

My life depended on the outcome.

Far to the east, the horizon darkened with clouds. Another storm. How strong would the winds be and how violent? The rain squall seemed distant, but if it hit us, we would be in trouble. I could not deploy the sea anchor or steer, and our chance of capsizing would become all too real.

The sun took a lifetime to reach the horizon; a lifetime of sizzling flesh; a lifetime of thirst; a lifetime listening to Brad below. Furious Brad. Rabid Brad. I could not think of him as my husband anymore. He had morphed into a devil, a demon from my nightmares. The sun touched the horizon and spread out, shimmering at the edges of the earth. It melted into the ocean and the sky changed from pewter to black.

I slid the case onto my lap, opened it, and loaded another flare. Two shots left. I aimed the gun toward the distant mast light and pulled the trigger. The flare rode high into the sky and burst like another sun, much brighter than before. I allowed myself to hope.

I stared at the green mast light flickering in the distance as the sailboat bobbed on the rising swells. The ocean heaved, like the chest of a giant beast. The wind died. Brad watched me from the deck below.

I waited.

CHAPTER FIFTY-SIX

Day nine.

I leaned my face against the mast, hovering between consciousness and sleep. I thought of Emma and my daydreams took on a life of their own. My head bobbed, and I forced myself awake. The sky turned steel blue signaling the approach of sunrise. I shook my head. The sail had filled, and the yacht pitched as it cut through the waves. I estimated we heeled fifteen degrees to starboard, and if the winds shifted any more, I would need to ease the boom out or turn the boat away from the wind. An unmanned sailboat was doomed.

The sun cracked the horizon and turned the water to golden honey. I raised my hands over my head and stretched my aching body. The sky had cleared to the east, so the storm had missed us. I twisted my torso to crack my back and froze. The other sailboat looked closer. Was the boat heading toward us? I rubbed my eyes and checked again. I detected the thin dark line of the hull and the red and green lights on the mast. It was not my imagination. The sailboat had turned toward us and closed the distance.

The crew must have seen my distress flare. The sailboat looked to be approximately ten miles away, and the wind had strengthened, blowing out of the east and propelling us forward at a minimum of five or six knots. We could go faster if we trimmed the sails and jibbed away from the wind, but since we failed to maximize our sails, the other boat should cruise faster than us. If their crew managed to milk a few more knots out of the wind, they could close the gap, assuming they took the right angle to intercept. However, the perfect angle was unlikely to be an ideal angle to the wind, which would slow them. I also did not know what kind of boat they had, or if they faced stronger currents or rougher seas, or how proficient they were at sailing. Many variables would determine their speed, but I estimated they would reach us during the night.

My head spun, my stomach ached from hunger, and pain radiated through my temples. Either dehydration caused my symptoms, or I was infected with rabies. I shook the notion away. Some things were out of my control.

Would I be conscious when help arrived? I needed to warn the other crew about the rabid nightmare lurking below. If I could slow our yacht, they would overtake us sooner. I could deploy the sea anchor, but I had stowed it after the storm. The most obvious solution was to furl the sails or turn into the wind, but I needed to be in the helm to do either of those maneuvers.

I looked over the bosun's chair at Brad sitting on the deck below. He raised his head and met my stare. I would never make it to the helm alive.

"Hey Brad, there's something I've been meaning to tell you. I want a fucking divorce."

He cocked his head and bared his teeth.

I watched the other boat. The sea was a dangerous place and thousands of years of sailing had created a culture where mariners helped others in distress, and with or without legal compulsion, most captains rushed to the aid of sailors in need. That had to be why the other boat had changed course. The crew must have found it odd we had fired a distress flare, but kept our sails raised and continued away from them. What if they decided we were not in trouble? What if they changed course and left us alone? I had to lower our sails to slow us or risk the other crew abandoning their rescue effort.

The luff edge of the mainsail clipped to the halyard with shackles, which were enclosed along a metal track inside the aft portion of the mast. I could squint and see them in there, but I could not reach them.

The yacht's enormous sails were meant to be controlled from the helm, not by a novice swinging off the mast like a monkey.

I leaned away and examined the sail. My goal was to drop the sail, so I did not have to furl it like I would under normal circumstances. I only needed it to lose the wind. I unclipped the Swiss army knife from my tee shirt and ran my hand across the mainsail. It was constructed from heavy cloth, probably Dacron or some other man-made fiber, and covered with laminate.

I opened the largest blade and pressed it against the sail, but the knife would not penetrate it. I stood in the stirrups and grabbed the head of the sail. I pulled the luff edge as taut as I could. The fabric wiggled in my hand as the wind tugged it. I swiveled the knife in my hand, angled the blade down, and raised it over my head.

I stabbed the sail, and the knife punctured the fabric with a pop.

I changed my grip and yanked the knife downward, but it was not sharp enough to cut the cloth. I closed the blade and fingered through the other tools. I opened a small saw with jagged teeth, inserted it into the hole, and sawed until it chewed through the sail.

Sweat beaded on my skin, rolled off my forehead, and burned my eyes. I cut a three-foot incision. Wind blew through the opening, pulling the sail and making it easier to saw. I lowered my bosun's chair a few more feet and continued to slice away. The sail fluttered as wind poured through the opening between the sail and the mast. I kept going, and the sail flapped wildly, slapping and stinging my arms.

I lowered the chair and cut for thirty more feet. The sail flapped out of control, striking me when I leaned too close. The wind slipped off the torn edge and slowed the yacht and decreased the angle of heel.

The hole in the sail reached a tipping point, and when the wind tugged at it, the weight of the fabric ripped on its own. I clipped the knife onto my shirt and swung the boson's chair forward, away from the snapping fabric. The wind completed my work and tore the edge of the mainsail all the way to the boom.

The sail billowed across the deck, causing the yacht to flounder and rock side to side. I had slowed our momentum to one or two knots, and from a distance, our damaged sail would be visible. If the other boat came within sight, they would know we were in trouble, but if they abandoned the pursuit, I had destroyed my best option for navigating to port.

Exhausted, I leaned against the mast and waited. Movement caught my eye. A dorsal fin appeared fifty yards of the port side. The shark had returned, if it had ever left. It swam around the boat in a lazy circle, then submerged into the depths.

Minutes turned into hours and the day slipped away. I dreamed about water, not the ocean, but large glasses of cold beverages—lemonade, apple juice, iced coffee—anything to hydrate. My lips cracked and bled in the sun. I licked them and my mouth filled with the taste of iron. My skin burned wherever it was not covered by the tee shirt. I wanted to vomit, a sign of heat exhaustion.

Brad waited below. He did not move out of the sun. He did not go to the bathroom. He sat and watched. Every few minutes he growled and pounded his hands on the deck. Once, he flopped around like he was having a seizure. Even from atop the mast I could see his skin had burned and blistered, but he did not appear to care. His sole focus was me. He wanted to catch me, hurt me . . . murder me. He was an animal on the hunt.

I hoped he would die soon.

What would I do with Brad when he passed away? His rabies-riddled body posed a biohazard, and heat would hasten his decomposition. It was a morbid thought, but I had been around enough cadavers to know what would happen. His body would bloat, burst, and liquefy. The smell would become unbearable and it would turn the yacht into an unlivable environment in two days. I would have to drag him over the side, but if he died below deck, I would not have the strength to carry him upstairs. If I got him into the water, the great white would eat him and draw more predators to the yacht. Would I be able to feed the body of my deceased husband to the sharks?

I shuddered. How would I explain that to the police? To his parents?

The waiting drove me to madness.

"What's happening to me?" Brad said.

I twisted in my seat and looked at him. Was he speaking to me? Those were the first coherent words he had uttered in days.

"Brad?"

"What is this?" he said.

"Brad, do you understand me?"

"Stay away from me, Dags. I'm . . . I'm so sorry."

I could not believe he was talking again. Was he beating the rabies?

"Are you okay?" I asked.

"Aargh," he yelled, and snapped his teeth at me.

Eric had said some patients experienced periods of lucidity near the end. What an evil virus. Brad must be in hell. I averted my eyes.

The sun beat on my face.

I stopped myself from staring at the other sailboat and trying to estimate when it would arrive. I checked hourly to see if my salvation drew near or if it had changed course and abandoned me for dead. My stomach tightened before I would look and then I would see it—larger, closer, coming to save me. By nightfall, I estimated it was two or three miles away. It would reach us before dawn.

What would happen when it did? The sailboat was coming to help because the crew had seen the distress flare, and I had a duty to warn them about Brad. He was violent and highly contagious, and if he bit someone, he would infect them. They would never hear me yelling over the wind and waves, so how could I signal the boat to tell them I had a rabid lunatic onboard? I could flap my arms and point—like a horrific game of charades—a game where the losers died.

I inspected the lights on the masthead. I could use them to signal, but the only Morse code I knew was SOS. It had been in the sailing book I had read on the plane. Dot, dot, dot—dash, dash, dash—dot, dot, dot. Simple enough to remember.

I held my hand over the red light for two seconds then removed it. I covered it two more times, followed by three long exposures, then three short ones. I repeated the sequence again and again. If anyone was watching, they should recognize the international distress code.

I held onto the mast and rested. Even the slightest physical exertion tired me. I untied the sheet from the gun case and used it to lash myself to the mast to avoid falling to my death hours before help arrived. I balanced the flare gun in my lap. I needed to get fuel into my body soon. I imagined a large plate of spaghetti Bolognese, the tomato sauce dripping over angel hair pasta, shredded parmesan cheese melted on top, and a piece of buttered garlic bread beside it. A hunger pang tweaked my gut.

I closed my eyes, leaned against the pole, and dreamed about food.

CHAPTER FIFTY-SEVEN

The bed sheet tugged at my wrist where I had tied it to the mast, and I jarred awake, not knowing where I was or what was happening. Lack of nutrients, dehydration, and physical exertion had exhausted me, and I must have passed out. I untied my hand and shook it to get the blood flowing. I reached in my lap for the flare gun, but it had fallen during the night. I saw the case lying on the deck, but no sign of Brad.

The sun rose over the horizon, turning the sky orange. Day ten of acute symptoms. My nightmare would end soon—one way or the other. I searched the horizon for the other sailboat but did not see it. Had it turned in the night?

I heard something faint, something new, and I cocked my ear to the wind. The low, throaty rumble of an engine in neutral chugged nearby. I rotated the bosun's chair and stared aft. The other sailboat floated ten yards off our starboard side. Its sails were furled, and it bobbed on the ocean swells. My chest filled.

When had it arrived? I had lost consciousness before dawn, so the boat could not have been there for long. If they had tried to hail me, I had not heard them. No one was visible onboard the forty-foot sailboat. "Sun Odyssey 419" adorned the white hull, under the beige gunwale. I did not see the crew. Or Brad.

"Hey," I shouted, but only a squeak came out.

My throat parched. I smacked my lips and tried to salivate but could not.

"Help, help, help," I yelled.

I stared at the boat's empty deck. No one responded. They could not hear me. I unclipped my knife from my shirt and banged it against the mast. I sent the SOS code. Clang, clang, clang—clang . . . clang . . . clang—clang, clang, clang.

Nothing.

"I'm up here. Somebody, help me."

No response.

My chest ached, and I cried a tearless sob. I had entered the recurrent dream I had as a child where I tried to call my mother but could not utter a sound. Salvation lay within sight, but I could not yell loud enough for anyone to hear. I banged the knife on the mast again and the clanging echoed through the air.

Why could no one hear me?

I scanned our yacht, but the sail obscured the cockpit. Had Brad gone below?

The sun glinted off something, fifty yards to port. I shaded my eyes and recognized the profile of a white dinghy—unoccupied. It must be the Sun Odyssey's lifeboat. It bobbed on the surface, drifting away, and trailing a line in the water. Why was their dinghy floating away?

I turned back to the Odyssey.

"Help me."

The wind carried my voice over the bow and across the ocean. The crew must have seen me hanging from the mast. Were they below deck? What the hell was going on?

My frustration gave way to anger. I had to get off the mast and find them, warn them about Brad. If he was still alive.

I lowered myself down the line toward the deck. The sail ruffled in the early morning breeze and I pushed off the mast with my feet to avoid it. Our yacht drifted away from the other boat as we rolled over long swells. I hesitated ten feet above the deck. I did not see anyone. Something was wrong.

"Hello? Is anyone there?"

No answer.

"Brad?"

Nothing.

I scanned the deck a final time. This was it. All of my efforts had gone toward signaling the sailboat, my last hope for survival. Now it had arrived, and I needed to get help.

I lowered myself to the deck.

My swollen foot throbbed with undulating waves of pain. I eased my weight onto it, as if I stood on a partially deflated balloon. I slipped out of the harness and scanned the deck, expecting Brad to emerge from below and finish me.

"Hello?" I said, my voice soft, tentative.

I moved along the gunwale, sidestepping around the sail, which flapped over the deck like a wounded bird. I walked to the edge of the cockpit, leaned over, and peeked inside. Nothing. I looked back at the other sailboat. It appeared abandoned.

The great white's fin cut through the water between the yacht and the other sailboat. I shivered. Where was Brad? Where was the other crew? Gooseflesh covered my arms. My lips trembled.

This feels wrong.

I knelt on the deck and pressed my face against the small cabin windows. The interior was dark, and I could not see though the tint. I walked to the stern and peeked around the helm. The companionway was open.

"Hello?"

No answer.

I rounded the steering wheel and stepped into the cockpit. I saw nothing in the darkness below. I glanced back at the sailboat. It bobbed silently, like a ghost ship.

"Ahoy on the Sun Odyssey," I yelled.

No response.

I took a step. My hair rose on my neck. I took another. My hands shook. I moved to the stairs, bent at my waist, and looked into the salon.

Empty.

I held the handrails and stepped onto the stairs. What else could I do? I had to find the other crew. Maybe Brad was dead. I hesitated on the top step. My entire body trembled.

"Brad? Are you in there? Please answer me."

The ocean lapped against the hull. The sail fluttered. I took another step. I looked right and left. Shadows veiled the stern berths. My bloody footprints had dried and turned a rusty brown. I climbed below. I held my breath and listened. A faint cracking sound came from somewhere below.

"Brad?"

Had he succumbed to the virus? After ten days of acute symptoms, he must be near the end. I moved to my left and peeked into the port berth. Empty. I checked the starboard berth, which was empty too. The broken door lay on the floor.

Another noise came from the stateroom.

What is that?

I glanced at the companionway, my every instinct urging me to flee, but where would I go? I turned and faced the bow. I limped forward, past the salon and galley. I stepped into the corridor outside the stateroom. The door hung open a few inches.

A wet slurping sound emanated from the room. Someone was in there. Was Brad snoring? I pushed the door halfway open, rested my palm on the doorjamb, and leaned into the opening.

An older man lay on his back, sideways across the bed, with his hands and legs dangling over the edges. His face had contorted into a mask of horror, and his dead, unblinking eyes stared at me. Brad hunched over him like an animal. The man's stomach splayed open and two broken ribs stuck out at odd angles. Blood soaked the bed and dripped off the saturated sheets onto the deck. Crimson liquid rolled across the floor, sloshing against the bulkheads and splashing the walls. The room stank of feces, blood, and death.

Brad dug his hands inside the man's abdomen and yanked a long string of intestines from the cavity—gray and slippery, like uncooked sausages. He jammed them into his mouth and bit into them. Blood squirted over his chest. He jerked his head, ripping a chunk off, and chewed it. He gnawed and slurped as the entrails slid out of his mouth.

"Nooo," a groan escaped my lips.

Brad jerked his head up and glared at me with yellow eyes—wild, inhuman. The intestines squeezed through his fingers. He growled and bared his teeth in a demonic smile.

CHAPTER FIFTY-EIGHT

I yanked my head out of the stateroom and slammed the door shut. My mind went black. I fled, driven by instinct. My legs moved by themselves and carried me through the salon. I reached the companionway and grabbed the rails.

Something thumped behind me.

I looked over my shoulder. Brad stood in the salon, drenched in the sailor's blood. Six feet of intestines dangled from his hands and trailed on the deck behind him. His eyes bore into mine and he bared his teeth. A flap of torn villus hung from the corner of his mouth. He moved toward me, dragging his broken leg behind him.

I turned and bounded up the steps, pain radiating from my lacerated foot. I shuffled through the cockpit to the starboard side and paused.

Where could I go?

The sailor—my savior—was dead. His sailboat drifted thirty yards behind us. I grabbed the lifelines between stanchions. I needed to get on his boat, but did I even remember how to swim?

The stairs creaked under Brad's weight.

I had to jump. I bent my knees and coiled my body, ready to leap over the side. My hands shook, almost out of control. My legs had gone numb, as if they belonged to someone else.

The dorsal fin passed five yards in front of me. If I jumped now, the great white would eat me alive.

Brad took another step and growled.

I sprinted for the mast.

I climbed onto the cabin top, took a step, and slipped on my bloody bandage. I crashed hard onto the deck and skinned my knee. Brad's head appeared in the cockpit. He whirled around and his eyes found me. I regained my footing and stepped into the harness. I did not stop to tighten it. I raised the top ascender and sat into the chair.

Brad rounded the corner and moved along the gunwale, toward me. He dragged his leg behind him like a piece of luggage. His broken leg slowed him, but his body radiated intensity. If he got his hands on me, it was over.

I raised the lower ascender and mounted the stirrups. I stood and lifted the top ascender in one motion. I sat in the seat and glanced at Brad. He was halfway to me and I dangled only four feet off the deck. I would not make it—not even close. He would grab me, pull me from the harness, and kill me. I needed an alternative plan.

I slipped out of the bosun's chair and dropped to the deck.

Brad slung the intestines to deck, growled, and flashed his teeth. I smelled the decay on him. He clambered onto the cabin top.

What now? I took a step backwards, tripped over an object, and landed hard on my side. The flare gun case lay beside my foot. I grabbed it and ran toward the bow, my nerve endings screaming with pain.

Brad twisted his body and swung his arms as he dragged his broken leg. He stepped with a thump, stopped, and pulled his leg behind him, scraping it across the deck. He continued toward me. Thump . . . scrape . . . thump.

I reached the bow and turned.

He pursued me across the deck. Thump . . . scrape . . . thump.

My fingers fumbled over the latches. I snapped the case open and removed the flare gun. One flare left.

Thump . . . scrape . . . thump. Fifteen feet away.

I tried to rip the plastic package around the flare, but my sweaty hands slipped off it.

Thump . . . scrape . . . thump. Ten feet.

I stuck it in my mouth and ripped it open. I removed the flare.

Thump . . . scrape . . . thump. Brad was right in front of me.

I dodged to the side away from his reach. I grabbed a stanchion and climbed onto the bowsprit. I balanced on the four-foot-long and one-foot-wide piece of metal, which pointed off the bow like a gangplank.

Thump . . . scrape . . . thump. Brad made it to the edge.

I wobbled on the slippery surface and looked through a slit at the anchor hanging below. The shark's fin sliced past, twenty yards to port.

The yacht rocked in the surge and Brad hesitated before stepping onto the bowsprit.

I snapped open the breach and turned the flare in my hand to insert it into the barrel. The bow bounced over a swell, and I lost my balance. I flailed my arms, trying not to fall, and dropped the flare. It clanked against the bowsprit. I moved my weight forward over my knees and regained my footing.

The yacht pitched over another wave, and the flare rolled to the edge. I leaned forward and reached for it. The flare bounced off the bowsprit and slipped over the lip. I lunged and caught it in the air.

I sat on the bowsprit, with my feet dangling over the edge.

Brad growled and crawled forward, dragging his leg behind him.

I slid the flare into the gun and slammed the breach shut. Brad reached for my throat.

I pointed the gun at his chest and pulled the trigger.

The flare fired out of the barrel with a whoosh. A white trail of smoke obscured the space between us. Brad's chest lit up with a bright red flame. He screamed and bolted upright, then scampered onto the deck clutching his chest. His shirt burst into flames with white phosphorus burning hot and bright. He stumbled backward, swatting at it.

He met my eyes, his face a mask of pain and rage. He snarled and took a step toward me.

The flare exploded with the secondary burst and red tracers flew out of him.

My leg burned, and I swatted at a flaming tracer embedded in my thigh. I dug at it with my fingernails, burning myself. It popped free, fell, and sizzled on the surface below.

Brad ran screaming across the deck, with the flare stuck in his skin, and the deck smoking in his wake. He ran aft and disappeared into the cockpit. He screamed and banged around below.

A loud whoosh erupted above me as the main sail burst into flames from the tracers. Fire crawled up the sail, burning and melting the Dacron. Black smoke billowed high into the air. A wide sheet of fabric, alive with flame, broke off and curled in the air. I ducked as it floated over me and drifted off to sea. Dark ash fluttered down and smoldered on the deck. Flames caught in a dozen places, and the fire spread.

I tossed the empty flare gun into the ocean and held the bowsprit with both hands. I moved my good foot behind me and hooked the metal. I knelt on one knee and walked my hands in toward my body to stand up. The bow pitched over a wave and the yacht canted to port. The weight of my upper body extended over the bowsprit.

I fell.

I hooked my arms around the bowsprit, and my legs dangled beneath me. Blood dripped off my toes. I looked left and right, but the shark was not in view. The metal dug into my arms. I tried to pull myself up, but I did not have the upper body strength left. Blood formed on the surface below me. I took a breath to compose myself.

Mind over matter—think it through.

I was not strong enough to climb up, but I could use my body weight to help. I twisted my torso and swung my legs beneath me, like a pendulum, reaching higher each time. At the apex of the arc I slung my left leg over the bowsprit and used my momentum to pull my body on top. I righted myself and tucked my knee underneath me.

I waited until the yacht lifted over a crest and plummeted into the trough. I put my weight on my knee and stood. The yacht climbed the next swell. I took two quick steps forward, grabbed the lifelines, and tumbled onto the deck.

I ran toward the stern. I slipped on a wet pile of the sailor's intestines and grabbed the lifeline to stop myself from toppling overboard. The shark swam close to the yacht, probably drawn by my blood. Smoke wafted across the deck.

I had to get to the Odyssey. The Karna's owner had stored the emergency life raft under the port berth. I limped through the cockpit, but the cabin was ablaze and acrid smoke poured out of the companionway like a chimney. I climbed onto the top step, choking on the heavy chemical smell. Brad banged around somewhere behind the smoke, screaming like a madman. Even if I could get to the berth without burning myself or being attacked, I could never drag a heavy life raft up the companionway alone.

I stepped into the fresh air. The deck burned in a dozen places. The sunscreen on the Bimini top burst into flames. I retreated to the stern. The Odyssey had drifted forty yards behind us.

What could I do?

I leaned against a stanchion and watched the shark swim past, making slow circles around the yacht. My eyes drifted to the transom beneath me. The rigid hull inflatable motorboat was in the tender garage. I could lower the dry dock, push the inflatable across it, and motor to the Odyssey. I had to hurry before Brad emerged from below or the fire consumed me.

I turned to the helm to lower the transom and open the dock, but the digital screen was black. The lightning had fried the electrical system, and I could not manually open the garage.

The deck below me warmed as both berths burned. Black smoke poured from below, and Brad's screams resonated out of the stateroom. A wisp of flame licked the cabin top around the companionway. I stepped onto the deck, now hot to the touch. The yacht groaned and something exploded in the galley. When the flames hit the fuel tanks, the yacht would disintegrate.

The fuel!

I could turn the engine on, motor close to the Odyssey, and leap onto its deck. I jumped back into the cockpit and reached for the ignition.

Brad had taken the key.

CHAPTER FIFTY-NINE

I had to swim to the Odyssey. There was no other way. The fuel tank could ignite at any time and blow the yacht into a million pieces. Even if the fuel did not explode, the fire would breach the hull and sink the yacht, and then the shark would have me. Unless I burned to death first. I did not have much time.

At least I had a chance in the water. My God, the water. The image of my father's pale, still body flashed in my mind. The Odyssey drifted fifty yards away. Could I swim that far? I was fatigued more than I had been after childbirth, but I had to try. I would not die here, afraid to act.

I climbed onto the deck and stepped over the lifelines. I balanced on my toes, ready to jump. Where was the shark? My foot slipped on the gunwale and I held the lifeline for support. Blood dripped down the hull. My foot bled, worse than before. The blood would attract the great white and draw it to me like a trail of breadcrumbs. I had to distract it and buy time to swim to the Odyssey. I looked at the yacht and my gaze fell upon the pile of intestines.

It has to work.

I climbed back over the lifelines and ran forward, I knelt, held my breath, and scooped the intestines into my arms. They squished and unraveled as I gathered them against my chest. The stench of death enveloped me. The intestines slid through my hands, like slithering snakes. Blood soaked my shirt.

I stepped gingerly across the wet deck to the port side. I leaned over the side and heaved the intestines into the air. They hit the surface with a sickening flop and blood and bile spread across the surface. A demonic chum. Seawater seeped into them and they started to sink. No sign of the shark.

I reached between the safety lines and slapped my palm against the hull to lure the great white. Still no shark. I balled my hand into a fist and banged with all my strength against the side of the boat.

The shark burst out of the water beneath the intestines, filling its mouth with the sailor's remains. Its jaws gnawed on the meat as its nose soared high into the air. It hung there for a moment, intestines dangling from its mouth, then plunged beneath the white foam. The impact splashed cool water over the gunwale, drenching me.

It had attacked from below—without warning.

Blood dripped off me onto the deck and ran over the gunwale. It was now or never. I jumped into the cockpit, grabbed a cushion off the couch, and hurled it over the transom.

I climbed over the lifelines, hesitated, and then ripped off the bloody tee shirt. I wadded it into a ball and threw it over the port side near the stew of intestines. I gazed into the black, bottomless abyss below me.

I jumped.

The water hit me like a slap in the face. Cool water tingled my legs below the surface. I kicked my feet and scooped my hands trying to doggy paddle. I flailed, barely keeping my head above the surface. The shock from the temperature change snapped me out of my panic and focused my mind. I had committed and there was nothing left to do but swim.

I swept my arms through the water toward the cushion. I reached it in two strokes and pulled it under my chest. It kept me afloat and subdued my fear. The Odyssey was almost fifty-five yards away. I aimed for the stern which was low enough for me to climb on board—if I made it.

I balanced on the cushion and kicked, trying to keep my knees locked as my father had taught me. I paddled with my arms, reaching in front of me.

Forty-five yards.

I focused on the sailboat and did not look back. There was no point. The Odyssey drifted away from me, but I gained on it.

Forty yards.

The cushion maintained its buoyancy, no doubt designed to serve as a flotation device, and it compensated for my lack of form. I chose not to think about how much my arms thrashing on either side of the cushion resembled a seal from below. I skimmed across the surface, driven by terror.

Thirty yards.

Something splashed beside me and my heart leapt. Another splash and then another. Small, gray fish jumped out of the water. Scared fish. Fish running from a predator below—something big.

Twenty yards.

The fish flew around me, into me, bouncing against my body. Terror drove them into the air as the great white neared.

Ten yards—so close.

"I love you, Emma," I shouted.

Fish swirled in a jumble of fear. They bounced off the stern and around the boat. I kicked as hard as I could, but I needed to be faster. I sensed it beneath me.

I dove off the cushion and swam for the boat.

I reached above my head and touched the Odyssey, grasping the transom with both hands. I scissor kicked, propelling myself out of the water. My chest landed on the gunwale. I reached for a sheet and pulled myself onto the deck, lifting my feet over the transom.

Behind me, something slapped the surface, splashing me. I turned and looked. The surface foamed white. The cushion had disappeared.

I crab-walked away from the edge until I backed into the steering wheel. I pulled my knees against my chest and rubbed my legs and feet. Everything remained attached and intact.

I made it.

CHAPTER SIXTY

Brad's screams echoed across the space between us.

I stood on the Odyssey's deck and watched the Karna burn. Flames burst through the windows and reached high into the air. The breeze carried a toxic, chemical odor. There was nothing I could do—nothing I wanted to do.

Hearing Brad burn to death was awful, a fate I would not wish on anyone, but the Brad I had known—my Brad—no longer inhabited his body. The virus had eaten away his brain, leaving a homicidal, flesh-eating monster in its wake. Watching the creature he had become feast on that innocent sailor had numbed me. My Brad could not have done that. No human could.

Rabies had released something wicked and heinous inside Brad—traits he had kept hidden. Maybe his violent tendencies had always been there, waiting for a physical or societal trigger to escape. Maybe the virus inside him had eaten away his nerves and removed his capacity to control his primal instincts. The Indonesian government needed to destroy every bat inside the Pura Goa Lawah cave, before it transformed more people into demons.

Long, orange tendrils of flame burst through the stateroom hatches and Brad's screaming stopped. His nightmare had ended. A huge plume of black smoke poured from the yacht, rising high into the air. A blinding flash forced my eyes shut and a wall of pressure knocked me off my feet.

My ears rang, and I shook my head to clear my mind. I grabbed the gunwale and pulled myself to my knees. The yacht's cabin top had disappeared in the explosion. Fragments rained onto the surface as flames consumed the yacht.

A loud crack reverberated across the water. The yacht's bow tilted at a sharp angle and slid stern-first into the ocean. The fire sizzled and popped as the cold seawater extinguished it. The yacht slipped below the surface, and only the mast remained visible, as if the Karna was giving me the finger.

The yacht sank.

The surface bubbled with air released from below. A billow swept away the disturbance, and the ocean turned placid, as if the yacht had never existed. Only a black cloud of smoke and scattered debris remained.

The yacht was gone. Brad was gone. The poor sailor was gone. But I lived.

I soaked in the thousands of miles of blue ocean. The only sound, the splashing of the sea against the hull. I ran my hands over my legs again to reassure myself I was in one piece. How had I made it off the yacht? How had I escaped the shark? My chance of survival had not been high.

I descended the companionway and walked through the cabin, feeling like an intruder. The elderly sailor had sailed the ocean alone and come to my rescue, only to be savagely murdered. I hoped he had died quickly and not suffered. A pang of guilt tugged at me, weighed on my soul. I had not intended to hurt anyone. I had meant to warn whoever came, but I had pushed my mind and body beyond my limits of endurance and had passed out on the mast.

I would have to live with that.

On the yacht, I had faced my worst fears and insurmountable odds, the sum of all of my life's tragedy, but I had persevered. I had confronted all of it and won. Beneath my depression, a fire still burned inside me. I would learn how to live with Emma's death. Her loss was a part of me, but it did not sting the same way it had a few weeks ago. I would be happy. I did not know the exact path I would take, because the future remained a mystery, an unending adventure full of sorrow and joy. But I knew one thing.

I wanted to try.

The Odyssey had an electronics system beside the chart table. I opened the navigation screen and the boat's position displayed on the map. I zoomed out. We had come within one hundred miles of the Maldives.

A light on the marine radio glowed green, and a list of frequencies had been taped above it. I plugged in the emergency maritime channel, lifted the handset to my mouth, and hesitated. If I notified the governments of the Maldives or India, would they allow me to dock or would they deny me entry as a potential rabies carrier?

I could sail the rest of the way by myself, dock in the Maldives, and fly home. But, two people had died, and I needed to notify the authorities. If the sailor had a family, they deserved to know. I also needed to warn the Balinese authorities before they had another rabies outbreak. And Eric worried about me. Everyone deserved to know what had happened. I had a moral duty to report it, even if it meant they would deny me entry.

I had an obligation to the dead. And to the living.

I lifted the receiver to my mouth.

"Mayday, mayday. This is the sailing vessel Odyssey declaring an emergency."

CHAPTER SIXTY-ONE

Four Years Later

I stood over Emma's grave. It had been four years since she passed. It seemed inconceivable how someone that small, whose life had been ephemeral, could have had such an impact. Her death had shaken me to my core, made me wonder if I could ever be happy again. Emma's death had also led me to Bali and put me on that yacht. It had impelled me to confront my demons and something more elemental. It had forced me to decide if I would submit and die or refuse to surrender and choose life. Emma's life had led me on a journey to discover who I was and what really mattered. It had been a quest to save my soul.

The early spring air smelled of buttercups, lilac, and hope. Another hard New England winter had ended, and the sun warmed my skin with the promise of summer. I knelt in the soft grass and laid a bouquet of tulips against the gravestone. I kissed my hand and touched the granite.

"The flowers are beautiful," Eric said.

"Beautiful flowers for a beautiful girl," I said.

I turned and smiled at him. Seeing him made me whole.

Eric bent over, took my hand, and kissed my cheek. "Spenser and Sophie are playing with Treasure in the car, but they're eager to get to the park. Do you need more time?"

"I'm ready now."

Eric helped me to my feet, and we walked to our vehicle. He had asked me on a date six months after I returned from my voyage. He had waited long enough for me to recover from my physical, psychological, and emotional wounds, and given me sufficient time to mourn Brad.

After arriving in the Maldives, I had spent twenty-four hours in quarantine, until a doctor confirmed I was not symptomatic. I received fourteen days of post-exposure prophylaxis; in case Brad had infected me with the rabies virus. During that time, authorities conducted a death investigation. Eric's testimony describing my frantic calls helped corroborate my story, and the Balinese Department of Health discovered hundreds of infected bats in the Pura Goa Lawah cave.

They averted a rabies outbreak, and the police cleared me of any wrongdoing.

Authorities identified the sailor Brad had killed—a retired engineer named Robert Mathis. His wife had passed away years before and they had no children. I tried to find other family members, but he had no living relatives. I made donations in his name to Boston Pediatric Surgical Center and to a rabies awareness group in Indonesia. I vowed to make those annual gifts to keep his name alive.

Brad's death devastated his parents, but when I had tried to console them, they pulled away. Maybe they blamed me for what happened or perhaps seeing me reminded them of their loss. Maybe they refused my sympathy, because they had never liked me, never thought I was good enough for their son. They hired a lawyer to enforce the prenuptial agreement I had signed, but I did not need any of Brad's things. I had been happy to move back into my family's brownstone in Boston, happy to return to my fellowship, happy to resume my life. I had signed a paper agreeing not to contest the prenuptial agreement and left their house for the last time.

I would never know if Brad had caused Emma's death. If he had hurt her, he was a monster, and I was not to blame—not a bad mother. If he had killed her, I would hate him forever. I wanted an answer, but that craving could turn into obsession, and either way, Emma was dead, and nothing would bring her back. Maybe it was better not to know.

I had finished my pediatric surgical fellowship six months after I returned to Boston and became a board-certified pediatric surgeon at Boston Pediatric Surgical Center. Eric and I had seen each other every day and spent all of our free time together. He had asked me to marry him a few months later and I had accepted with none of the second-guessing or internal conflict I had experienced with Brad. I knew it was right.

Eric was my soul mate and everything I ever wanted in a man. His kindness and his intelligence reminded me of my father. His passion for helping children and his drive to be the best doctor possible reminded me of myself. We shared a common outlook on life, a rational approach to problem solving, and most importantly, the desire to find happiness and meaning in every moment.

Eric and I had married less than a year after he proposed, and we had twins, Sophie and Spenser, two beautiful, healthy children. They were two years old now, and we planned to give them a brother or sister soon.

We arrived at our SUV and our dog, Treasure, stuck her head through the window. She was the golden retriever I had always wanted, the dog I had dreamed about and thought I would never have. We lived in my family's brownstone, and I took her for daily walks along Commonwealth Avenue.

Inside the SUV, Spenser and Sophie clung to Treasure and screamed with delight. I belted the kids into their car seats, and Eric drove us downtown to the Boston Public Garden.

We spread our blankets and opened a picnic basket near the lagoon. The trees along the shore hung over the water, their buds open, revealing white and pink flowers. Spenser pointed at two swans floating a few feet away and laughed, with the infectious sound of unbridled joy only a child can make. Sophie ran around the blanket giggling, and Treasure lay beside me watching a flock of ducks paddle across the surface. Eric flashed a loving glance, warming me and filling me with happiness. Only Eric could do that.

My life had changed in four years. Since childhood, I had focused on my career, somehow trying to compensate for the tragic death of my father. My pregnancy with Emma and marriage to Brad had changed my life overnight and made me abandon my identity.

Then came the voyage.

Facing certain death had realigned my priorities and allowed me to gain perspective on my life. I realized my altruistic dedication to saving children was noble, but it had also been a coping mechanism, a way to overcome childhood trauma. Expecting my life to end on that yacht had made me rethink how I would spend the remaining time I had left on earth. I still cared about my career and helping others, but I knew I had to focus on my happiness first, which meant marrying the man I loved, having children, and enjoying every moment.

That voyage had changed everything.

Treasure lifted her head and sniffed the air. The hair on her back stood at attention, and she leapt to her feet, wide-eyed and alert. I thought she would run after the geese or ducks, but she faced away from the pond toward something in the garden.

A horrible growling rumbled behind us—visceral, angry, close. My body turned to ice. I flashed back to the yacht, to the monster.

I whirled around and faced a two-hundred pound mastiff. It stared at Treasure then turned its head toward Sophie, Spenser, and Eric. It curled its lips and bared its teeth. Drool dripped from its fangs.

In my mind, I saw Brad on his knees, hunched over the sailor and eating his intestines. Brad standing below the mast, clawing at the air, waiting for me. Brad with flesh hanging from his mouth. He had died, but the monster would never be completely gone.

Eric jumped to his feet and scooped Spenser and Sophie into his arms, shielding them with his body. Treasure lowered her head, ready to pounce.

A low guttural growl rolled out of the mastiff's throat and its shoulders tensed.

I planted a foot beneath me and charged the mastiff, waving my hands in the air. The beast turned toward me.

"Get the hell out of here, you bitch," I yelled.

The mastiff backed up, surprised by my aggression. It turned its head and trotted away with its tail between its legs.

I looked at Eric and he smiled. He set Spenser and Sophie on the grass and they ran to watch the ducks, unperturbed by the mastiff's attack.

"I thought it was my job to protect our family," Eric said, grinning.

"We can protect each other. I won't let anything hurt my family. Not ever."

Eric took my hand and kissed me.

Four years ago, I had been afraid of many things. Now, I feared nothing. The voyage had given me that gift and I would always be thankful. I had much left to do, and I was capable and ready. I had patients to heal and children to save. I had a husband to love and twins to raise. I closed my eyes, letting the sun warm my face, and I smiled.

I had a life to live.

• • • • •

ABOUT THE AUTHOR

Author photo by Rowland Scherman
https://www.rowlandscherman.com

Jeffrey James Higgins is a former reporter, former elected official, and retired supervisory special agent, who writes creative nonfiction, essays, short stories, and thriller novels. He has wrestled an IED away from a suicide bomber, fought the Taliban in combat, and chased terrorists across five continents. He received both the Attorney General's Award for Exceptional Heroism and the DEA Award of Valor. He lives with his wife in Alexandria, Virginia.

Learn more at http://JeffreyJamesHiggins.com.

NOTE FROM THE AUTHOR

Word-of-mouth is crucial for any author to succeed. If you enjoyed *Furious*, please leave a review online, even if it's just a sentence or two. It would make all the difference and would be greatly appreciated.

Thanks!
Jeffrey James Higgins

Thank you so much for reading one of our **Horror** novels.

If you enjoyed our book, please check out our recommendation for your next great read!

Doll House by John Hunt

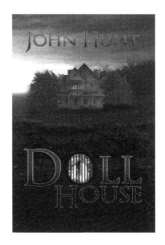

"Scary, disturbing, creepy, suspenseful. It might be too intense for some people."

—Amazon Review

Made in the USA
Monee, IL
27 September 2021